RUN
AGROUND

by
Annie DeMoranville

Deco Skyline Publishing
Boston, MA

Copyright © 2017 by **Annie DeMoranville**

www.AnnieDeMoranville.com

Deco Skyline Publishing
Boston, MA

Publisher's Note: This is a work of fiction. Names, characters, places, and incidents are a product of the author's imagination. Locales and public names are sometimes used for atmospheric purposes. Any resemblance to actual people, living or dead, or to businesses, companies, events, institutions, or locales is completely coincidental.

Cover by Keri Knutson • Alchemy Book Covers • www.alchemybookcovers.com/

Run Aground Author Annie DeMoranville. -- 1st ed.
ISBN 978-1-7325070-0-5

To my Gram
For encouraging all of my crazy adventures
May you bless this one from the heavens above

I just kind of conjured them up out of my subconscious and put them in order of ascending peculiarity.

Edward Gorey

ONE

*There is nothing more intimidating than a clean white
canvas and a palette of colors.*
− TJ Wilde

I'm TJ Wilde-Mason, soon to be simply TJ Wilde again −
Tammy Jean Wilde to be exact. My mother was a big
country western fan. No one, and I mean *no one*, calls me
Tammy Jean, not even my mother. Before I entered
kindergarten I began the resistance. I would only answer to
TJ. It was an epic battle.

"Tammy Jean, I just spoke to your teacher. Misbehaving
and it's only the first week of kindergarten, what am I going
to do with you? Tammy Jean? Tammy Jean, don't you give
me that silent treatment. Stubborn as your father, may he rest
in peace. Tammy Jean?"

It was TJ or nothing. I refused to end up a big-haired
country western singer with fake eyelashes and even faker
boobs…or working a stripper's pole. You know, like my older
cousin Kelli-Jo Kelley. I had definite ideas as a child. Not
much has changed.

I bet you're wondering what I'm doing standing in the
dark with my ear pressed against this door. Fair question. I'm

afraid the answers are more complicated than I have time for right now, considering I'm running for my life at this precise moment. But, I'll give you the highlights.

I'm standing in the dark because this is embalming room number two at Butterfield Funeral Home and Crematory. If I turn on the light, what I will see is Mr. Frank Absom in all his glory laid out on table one. On table two, depending on whom you believe, a Deputy U.S. Marshal who died in the line of duty or a dirty cop who got caught up in a gambling ring in the heart of Peoria, IL. He's naked as the day he was born and since I almost went out on a date with him, I'd rather not see him in that condition. Don't get me wrong, naked is fine when your equipment still works, but he's long past that point.

If I sound cold and disrespectful, it is only because if I stopped to think about what that really means, I wouldn't be able to breathe. In a situation like this, denial is your friend. At least that's what I keep telling myself.

The first thing you realize when you work at a funeral home – oh and I do work at this funeral home, temporarily, until my divorce is finalized. Well, actually, until my Soon-To-Be-Ex: (a) finally decides to sign the papers, (b) comes out of the closet, and (c) gets on with his life. Then I am out of here, never to be seen again. That is if I make it out of this room without needing this room. Anyway, as I was saying, the first thing I realized after I began working here, there is no dignity in death. No matter how much an undertaker tells you that your deceased loved one will be treated with dignity and respect, I rapidly learned there is no such thing. It's not that they are lying to you. It's that the business of death is messy and clinical. The dead are laid out naked on a shiny metal table, their neck elevated on a wooden block. Depending on the family's wishes, they are either placed in a giant oven, baked to very well done, or a tube is stuck into a femoral artery and all their bodily fluids are drained out and replaced with embalming fluid. Don't even ask me about the horrors if rigor mortis has set in.

Now Mr. Absom, he's an interesting story. Eighty-four, died in the arms of thirty-year-old Maggie Smith. Not his wife. Cliché, I know, but if you have to go, that's the way to go. Scuttlebutt around town is he was quite the womanizer and no one, including his wife, was surprised by the manner he shuffled off his mortal coil. Deputy U.S. Marshal Michael Fraser, on the other hand, is the reason I'm running – okay hiding – for my life right now. How I became tangled up with Mike in all of this I'm not quite sure, I'm still trying to suss out that one.

To my current dilemma, I'm hiding from some really Scary Dudes. I figure that if I can stay hidden here until seven thirty when Jim Johnson arrives to open up the funeral home, I might stand a chance. He's the groundskeeper and handyman. He comes in, turns on all the lights, starts the heat or air conditioning and begins to tidy up before everyone else gets here around eight thirty. If I can remain undetected until he arrives, I may make it out of here, still breathing.

Generally, I'd say I could take care of myself. I'm a first degree black belt in Kendo. Recently, to work off the stress of divorce, financial insecurity, and my sexual frustration, I've become a hardcore kickboxer. However, my instincts tell me Scary Dudes are serious. Considering everything that has transpired in the last few days, I'm subscribing to the safety in numbers philosophy – unless the other team is armed, then no one is safe. I think it must be about six, maybe even six thirty, now. With all that's happened, I've lost track of time, but I bet I have been hiding here for over an hour. There is no clock in the room, it's not like the occupants have any pressing need for one. I don't have a watch and my cell phone is in my purse. My purse, unfortunately, is in my car.

My car, a cute little black and yellow Mini Cooper, is in a ditch about two miles from here. I had to leave it there after being deliberately run off the road by Scary Dudes in their big, black Cadillac Escalade. In my haste to get away, I left my bag under the driver's seat. I'm hoping they were distracted enough chasing after me that they didn't think to steal it. It's a bitch having to cancel all those credit cards and get a new driver's license. Although, I could use a new picture and maybe I could change my name back while I was at the DMV. There's always a bright side, right?

Luckily, I managed to grab my car keys, which also had the keys to the funeral home on the ring. I was on my way here anyway, so I continued on foot, running through the trees, between houses, avoiding street lights. A regular secret agent. I was congratulating myself on my stealth and physical fitness because I arrived at the funeral home in what I believed was record time.

That was until I turned the corner, breathless and sweaty and saw the Escalade in the parking lot, lights off, engine running. That was ominous. They appeared to be waiting for something or someone. In case it was me, I decided sneaking in would be prudent. The back door to the funeral home is not visible from the parking lot or the street. It's tucked away between the garage and tall lilac hedges. The perfect location for bringing in the dead without drawing attention, also, not a bad way for a regular Ninja Girl to sneak in without tipping off Scary Dudes.

Why does everyone want to be at the funeral home before dawn on a Monday morning? I doubted it was to see Mr. Absom. I knew why I was here. Late yesterday, I had an epiphany. A key piece of evidence, one that could end this whole nightmare, might be in Mike's personal effects. What I couldn't figure out was how Scary Dudes knew where I was going in the middle of the night. Had they been following me for a while without my notice? Were they somehow monitoring my conversations? Or, nightmare of nightmares, had I been betrayed by the only person I've trusted since Mike's murder?

I've been pushing that thought out of my head for hours. However, it's persistent and keeps coming back, like a wasp at a picnic. You know the one. It hangs out by your soda can. You swat it away, but it keeps coming back until you absently take a sip and get stung. I'm waiting for the stinger.

The only person I had confided in since Mike turned up dead, the only person who had seen me naked in months, the only person I have *wanted* to see me naked in months, is also the only person who knew where I was headed: Deputy U.S. Marshal Colby Marcus Jameson, III. I knew I was in trouble when he arrived on scene. Tall, mocha skinned, with vibrant green eyes, he hit me straight in the heart. Unexpected, unnerving and unavoidable, every cell in my body said he was different, special. Before he even spoke a word, his eyes met mine and I knew. I knew he was that soul connection we are all looking for and if I wasn't so busy running from Scary Dudes, I'd be running from him at breakneck speed. The last thing my fragile heart needed was *that* type of entanglement.

Of course, all that could have been the adrenaline talking, because Colby was first through the door after I discovered Mike's body. Without a word, he gestured for me to be still and quiet while he assessed the situation. He took control, offered comfort and looked down my shirt, all without missing a beat. He was all that stood between me and the hysteria that threatened to overwhelm me. Before the day was out, he had saved my life, twice. Last night when inspiration hit, he had been my first and only call.

"Colby, it's me. Where are you?"

He answered with his unmistakable deep growl of a voice. "On a stakeout with the State LEOS. Everything okay?"

"I've been going over and over the last night I was with Mike...Marshal Fraser. I think we missed something. I remembered he kept a flash drive on his keychain, but I don't think it was there that last night. We were at my apartment so we could go over the funeral service in detail. He brought take-out..."

"TJ," he interrupted. "A little busy here..."

"Right...right. The flash drive, you didn't find one when you went through his stuff, did you?" There was a beat, and I imagined him mentally taking an inventory.

"No. You think it's important?"

"I do. Nothing concrete, simply a nagging feeling, I'm not even sure why I remembered it."

"Women's intuition?" he teased.

"Really? Mocking me?" I said, my voice unnaturally high. "I've been threatened, shot at, used as an operative, a decoy and the man I was sipping wine with two days ago is dead. And you want to mock me?!" I was little on edge.

"Sorry TJ. I didn't mean anything. Breathe," he added gently, "I was trying to lighten the mood. Clearly, I failed."

"I'm sorry. I'm a little on edge." To his credit, he remained silent. "I think I should look through his stuff at the funeral home, just to double-check. They have it locked down but no one has picked it up yet. Shouldn't the Marshals have it?"

"Jurisdiction issues, it gets ugly. No one wants to touch it when it might be a dirty cop."

"I don't believe he is...was dirty. I don't," I said adamantly. I fought back tears as I thought of my last moments with Mike.

"I know," he said in a tone that indicated he really did know. "Look, as soon as I can get away, I'll pick you up and we'll check it out okay?"

"Okay," I agreed and he disconnected. I probably should have waited for him, but after lying in bed and staring up at the night sky for hours, I made the fateful decision to get up and head here. Realistically, how could he have known? He couldn't have tipped anyone off...could he?

I refuse to believe he'd do anything like that. Of course, my judgment in regards to men could be compromised. What did I know? Maybe Mike had been a dirty cop. Maybe my Soon-To-Be-Ex wasn't gay. Maybe Colby was not to be trusted. Then again, maybe I'm a little jumpy because of everything that's happened over the last month. Month? It felt like a year.

Maybe I should start at the beginning. When my life began to unravel...

TWO

The greater danger for most of us lies not in setting our aim too high and falling short; but in setting our aim too low, and achieving our mark. – Michelangelo

Running out of money weeks after my life came crashing down around me and unable to convince Peter, my Soon-To-Be Ex, to sign our divorce papers – a divorce he had asked for I might add – I took the only job I could find in a bad economy with a Master's in art history and museum studies. I became the marketing director for Butterfield Funeral Homes. Making it clear to my lascivious boss that as soon as my divorce was final, I'd be leaving. Heading as far away from the Midwest as humanly possible and getting a job in the biggest museum I could find, preferably within driving distance of an ocean. It was win-win. They needed someone cheap and temporary, I needed the money.

I had other plans, so many other plans. When Peter and I first moved to Peoria for his new job almost ten months ago, we bought a cute little bungalow in less than ideal condition. It was all we could afford and I had meticulously renovated and restored it over the first six months. I had hoped to turn our showplace into a walking advertisement for my small business idea as a project manager for other homeowners. There were a plethora of rundown bungalows and Victorian homes all over Peoria that needed tender loving care. That idea went up in the same blaze as my marriage. So now I was renovating the reputation of the local funeral home empire instead.

Butterfield had recently acquired the second largest funeral home in a three funeral home town, Suggs-Haney. This now made them the largest funeral home in Peoria and earned them the ire of many in the community. They were seen as predatory, greedy and suspect. My job was to put a compassionate, community-centered face on things. That proved to be more difficult than it sounded. Butterfield was now in the hands of Nick Butterfield, the son of Alton Butterfield, Jr. (semi-retired) and grandson of Alton Butterfield, Sr. (deceased) who founded the Butterfield conglomerate.

Nick does not have the family passion for the dead nor the family work ethic. He has dreams of being a musician. Many nights he could be found in the basement of the old Victorian mansion that houses the business – smoking a fatty and rocking out on his Gibson guitar. Luckily, the overnight guests are dead. He's also growing a small crop in the old carriage house at the back of the property. If that weren't enough, he has a reputation for being handsy with the help and maybe a few grieving widows.

Yup, this was the guy I had to make compassionate and respectable. Good thing I liked a challenge.

"We interviewed quite a few people for this job, TJ, but you were definitely the hottest. It'll be nice to have a pretty face here every morning," he told me on my first day. "Coffee?"

"Did I mention in my interview I'm a first degree black belt?"

"You did. Think you can take me down?" he asked suggestively. To my credit, I did not slug him.

Two weeks into the job I knew I needed a raise when he told me I should wear my "skirts tighter and flirt with the old guys." This was my penance for giving up painting.

That same day, I watched a beautiful, dark-haired man step out of a navy blue Hyundai. I was sitting in my office, a lovely windowed alcove off the main floor. It was an Impressionist dream. Full of light, the windows perfectly framed the grand porch that served as the front entrance. I had a splendid view as he walked up the front steps.

I took notice because ever since Soon-To-Be-Ex-Peter had cracked open the closet and decided to let some light in and announced, "Honey, I think I might be attracted to men, but that doesn't mean I don't still love you," and then asked for a divorce, I needed a beautiful man in my life. And here he was, walking through the big hundred-year-old double doors and into the foyer.

On my first day at Butterfield, I discovered that if I opened my door a crack, I could hear everything in the foyer, hallway and reception area. This came in handy on several occasions, as I was able to anticipate the next Nick-centered public relations crisis. I was about to open said door in order to eavesdrop when there was a knock on it. I leapt like a startled cat, took a deep breath to gather myself, and opened the door to Deep Blue Eyes smiling at me.

He was easily six two, filling the doorway as he asked to come in. He was no Michelangelo's David, but then, who was? He was pretty fine on his own. He showed me his badge and I caught a glimpse of his big gun. I learned that Deep Blue Eyes was Deputy U.S. Marshal Michael Fraser. He was there to inquire about Mr. Arthur Shiedeger, a prominent member of the Peoria River Dogs minor league baseball management team. Mr. Shiedeger was currently in embalming room two, waiting for family instructions. The family was waiting on the report from the coroner. The coroner was waiting to meet with police. Seems Mr. Shiedeger was a victim of foul play.

The Marshals had Mr. Shiedeger under surveillance and were about to serve him with a felony fugitive warrant when he turned up dead. The rest of the River Dogs management team were under suspicion of racketeering, money laundering and interstate gambling. It appeared that while the River Dogs were suffering four straight years of financial losses, despite record attendance, some members of the management team were seeing record profits. The State Police had been investigating the possibility of fraud, gambling and embezzlement when Mr. Shiedeger decided to take a trip to Vegas.

While in Vegas, he met up with some not-so-nice people and engaged in alleged criminal activity. This alleged activity included expanding the sports gambling and money laundering from small-town Illinois to big-time Vegas. That's when the Marshals had to get involved. That led Marshal Fraser on the hunt for Shiedeger's killer and to my office looking for my help.

I was eager to help. He was sitting close and whatever he was wearing was intoxicating. I asked Marshal Fraser why in the world he would enlist my help, even while thinking I would be the best damn Girl Friday he had ever seen if he'd just keep smiling at me like that.

"Call me Mike," he said with a smile. "Look, it's unorthodox, I know, but I've done a little checking and you're not from around here. My guess is you have no ties and no one to gossip to about what I'm going to ask you to do."

"You've been checking up on me? Creepy."

"My job, sometimes it's creepy," he said, his eyes twinkling.

I took a deep breath to calm my overzealous endocrine system and asked him what he needed me to do.

"Watch. Take notes. Let me know who is coming and going. Who looks in on Shiedeger. Be discreet."

Okay, I was totally hooked on the idea of spying for the federal government. How insane is that? And, I got to report back to Deep Blue Eyes? Yup, this did not suck. We spent the next hour discussing the task ahead as I ignored the work piled on my desk.

I'll admit it, this was exactly what I needed to shake things up in my life. Sure, I was sorry about Mr. Shiedeger lying naked in limbo on a cold steel table, but since I had no emotional connection to him or his family, it was relatively easy to push away any remorse to the dark recesses of my mind. Remorse would have a lot of company: denial, confusion, and self-doubt were currently visiting that section.

Mike had suggested we meet at a pizza parlor near his hotel that evening so I could debrief him. Oh, look at me, I'll be doing a debriefing. Hot damn. I kept an eagle-eye out the rest of the day, but unfortunately, with the exception of the Widow Martin coming to collect her husband's cremains, the day had been a dud. I discretely inquired about Mr. Shiedeger's disposition and was told he was in limbo for the foreseeable future. He'd been transferred to a refrigeration unit. I managed to dig through his paperwork and found who was listed as his next of kin. I was surprised to see that instead of a spouse, it was his brother. Maybe this information would be helpful to my Beautiful Marshal, but I had my doubts. I was afraid on my first day of surveillance I was neither brilliant nor successful.

At home after work, I touched up my makeup and threw on what I hoped would be a cute-casual-pizza-bar look of jeans and a pink tee. I pulled on my favorite three-inch heeled Coachella boots. I finished up with a delicate pair of silver and pink dangle earrings, stepped back and took a long look in the full-length mirror on my closet door. I might be damaged goods but I could still pull off cute and fresh. At least I had that going for me. I grabbed my leather jacket and headed to the pizza parlor on Sheridan. Over pizza and a local brew, I filled Mike in on my day.

"Not much help I'm afraid."

"It's early yet. And you've learned one of the first lessons of investigative work: tedium."

I sighed heavily. Tedium was not what I was looking for.

"Why the big sigh?" he asked as he grabbed another slice.

"Honestly? I was looking for a little excitement to distract me from my disastrous personal life."

"Careful," he said with a smile, "you might get more excitement than you can handle."

I almost choked on my beer. Hey, look at me I'm flirting. I might get through this divorce yet. Excitement indeed.

I didn't know how much I would come to regret that desire.

"So," Mike said as he poured more beer into my glass, "tell me about this disastrous personal life."

I laughed, sipped my beer and did just that. I told him about lecherous Nick, Peter's awakening, the nightmare of disentangling our finances for the impending divorce and my hopes for the future. It was nice to have someone to talk with, not realizing how lonely I had become after moving out of the bungalow and into my own apartment.

By day three, I was beginning to think we were going to have to flash freeze Mr. Shiedeger since no one, and I mean no one, wanted to take responsibility for his remains. The police had officially released his body to the family, but repeated calls to his brother went unanswered. Mike postulated that everyone wanted to lay low until they were sure they wouldn't be implicated in his criminal activity. Mike had a deep reserve of patience, and not only in his work.

Despite multiple evenings of heavy flirtation, there were no multiple orgasms. Other than occasionally brushing the curls away from my face, he kept his distance. I assumed work came first, and I was fine with that. In reality, playing Undercover Girl was more enticing than being under-the-covers-girl. My life was complicated enough. Besides, maybe he had a wife and five little Mikes waiting for him in a tidy house with a tidy yard. I never got the chance to ask him.

After days of inaction, one afternoon there was suddenly a flurry of activity. Mr. Shiedeger was to be cremated and a memorial service held for him on Saturday. Since word of his criminal activities had leaked and was all anyone talked about, not to mention he was a prominent and now infamous member of the River Dogs, the service was going to be packed. Nothing brings out the bereaved like a good scandal. It would be all hands on deck. Nick asked me to work the service, to be on tissue box duty. No problem, I doubted there would be a big demand.

"Do you think it will be dangerous, at the funeral I mean?" I asked Mike as he gave me instructions the Friday night before the service. We sat in my dining room, sipping wine, tackling the logistics while eating dinner. When things had started to heat up with the funeral, we began having dinner at my place for maximum privacy as we discussed the details. That night, Mike had brought over Lebanese take-out from Khoury's. I provided the wine.

"If I thought there would be any chance of that, I wouldn't let you anywhere near it. Not even to hand out tissues," he replied protectively, his face serious. "You'll be people watching and I'll be half a block away in the van, taking notes." He lifted his wine glass and took a sip before continuing, "Another day of tedium, I'm afraid." He smiled at the joke and then began to lay out the plans. I suppressed a sigh.

He gave me a nifty pin camera that doubled as a pretty brooch. With it, he could see everything that was going on around me. My next fun gadget was an earpiece. He would be able to direct me on where he needed to look. He could even whisper questions he might want me to ask someone. I was feeling all *Mission: Impossible*. I thoroughly expected to hear theme music and see Mike slide across the hood of his Hyundai.

I asked him if there would be other officers with him in the van. By this time, I knew he worked closely with the State Police. Federal Marshals have a broad, but limited scope of duties he told me over hot wings and tequila one night.

"U.S. Marshals are sworn to protect the courts, transport prisoners, protect witnesses, seize assets and chase down fugitives from the law," he instructed me, "but we don't have local jurisdiction." Marshals are an elite group of about four thousand agents, he continued, chosen to serve and protect the country on a federal level. And, while it was a dangerous job that kept Marshals in risky situations, only two hundred Marshals had ever died in the line of duty since its inception. That was in 1789.

Mr. Shiedeger might have been a fugitive, but he was also an asset. The State Police were hoping he could lead them to the core of the illegal gambling operations in Peoria. This complicated Mike's job.

"The Marshals work directly with the Troopers," he told me. "When it was all over Shiedeger was to be brought in. I'd hoped to be part of the team that seized all the financial assets of those involved."

But then, Shiedeger turned up dead and everything was thrown into disarray. Mike and the State Troopers were struggling to put the pieces together and not lose the progress they'd made up to that point. They were all hoping something would turn up before Shiedeger, and their entire case, was turned to ash.

To keep the funeral surveillance discreet, Mike had said there wouldn't be any other officers. He'd be the only one in the van and it would be parked out of sight. He'd anticipated an uneventful afternoon followed by burgers and beer. I wished he'd been right.

The Saturday of the memorial service turned out to be forty-eight hours long. When it was over, Mike was dead and I realized my life was also in danger.

The more I thought about what had happened since Mike had been shot, the more I began to suspect that the Scary Dudes who ran me off the road this morning were not the only ones I needed to be worried about. In the last two days, there had been three attempts on my life. Deputy U.S. Marshal Colby Jameson had been present at two. He saved my life both times. At least that's how it had appeared.

I would have to agonize about all that later because right now, trapped inside this dark embalming room, I was determined to solve Mike's murder. Remembering his pride as he told me about becoming a Marshal, of belonging to that elite group, I felt my chest tighten. I had to push those thoughts aside. They were not going to help me. Maybe later I'd have the luxury of grief.

If I was going to find anything I was going to have to turn on the lights so I could look for the keys to the personal effects locker. Going through Mike's stuff was a long shot, but I was desperate. I wanted to be the one to find the flash drive, to be in possession of it, to turn it over to…to whom? Colby? The State Police? The truth was, someone tipped off the killers about everything – Shiedeger, Mike, me – and I hadn't a clue whom to trust. I slammed my head back in frustration, making what sounded like a sonic boom as it connected with the hollow core door. "Damn it," I cursed quietly. I had to stop reacting and start acting. "Be smart," I told myself. The stress and the smell of formaldehyde were beginning to take a toll. Colby was a good man. He was not trying to set me up or kill me and I'm sure I was not being influenced by his stated desire to see me naked...again. Mostly sure.

I was leaning on the door, wishing it had a lock. I was trying to feel along the wall for the light switch, all while listening intently for signs of Scary Dudes or Jim – praying for Jim. Suddenly the doorknob turned and the door began to scrape open, meeting with 130 pounds of resistance, as I stood frozen in fear against it.

THREE

Life is intrinsically, well, boring and dangerous at the same time. At any given moment the floor may open up. Of course, it almost never does; that's what makes it so boring.– Edward Gorey

"TJ? Are you in there? Let me in." I pulled the door open, flinging the inquisitor into the room.

"Jesus-fucking-Christ you scared the shit out of me, Jameson," I said in a terse whisper as Colby came into full view.

"That is some mouth you have on you, TJ." He moved in close. "And as soon as we figure this mess out, I plan on feasting on it." He made a point of looking down my loose t-shirt and sports bra, dimly lit by the light from the open door.

I wasn't sure if I wanted to kill him or kiss him. I pushed him aside, closed the door and flipped on the light. I was growing accustomed to his salacious quips. I suspected they were his coping mechanisms. Much better than my coping mechanisms, which fluctuated wildly between barely controlled rage and unrelenting nausea.

The light revealed a spotless interior. I looked everywhere but at Mike. I knew he was embalmed and ready to be prepped for a viewing. His autopsy wounds would be carefully sewn shut and he'd be cleaned up, but that didn't matter. It was still too much for me. Right now I needed to focus on finding out why it happened. Later today, they would dress and casket him. Then ready him for transport back to his hometown, where he was set for viewing, a funeral and burial with full honors. Maybe before they closed the casket this afternoon I'd be able to say goodbye. For now, I focused my attention on Colby, who was standing too far away.

"I was run off the road by these Scary Dudes in a black Escalade," I started in a breathless whisper, "about two miles from here. It was too dark to see who they were. I ran the rest of the way on foot. When I got here, they were parked in the front lot."

"Dammit, TJ, what were you thinking?" he asked, as he closed the space between us. "Going out in the middle of the night without any backup? You should have waited for me." He seemed exasperated, or maybe it was concerned. I was too tired to make the distinction.

"I couldn't sleep and you were working," I responded defensively. He scowled, but then put his arms around me. "Look, I'm sorry," I said, as I leaned into him. "I didn't think anything would happen. Up to this point, nothing in my life had prepared me for a time when I might need backup."

Colby pulled me tightly into him, shaking his head before tucking me under his chin and wrapping me in his arms. "You're right. You should never have been put in this situation."

"Well, I'm in it now," I interrupted – afraid he was going to cut me from the team. He didn't know it yet, but I was going to work hard to make sure I stayed a part of this. Seeing

Mike, slumped over and bleeding, his life slipping away had galvanized me. I would do whatever it took to find out who murdered him. "What do we do about the guys in the parking lot?"

"They're not there. I scouted the entire perimeter before I came in. There's no one out there. I also checked out the first floor before I came down here looking for you." His voice was deep, vibrating his chest as I pressed against it. For a fleeting moment, I felt safe.

"How'd you know I'd be here?"

"You weren't at the apartment when I got there. You weren't answering your cell. I assumed you came here. When I didn't see your car, I really started to worry."

"How'd you get in?"

"Picked the lock."

"Talented."

"Trust me, that's not my only talent."

Reluctantly, I pulled myself away and walked over to the lockers. That nagging feeling had edged its way back even as Colby tried to reassure me. Who was this man I was trusting with my life? For that matter, who was the man dead on the table across the room? I didn't have an answer to either of those questions, so I took a deep breath, swallowed the rising panic, and resolved to focus only on the task in front of us. "Let's see if we can find the flash drive."

We worked in silence as I unlocked the locker with Mike's personal effects in it. Most of it was neatly compiled in a large paper bag. The rest was in his duffle bag. I listened for Jim as I worked. "What time is it?" I asked distractedly, as I pulled Mike's badge and ID from the bottom of the bag. I opened it and ran my thumb across his picture, those deep blue eyes staring back at me. No one, including Colby, was going to deter me.

Colby pulled his phone from his pocket to look at it and replied, "Six forty-five." Jim would be here soon. It would be better if we were gone when he arrived, fewer questions to answer.

We had everything laid out on the expanse of counter between the sink and the lockers. There wasn't much. Jacket, badge, a brown case with a few unimportant papers in it, a shaving kit, and a change of clothes, that was it. A heartbreaking testament.

"It's not here," I said quietly. It wasn't that I was surprised, it had been a long shot at best. What did surprise me was that there was anything here at all. I thought the police would have taken everything and then the crime lab would swab it all for trace evidence. That's what I get for trusting CSI reruns. "I don't get it. Why is this stuff still here? Why don't the State Police have it? Why didn't the Marshals take it?" I asked.

"The State Police were mostly concerned with the crime scene. Everything there was cataloged into evidence. I've been over all of it. There was no flash drive. There wasn't really much of anything personal – his watch and cell phone, surveillance equipment and his service weapon. All they took from his hotel room was his laptop. This stuff," he gestured across the counter, "from his car and his room, it wasn't deemed important. They pulled it before the car was returned to the rental company and the hotel room was released. The agency will most likely ask the funeral home to return it to his next of kin."

"Who is his next of kin?" I asked, saddened. Reminded once again that Mike and I never had a chance to talk about his life outside this case. Colby was behind me now, gently touching my shoulders, sensing my tension. I was holding everything together with adrenaline and caffeine.

"I don't know for sure. We list it on our paperwork. It could be his parents or a sibling. He wasn't married that I know of, I can find out if it's important to you."

I shook my head. Exhaustion had caught up with me. "I need to get home, I have to shower and get back here. I have a meeting at nine."

"You're going to work? Today?" He let me go. I immediately missed his warmth. I turned around and could see the concern filling his green eyes. "You've barely slept in two days."

I had to go to work, had to have some moment that wasn't surreal. A moment that wasn't filled with blood, terror, or doubt. And oddly, I knew I was going to find it in an alcove office at a funeral home. I began to put Mike's belongings back in the locker, then stopped. "Wait, where are his keys?" I asked abruptly.

"I suppose they were turned in with the rental car."

"No. Not the rental car key. His keychain. It was a small, black and silver carabiner and it had a ring with keys attached to it," I was getting excited now. "I remember it because he was teasing me about all the keys on my key ring one night. He pulled his keys out to illustrate his point. His key ring only had two keys and the flash drive." I laughed at the memory. "Then he made me explain every key on my ring and why I needed it." I paused, trying to focus. "The flash drive wasn't there Friday night, because he used one of the keys to open the case with the earpiece and camera in it. I don't remember seeing it then." I futilely ran my hands over everything on the counter again. "Do you think the key ring was booked into evidence? Maybe he put the flash drive back on it, or maybe the other key could lead us to where he stashed it."

Colby stood quietly for a moment. I knew he was once again going over the items booked into evidence in his mind. He looked at me. "There were no other keys. Not even his hotel keycard. We had to get one from the front desk in order to search his room."

I looked over everything spread on the counter. Where was it now? I was beginning to feel stupid for even thinking the flash drive could be important. It was probably filled with his favorite songs instead of crucial evidence in his investigation and was left in his rental car. But it had stuck in my mind...why? Did Mike say something about it? I was too tired to think anymore so I continued to put Mike's things away.

"This is a needle in a haystack. I'm probably wrong," I said after I'd put everything back into the locker. I was discouraged and I needed a shower. "Let's go."

Colby took my hand and pulled me close. "The first lesson in police work is, don't ignore your gut."

"I thought the first lesson was tedium," I said quietly as I leaned into him and fought back tears.

My apartment was the best thing about being stranded in Peoria. I saw it for rent two days after Peter's proclamation. Determined to get on with my life, I snapped it up. It was a funky three-story stone castle in the historic district, about a mile and a half from the riverfront. The streets were tree-lined and most of the stately older homes and mansions had been turned into apartments or condominiums. The castle stood out, with her rough-hewn stone and turret, sitting on the corner, proud and regal, overseeing her kingdom. I was the princess who lived in the tower, looking out upon the land. Every day I climbed up three flights of stairs. Past Jeff Avery's apartment on the first floor, where often I could hear him practicing his cello. Past Mrs. Cavaleri's apartment on the second floor, envious of whatever aromatic food she was cooking. Then up the narrow stairs to a tiny landing and my door.

Behind it was a true treasure. An expansive apartment, windowed on three sides and a spiral staircase in one corner that led to my bedroom, at the top of the turret that stood guard over the entire block. I loved that room with its 360-degree view and vaulted ceiling. It was tiny, but it didn't matter, at night I had a view van Gogh would have envied. I could see the city lights, the moon and the stars. Every morning I was awakened by sunlight streaming through the trees.

The main floor was equally beautiful, with wood floors and large windows. The living room looked out onto the quiet street and in back, a sunny kitchen faced a large oak tree filled with squirrels and birds. Mrs. Cavaleri, of course, put up feeders for both. There was a small room off the kitchen that served as both a laundry room and a landing for the back stairs. Below my tower bedroom, behind the stairs, was a curved alcove, perfect for my desk, laptop and easel. The bathroom was between the kitchen and the alcove. It had a big clawfoot tub, to which a shower had been added, along with a shower rod that encircled the tub. The sink and vanity looked vintage. Only the toilet had a modern feel, in deference to water conservation I had to assume.

Colby and I walked wordlessly up the three flights of stairs. I put the key into the lock and let us in. The rising sun cast long, cool shadows across the floor. I left Colby to make phone calls and went to turn on the shower. I stripped off my clothes and checked the temperature before stepping into the tub.

The steaming water cleared my head and when I finished, I felt revived. I wrapped a little flowered robe around me, stepped out of the bathroom and took a deep inhale of freshly brewed coffee. Colby had a mug waiting for me when I padded barefoot into the kitchen. He'd also arranged for my car to be towed to the funeral home, he told me as he rummaged in the refrigerator for milk.

"Do you feel like some breakfast? I make a mean omelet," he said as he pulled the milk carton out.

I shook my head no, as I took the milk from him and poured a dash into my mug. He was starting to grow on me. His phone vibrated, he looked at it and indicated he needed to answer. I watched him, sitting at my sunny kitchen table, talking on his cell, writing notes, smoldering with innate sexuality. He looked like he belonged there. I felt a pang of guilt, knowing I spent the morning suspecting him of betraying me. I poured myself another cup of coffee and laughed as I topped off his mug. He'd chosen the one with the tiny red hearts. He smiled up at me and I had to tamp down the urge to drag him upstairs. He continued his conversation, unaware of my lustful thoughts. He had to be one of the good guys, he just had to be.

I left to get ready for work. When I came downstairs, he was leaning against the sink, waiting for me.

"Ready to face the day?"

"Ready as I'll ever be."

"I'd try to talk you into staying home today, but I think you'll be safer at the funeral home."

"You think I'm in danger?" I teased, trying to sound brave. He wrapped his arm around me, kissed the top of my head and steered me out the door.

"I want you to stay there. I have to meet with the State Police and the Marshals on the case, but I should be done around one. I'll bring you lunch." He opened the truck door for me. He tried to hide his apprehension, but his eyes betrayed him as he watched me settle in my seat. I was the sole witness to the murder of a Deputy U.S. Marshal and that made me a target. It didn't matter that I knew nothing more than law enforcement, I was the last person to see Mike alive and that was enough.

We rode in silence to the funeral home in his very bad-ass black Silverado. It suited him. I was quiet. My mind, on the other hand, was in overdrive, rejuvenated by my shower, fueled by fatigue and caffeine. I couldn't stop replaying everything over and over, like one of those nightmares where you are running from danger but standing in the same spot, unable to get away. I laughed to myself at the thought. I was Scooby Doo trying to outrun the Headless Specter, feet moving at full speed, but going nowhere. Only my specter was real.

I tried to focus on the drive, but the film in my head was relentless. All I could see was Mike's blood, smell it, feel its warmth, and hear his labored breath. Then it was sensory overload, like I was there again. Dark red everywhere, with the smell of wet copper, burnt flesh and gunpowder hanging in the air. Waves of nausea hit. I rolled down my window, tipping my head out, breathing deep, grateful for the late summer smells of the tree-lined street.

"You okay there Kit-Kat?"

I pulled my head in and leaned back against the headrest. "Yeah," I replied none too convincingly. "Kit-Kat?" I inquired a moment later.

"It's safer than calling you a hot pus..." he stopped, cleared his throat and grinned as I rolled my eyes at him. He looked over at me, curled up in my seat, facing him, shoes kicked off, legs tucked under me. "You're a sweet treat," he said as he pulled up to a red light. He leaned over and kissed me before it turned green.

I smiled at him. A genuine, warm smile, something I hadn't done in days. Desire flooded over me, but there was something else. I was teetering precipitously close to the edge of very dangerous emotional ground. I unfolded myself and turned to face front, grateful we were close to the funeral home. Colby turned into the parking lot and parked near the big doors. I began to put on my sandals but realized I had kicked one under the seat. As I bent down to retrieve it, Colby got out, walked over to my door and opened it.

"Thank you," I said as I slipped on my errant slingback and stepped out of the truck. He closed the door and beeped the alarm. "You don't have to escort me to the door."

"I'm escorting you to your office. In case you have forgotten you were run off the road this morning by persons unknown." His phone vibrated again. He pulled it out and looked down at a text. "Speaking of, your car is on its way here. It looks like it's okay except for a few dings and a broken window. I'll have someone out to fix the window this morning."

Well, that didn't sound too bad. I knew it could have been much worse because there were no street lights and the road had been dark. It was sheer luck that my car ended up in an empty lot, between an office building and the houses lining the rest of the street. It was an older neighborhood and most of the houses were stone or brick. The trees were large and unyielding. There were low stone walls separating the yards from the street and on one side, a small lake. Somehow I managed to miss all of those obstacles when I was run off the road.

I hadn't even realized I was being followed until I turned onto that quiet residential street. If I had, I would have taken a more traveled route instead. This was my routine shortcut each morning to work. It was prettier than the more populated Knoxville Avenue. There were fewer stop lights and a slower pace. Many mornings I could see the ducks and swans out on the lake. I drove it out of habit, no idea I was in danger.

My first indication of trouble had been when the lights of the Escalade sped up and loomed large in the rearview mirror, almost blinding me. I slowed to let them pass, but that was not what they wanted. My heart raced as I suspected something was amiss. By the time my bumper took the first hit, I was already calculating my escape. The problem was I didn't know the roads around the area very well. I could make my way to the funeral home and not much else. However, I did remember that there was a fire station on Knoxville. If I could find a way to double back to the last intersection, I had some confidence I could get there. At the very least, I'd be on a busier street.

I decided I would turn left at the next intersection and swing around. Before I could turn, they hit me again, this time hard enough that I began to lose control of the car. I wheeled hard left and jumped the curb, hitting soft dirt and fishtailing as I went. The Escalade sped past unable to maneuver as quickly. My car continued forward, jumping a small ditch, sliding right and tipping precariously on the uneven ground. I jerked the steering wheel sharply again, slamming on the brakes, barely missing a low wall. I wrestled the car to a stop as a large oak appeared in front of me, illuminated by my headlights. Metal met wood, but without much force.

I put the car in reverse, thinking it was best to keep moving. At that moment, something shattered my passenger window, glass flying everywhere. Afraid it was Scary Dudes, I threw the car into park, turned it off, scrambled out the door, keys in hand, and started to run. I looked back only long enough to see the brake lights on the Escalade as it stopped. When the white backup lights glowed, I turned and headed to the funeral home.

Considering those events, I was pleasantly surprised when Colby said the damage was minimal. I was happy Scary Dudes hadn't backed all the way up and run over my car a couple of times before following me to the funeral home. I'd have to wait to see if they ransacked the inside.

True to his word, Colby walked me to my office. He leaned on the doorjamb as I flipped on my computer. I saw Dee Miller, the office manager, peeking out of the reception area, clearly interested in my newest suitor. Colby reached over and touched my arm. He reminded me I was not to go anywhere and he'd be back by lunch. Then he was gone.

When he left, the void was palpable as my cold reality swept in.

I settled into my morning routine of checking email and phone messages. I readied my notes for the staff meeting. I had set the agenda last week, two lifetimes ago, and my talking points seemed unimportant this morning. But in the interest of returning to normalcy, I diligently highlighted the most important ideas and crossed out the things that could wait. I had to remind myself that no one here had any idea what transpired this weekend. They knew only what the Marshals Service had released to the public: a Marshal had been killed in the line of duty. They didn't realize how close he was when it happened or that I was the one he was protecting when it did. As far as I know, they didn't even notice I left the service early.

I gathered my notes and stood up to leave when my office phone rang. It was jarring and I jumped as the sound filled my tiny office. Taking a deep breath to slow my breathing and bring my pulse rate back to normal, I picked it up. "Butterfield Funeral Home, this is TJ."

"TJ, we have to talk."

FOUR

In love, the one who runs away is the winner. – Henri Matisse

"Hi Peter," I replied coolly to my Soon-To-Be-Ex. I was about to cut him off with a "too busy to talk right now" when I remembered I really needed to talk with him. We had unfinished business and it was interfering with my ability to take advantage of the man who was currently sharing my apartment, if not my bed. "Yes, we do."

"Can you meet me for coffee now?" He sounded almost desperate. But since I'd had my fill of drama this week, I wasn't inclined to inquire about his mental state.

"I have a meeting in a few minutes, but I can meet you in about an hour," I said, not even offering an alternative. I did a mental head slap as I remembered I was without transportation. I assumed whichever law enforcement agency Colby called in to rescue my car had more important duties that day, so I had no idea when it would appear. "One thing, Peter, my car is…getting a replacement window, so you'll have to come to this end of town. There's a Dunkin' Donuts within walking distance, why don't we meet there at ten-fifteen?"

"That'll work," he replied, a little too eagerly. "I'll order you your regular." I felt a twinge at the familiarity. No matter what we needed to do now, we would always have history. Late night study sessions with Mexican food from Rosita's two blocks from our college apartment, Dunkin' Donut mornings before important job interviews, sharing the sink before bed, and more I would honestly miss. Nevertheless, it was time to move on. I felt a pang as I wondered if there would ever be another who would share my love of both the Museum of Fine Arts and the Red Sox.

"And Peter – bring the divorce papers." He clicked off so fast, I wasn't sure he heard me or if he was ignoring the request. My urgency to meet with Peter and have him sign the divorce papers was not compelled solely by financial insecurity or feeling run aground in the middle of middle America. The urgency was precipitated by a startling realization that affected my ability to embrace my new life.

On the night Mike had been shot, I was overrun by grief, shock and enough adrenaline to power a small city. After hours of interrogation by every law enforcement agency in the Greater Peoria area, Colby had called a halt to it all. He'd made it clear they had all the information I had to give and whisked me to his truck. I told him my address and watched him plug it into his GPS. We drove in silence.

Numb and exhausted, I curled my legs up under me and leaned back in the generous leather seat. Colby reached across me, his impossibly green eyes looking cautiously into mine. "Seatbelt," he said while reaching for the strap and pulling it over and buckling me in. My breath caught as his hand lightly brushed across my breasts, clicking the buckle before moving away to his side of the vehicle. I leaned my head back into the comfort of the dark cabin and wondered at my libidinousness in the midst of such tragedy. Since at the moment my brain was the consistency of oatmeal, I decided it would be best to wait and chastise myself at a later date. No good would come of it tonight. I turned to the window and watched the city lights slide by, intermingled with persistent images of Mike. They created a surrealist nightmare. I sighed wearily. Colby reached over and placed a reassuring hand on my thigh. There was that electric shock again. I was going to hell.

It was well after midnight when we arrived at my apartment and I was spent. I was also covered in Mike's blood. The State Police had taken my blood-soaked white blouse, for reasons I couldn't bring myself to contemplate. They'd given me a navy blue shirt, two sizes too big, emblazoned with "Illinois State Police" across the chest, to wear. But my bra, my hands, my arms and my left cheek were coated in dried blood. Colby led me up the three flights of stairs and straight into the bathroom.

"Why don't you get cleaned up? I'll find my way around your kitchen and make you something to drink. Tea? Coffee? Alcohol?" I stared at him blankly, my mind unable to form words. "Okay," he continued as he stood me in front of the pedestal sink, "I'll figure it out." He left.

I stared into the mirror, not recognizing the person staring back. Somewhere in my brain, I knew this was shock, but it was too far back and I was unable to bring that information to bear on my actions. I took off the shirt and stepped back. I could see where the blood had soaked through my blouse, leaving a stain from my left shoulder, across my bra and down the right side of my ribs. A clear reminder of moving Mike from his chair to the floor in a futile effort to stem his bleeding and begin CPR, ending with me lying across him, in what must have been a primal response of protection and grief. Everything after that was a blur I would sort out later. In this moment, this irrational moment, this blood was all I had of Mike. I turned the water on and then slid to the floor, brought my knees up to my chest and began to shake.

That's how Colby found me. He turned the water off in the sink and turned on the shower. With gentle words and strong arms, he helped me to my feet, quietly undressed me and placed me in the shower. He put shower gel on a washcloth and handed it to me. He pulled the shower curtain with the giant red poppies on a white background closed, but stayed just on the other side. Somehow, I managed to wash away the remnants of blood, trying hard not to cry as the pink water swirled toward the drain. I turned off the water. As I stepped out of the shower, Colby wrapped me in a pastel green bath towel and held me close. He helped me dry off and handed me a well-worn pair of sweats and a t-shirt.

"These looked like they might be favorites," he said. I looked down and sure enough, he'd found my favorite kick-around-the-house-on-a-Saturday-night clothes. I guess that's why he's the Marshal. "I have tea steeping. Once you're dressed, come into the kitchen."

I put the clothes on, toweled my hair and went to the kitchen. Colby was sitting at my antique oak table, one of the few things I'd kept from my marriage. It had belonged to my grandmother and it was a cherished piece. Nothing that would make the Keno brothers swoon, but it carried with it fond memories of my grandmother and her bright yellow kitchen. Colby stood when I entered and pulled out one of the matching chairs for me. He brought me tea and dry toast. "I thought you could use a bite. I can't imagine how long it's been since you've eaten."

I looked at the plate of perfectly browned bread. I had no appetite, but there was something comforting about the smell of toast. The tea was peppermint. Smart man, anticipating my delicate stomach and providing the perfect antidote. I sipped the tea and Colby settled in across from me. He let silence breathe between us. I was grateful after hours of non-stop questions and chaos. I pulled my legs up and tucked them under me, leaning back and sipping my tea, letting the quiet wash over me. I wasn't ready to sample the toast yet, but I was reassured by Colby's strong presence at the table and his willingness to let me reenter at my own speed. He looked good in my kitchen, among the muted tones and Art Deco touches.

If I were painting again, I'd take inspiration from the light and colors in front of me, how they deepened his skin and intensified his strong jaw. Add a cigarette on the table, swirling blue smoke into the air and it would have been the perfect tableau. I looked past him, mixing colors in my mind. Hopper, Motley, maybe a little van Gogh, vibrant colors that created a mood.

"Are you cold? Can I get you a blanket?" Colby finally asked, watching me carefully. I had wrapped my arms around one knee, hugging it to my chest. I looked toward him, bringing him into focus, and shook my head before I returned to staring into space. "Maybe you should try and get some rest. I'm going to stay here with you," he paused when I looked up sharply – "until we know what's going on, I need to make sure nothing happens to you."

"You...you think I'm in danger?" I formed the words carefully, feeling much like a swimmer trying to ascend through murky waters. My brain was slow to put all the pieces together.

"Until we know what happened. It could be that no one but Marshal Fraser knew anything about you," he said trying to reassure me, but something in his manner betrayed him.

"But you don't believe that, do you?" I asked, already knowing the answer.

"My gut says I need to keep an eye on you. And I've learned it's better not to ignore that feeling. Besides, I don't think that second bullet was meant for Fraser and neither do you."

He was talking about the bullet that had shattered the windshield in the van as I was moving Mike to the floor. It had all happened quickly, yet time slowed and every detail was burned into my mind. I had Mike cradled in my arms, he was hard muscled and heavy and I had struggled to lower him. I felt his breath, shallow and warm on my neck. My heart racing, I'd pulled him in close, as if I could transfer the strength of my heart to his. I bent low over him, trying to move my arm from under his shoulders when I heard the glass shatter and felt something fly past me. I never heard a gunshot, only the whoosh of air.

A moment later, Colby had slid open the panel door, put his finger to his lips and motioned for me to stay down. I'd thrown myself protectively over Mike, my hands covering his wound, trying to stem the bleeding. Before I knew what was happening, Colby was over me, the full weight of his body had me immobilized.

"Stay down," he whispered in my ear. I heard tires kick up gravel on the asphalt as a car sped away and then distant sirens. "Are you hurt?" Colby asked as he slowly moved off me, still keeping us both low to the floor.

"No, but Mike is, he's bleeding…a lot…and…" and then I realized he wasn't breathing. Without a word, I was on my knees and giving him CPR. I heard Colby in the background declare "officer down" and requested an ambulance.

It wasn't until later, during the interrogation, that an officer had come in and confirmed that they had retrieved a 9mm bullet from the video/audio console above my head.

Colby was right. That bullet wasn't meant for Mike.

I sipped my tea in silence. I nibbled on the dry toast. I stared out the window, seeing nothing. I tried to shut out the images running through my mind. Mike proudly explaining all my fancy gear, as he laid it out before me. Laughing as I described the cast of characters from my day job, so he'd be up to speed as he did surveillance at the memorial. Whispering in my earpiece as I walked through the crowd at the service, telling me what a good job I was doing. Joking about Nick's lechery, the disingenuousness of the mourners and relaying the felonious nature of several of the guests. Then the explosion of shattering glass in my ear. Mike, slumped over the seat in the surveillance van, blood flowing across the console as I arrived breathless from sprinting across the back parking lot and down the alley. Mike, warm in my arms as his breath slipped away.

I looked up and Colby was kneeling in front of me, whispering softly as he took my face in his hands. I didn't realize it, but tears were flowing down my cheeks. I looked at him, into those intense green eyes looking back at me with concern. I let myself relax into his gentle touch across my face, his hand tangling into my hair. I looked down at his lips, full and slightly parted. I knew I needed to push everything out of my mind. I needed to forget, even if only for an hour. I bent forward, kissed those soft, warm lips and without hesitation, he kissed me back. He kissed me deeply, with all the pent-up heat I was feeling. Hallelujah, I wasn't imagining the electricity between us. I didn't care if it was all a reaction to the horrible events I'd witnessed. It didn't matter. What mattered were touch, heat and desire. Those would be enough.

Colby pulled back. I moaned in protest, trying to get back to those lips, so capable of distracting me from the real world. I didn't want him to second-guess himself. I didn't want a moment to reconsider what I wanted. I need not have worried. He stood up, reached a hand out to me and helped me to my feet. He led me to the spiral staircase where he stopped and bent down to kiss me again, with all the fire of the first kiss. He had me pressed against the iron railing, arms on either side of me, trapping me. I felt completely safe and totally aroused.

For the first time in hours my mind was thoroughly, blissfully, blank, except for thoughts of Colby naked and inside me. He pulled back again and it was sweet torture feeling him move away, taking his heat with him. He took my hand and led me up the stairs. I was dizzy with desire and the circular architecture as we ascended amplified the effect. By the time we reached my room, I was spinning.

Exhaustion, desire, grief, shock and passion collided and created a rush that went straight to my head. That was until Colby took me in his arms. He crushed my body against his, kissing me and reaching under my shirt. I shivered at his touch as he cupped my breast, teasing his thumb across my nipple. He pushed me gently to the bed. I pulled my t-shirt over my head. The cool air intensified my already aroused nipples. Colby's eyes went dark with desire. He stripped off his shirt, revealing chiseled abs. I ran my hand down his chest, down those rock hard abs and teased at the waist of his jeans. He sighed in pleasure and began to bend down to take my breast in his mouth when his cell phone rang.

It was like a siren, waking both of us from a dream state and throwing cold water on a five-alarm fire. He abruptly stood up and pulled the phone out of the pocket of his jeans. I couldn't help but notice how his erection was pressing against his zipper. Denying myself that pleasure wasn't going to be easy.

He answered the call, speaking softly and a bit breathlessly into the phone. I watched and realized how much I wanted him, not solely the sex, there was something more. Something I still wasn't ready to admit. But, the moment that phone rang, I also realized I was still married. Oh hell, I was *that* woman, the woman who could not be with this man until she had finished things with, well, with her husband. In my case, it meant I needed Peter to sign the divorce papers. *Immediately.* I put my shirt back on.

For his part, Colby had taken the news well. Although it had helped that the call meant he needed to get back to work. He returned the phone to his pocket. Then he slipped on his shirt, hiding those beautiful abs, and pulled me off the bed, into him, and held me tight. After kissing my forehead he'd sighed and said. "Get dressed. We have to meet with my boss." Yippee.

That's why Peter's request to meet today felt like fate. Despite everything that was going on, I knew I had to make the time. I needed those papers signed. I needed to get laid. I wasn't sure I could spend another night with Colby in my apartment and continue the chastity ruse. Besides, who knew when the next attempt on my life would be? I was learning the importance of living in the moment.

But for now, I needed to get this staff meeting off my to-do list. I entered the conference room, which doubled as a full kitchen, and found everyone but Nick and Tom Garner in attendance. Tom only worked weekends, so his absence was expected. Nick was just, well, Nick. There were fresh donuts and coffee, this week provided by young, sweet Jacob Malek, the newest funeral director in the Butterfield monopoly. He was smartly dressed in a charcoal suit that set off his dark hair and eyes. You'd trust him with your dead grandma if you met him downstairs. But up here, on the second floor, where everyone was allowed to let their guard down and burn off a little of the inevitable tension created by dealing with other people's loss, you'd see him as I did. He had a wicked sense of humor, a bit risqué, definitely not politically – or funeral home – correct. Any day I could sit across from him at lunch was a good day.

Dee was sitting at the head of the long table, dressed in her typical blue skirt, white blouse and red print silk scarf. I often wondered if she thought Butterfield was actually an airline instead of a funeral home. *Fly with Butterfield we'll make sure you arrive at your destination safely, whether it be heaven or hell.* She always seemed surprised she wasn't in charge and did little to disguise her annoyance when I was assigned to run the weekly staff meeting.

Jim sat on the couch sipping his coffee. I appreciated the fact that when we had these meetings, they made sure Jim was included. It was a sign of how they valued every member of the team, something Grandpa Butterfield thought to be very important. Of course, Nick seldom acted as a team member, more like a cross between petulant teen and Rockefeller heir. I wasn't surprised he was missing in action this morning. I poured a mug of coffee, added some cream and waved off Jacob's offer of a donut.

Butterfield had a staff meeting tradition. Employees alternated supplying the donuts for staff meetings. They even had a little chart on the refrigerator, so everyone knew who was in charge of them each week. Pity the person who forgot their week. They had to buy lunch for everyone that day. Ask me how I know this. Luckily, pizza is pretty cheap.

"Where's Nick?"

"You mean our fearless leader?" Jacob sniped. "He hasn't shown up yet."

"Dee, did he call?" I asked, passing her the donut box. She shook her head as she took a chocolate sprinkle. I went over to the phone and pressed the speed dial for Nick's cell. I could hear it ringing as he bounded up the back stairs.

"I'm here. I'm here," he chimed as he breezed in, poured himself a mug of coffee, and grabbed a sour cream glazed from the box.

I rushed through our meeting. Moving swiftly through my bullet list with laser precision, I gave everyone a task to complete, cutting short any discussion. I handled the latest Nick generated crisis with a quick phone call and a promise to have him at the next Peoria Historical Society fundraiser, dressed in 1890's garb and providing the horse-drawn hearse for historical accuracy. For his part, he agreed easily. I think he liked the theatrics of it and saw the opportunities an event like that provided. He might have some business sense after all. Once everyone was up to speed, I called the meeting to a close and hurried back to my office to grab my purse before remembering I had left it in my car last night. I guess Pete would be buying. I closed my office door behind me and called around the corner to Dee as I left, saying I had a quick meeting with my ex-husband and I'd be back shortly.

I went down the hallway, out the big double doors and down the steps to the parking lot. To my surprise, my car was there and so was the window repair truck. The technician was pulling all the broken glass out, so it looked like I would still be hoofing it. Good thing I wore comfortable shoes. I said good morning to the tech and ducked inside the driver's side, hoping against hope my bag would still be there. Woo-hoo! It was! Today was looking up. I breathed a sigh of relief as I did a quick inventory.

My phone, wallet, makeup and favorite brush were still there. My phone was almost dead, so I opened up the glove compartment to grab my charger. That's when I saw it, the blue vinyl folder where I kept my registration and insurance card was open and all the documents were missing. My name and address clearly printed on them. I shuffled through everything else, hoping to find them. No luck. I put my password into my phone and hit redial.

FIVE

I've come to the conclusion that it's not really possible to help others. – Paul Cézanne

Colby answered on the third ring. "Jameson."

"Colby, it's me. Something's happened and I thought you should know."

"Are you okay? I can get there in ten minutes...."

There was genuine concern in his voice. I wanted it to be more than professional obligation. I'd have to beat that desire down...with an enormous stick...and a shovel...possibly a backhoe.

"No," I interrupted, "I'm okay. It's my car. I mean it's my insurance and registration. They're missing. My glove box was rifled through and they're gone."

"Damn."

I knew exactly how he felt. He said he'd get someone over to my apartment and I was to stay put. He'd be back to the funeral home as soon as he could get out of this meeting. He sounded tense, so I felt it best not to mention the ten-fifteen with my ex. Unless someone had stuck a GPS tracker to my ass, I felt it was fairly safe at the local coffee shop. Except if they had run out of glazed chocolate donuts, then there would be hell to pay. I clicked off my phone, hiked my purse onto my shoulder and set out for Dunkin' Donuts. It wasn't far, even on foot, and I arrived a smidge after ten-fifteen. Peter was there, sitting in the corner with two coffees and two donuts, one looking encouragingly like glazed chocolate. He stood as I entered, looking put together in a dark designer suit, a deep blue button-down shirt that made his grey eyes sparkle, and a coordinated silk tie. Damn, he always knew how to dress. Business suit or jeans and a cotton tee, it didn't matter, he was a good-looking man. He hugged me as I came up to the table.

"Teej, thanks for agreeing to coffee."

I felt myself melt into his embrace. It was familiar and comforting. After the last few days, I needed it. I finally pulled away and sat down across from him. He slid the chocolate donut and one of the coffees over to me as I settled into my chair. I took the lid off the coffee, inhaled the deep brew and blew gently across the top before sipping it. Peter watched me intently. Since he called this meeting, I decided to wait and see what he had to say. We'd get to my agenda before I left, of that I was sure.

"You look great." Now I knew he wanted something, because after no sleep and weeks of stress, I looked anything but great.

"Thanks Peter. Did you bring the divorce papers?" Apparently, my desire for sex outweighed my resolve of patience.

"I did," he replied as he pulled them out of his bag and put them on the table. "I've even signed them. But I wanted to talk to you before we sent them in."

I pulled off a piece of donut, popped it into my mouth and let him speak. It was easier to practice patience when my mouth was full. I was savoring the sweet chocolate cake so I almost missed Peter's reason for arranging this meeting. He got right to the point.

"I think we should give things another try." I almost choked on all that chocolate goodness as he continued, "I miss you. I miss us."

I took a sip of coffee and looked at him. He was as handsome as ever, still sweet and charming. We did have fun when we were together. We were the best of friends. I'd be lying if I said I wasn't tempted. But, the reality was the sex had always been lackluster and infrequent. Amazing how many excuses you can come up with to explain away someone's lack of desire for you. It wasn't that sex was the deal breaker, it was more about the doubts it raised.

I suppose, if I was honest with myself, I wasn't all that surprised with Peter's confession on the heels of our fourth wedding anniversary. It brought clarity to a nagging feeling I'd had for far too long. After we'd moved here and I realized there were no job opportunities, I busied myself with managing our house renovations, ignoring Peter's late nights, his emotional distance and my own restlessness. I told myself his lack of interest in intimacy was more about a new job and the added stress of new responsibilities. All the while I felt undesirable and a failure as a wife, an adult and an artist.

Now here he was, sitting across from me, looking hopeful, ready to plead his case for our reconciliation. I'd have to nip that in the bud, for both our sakes.

"Peter," I paused, taking another sip of coffee, collecting my thoughts, hoping to find the right words. "Peter, you're gay. You like men." I was never known for my tact.

"In all fairness, I'm bisexual," he interrupted, then sat back, expecting the worst.

"Okay. That may be. However, I'm not into sharing. Man or woman. I don't really think you want to get back together, I think you're scared. So am I. We were together a long time, we have history. It's understandable that we'd be scared of seeing what life is like outside that bubble." Somehow, being a Marshal's sidekick, witnessing his death and having my own life threatened had dissipated most of the anger I felt toward the dissolution of my marriage and toward Peter. A month ago I wanted to eviscerate him and would have happily done it. Now I began to realize, as I explained to him why we should move on with our lives, that I was actually excited to see what the future might hold. If I lived that long. Being shot at makes you fearless.

"Are you sure you don't want to at least try?" Peter asked again, looking forlorn. The light from the window lit up his hair making it look golden and a bit angelic. I was sure he wouldn't be alone for long. I had a suspicion there was someone on his horizon, someone who helped him crack open the door to what he really wanted.

"Darling," I began, "we will always have a connection. And we'll always have Paris." This made him laugh, not only was it a line from our favorite movie, we honeymooned there. "But it's time," I continued gently, "I think there is someone waiting for you...isn't there?" He nodded ever so slightly, so I went on, "These last few weeks have shown me so much about myself, I can't go backward and neither should you.

You're a great guy. The best and I'll always love you. You deserve to have it all."

He reached across the table and held my hand. We both took in a deep breath and let out a simultaneous sigh. This made us laugh again. Peter grabbed my other hand and pulled them close. "I will always love you, too."

We stood up. Peter bent down, kissed my forehead and as he did, I caught glimpse of a black Escalade moving past the window and down the street. I hugged him, folded the divorce papers into my bag and told him I needed to get back to work. I scanned the street through the big front window as he walked me to the door.

"Can I give you a ride back to the funeral home?"

I thought about it for a second. It would be the quickest way back if my fan club had somehow followed me here, but I immediately nixed the idea, not wanting to put him in harm's way. "Thanks. But it's such a nice morning, I think I'll walk," I answered. I was probably imagining the Escalade anyway. No sooner had that thought flitted through my brain than I saw the same SUV slowly turn the corner and head past me in the opposite direction. Subtle they weren't. I turned to go back into the donut shop. "I left my phone on the table," I lied. I bid Peter to have a good day and told him I'd call him later in the week.

Once I was sure he had left, I looked around for a back entrance, hoping it let out onto an alley or a quieter street. I asked the cashier if there was a back door. She looked confused as she pointed toward the door near the drive-thru window. "Thanks," I said, "old boyfriend coming in the front door, don't want him to see me." She nodded knowingly, let me behind the counter and ushered me out.

The door led into a wide alley that served as the drive-thru lane. There was parking for the employees, a big dumpster and a short walk to Dechman Avenue. From there I would be able to take neighborhood streets back to the funeral home. I was fairly confident I could avoid detection, but my heart was racing anyway. Not only was I thinking of what danger I might be in, but also that I was going to have to tell Colby what had just happened. I think I would rather confront Scary Dudes than him. Colby, cranky and annoyed definitely trumped dudes with guns as most frightening, any day.

I took a deep breath and plunged into the alley, walking briskly to the corner. I stayed close to the brick building that housed Ned's Shoe Repair While-U-Wait. I peeked around the corner to make sure the coast was clear before turning onto Dechman and making my way toward the safety of my office. There were no cars on the roadway as I hurried down the tree-lined street, but I planned my escape regardless, looking ahead to which yard I might take refuge in if needed. All the while listening and scanning for any sign of the Escalade. When a car did approach from behind I jerked in fright, even though it was only a lime-green Volkswagen Beetle, driven by a red-headed teenage girl. I turned and made my way through several more neighborhoods before reaching the alleyway behind the funeral home.

Now I had a decision to make. Bring myself out into the open and use the front door, or walk down the alley and use the back entrance by the garage. Either way seemed to be equally perilous. I was hiding beside a big oak tree, unable to make a decision when my phone rang. My already jagged nerves shattered at the sound. I fumbled in my jacket pocket trying to extricate the phone and halt its persistent ringing. My hands were shaking so badly that once I pulled it out, I could barely push to talk. I looked at the caller ID. *Oh, shit,* I silently cursed, before I said hello.

"Where the hell are you? I thought I told you not to leave the funeral home until I got here," Colby said from the other end.

"Are you in my office?" I asked stupidly. I was stalling.

"Yes – where you are not. Where are you?" He did not sound happy.

"I'm nearby," I replied and closed my eyes before I asked him the next question. "Can you look out the front window and tell me if you see the black Escalade driving by?" There was deadly silence on the other end. Then a moment later, he replied.

"It's all clear."

"Good. I'll be right in."

I was relieved to be in the relative safety of my office, even with Colby standing and staring at me in stone silence.

"The good news is, I may have a lead for you," I said brightly. Then I held up my hand and said, "Let me check in with Dee before you start the lecture." I let Dee know I was back and that I was in a meeting for the next few minutes. She didn't sound pleased, but she had no urgent messages for me, so I chose to ignore her disapproval. I could only deal with one reprimand at a time. I turned and steeled myself for Colby next. He took a deep breath, let it out slowly and shook his head.

"Do you want to tell me what was so important you decided to go on a walkabout while men with guns are hunting you?"

"I got my divorce papers!" I said with a bit too much enthusiasm. I pulled them out of my purse and waved them triumphantly, as if to bolster my claim. "Look," I said with more gravity, "Peter wanted to talk, I wanted the papers. It was coffee a couple of blocks away. I didn't think it would be that big of a deal. Well, not until I saw the Escalade circling the block."

"Christ, TJ. Are you sure it was the same one?"

"Pretty sure. And guess what? It has Nevada plates. That can't be a coincidence."

"Did you see the plate number?" he asked hopefully.

"Not all of it. I was trying to stay inconspicuous. I could only see the last three numbers. 072."

"Well, that's something. But you have to be more careful. We don't know what's going on here. We don't know who is involved."

"You mean cops, right? You think there are cops involved?" I was already sure of this. There was no other explanation for how anyone knew of my involvement with Mike. Mike knew. Colby knew. The few Marshals who interviewed me knew. No one else knew. I mean even if they saw me in the van with Mike, there was no way anyone would think I was more than a bystander helping him. Why come after me, unless they thought I knew something?

"Someone thinks you have information," Colby said, reading my mind. "I don't know why, I don't know how, but they do. I don't think they are trying to kill you, they're trying to find out what you know."

"Then they'll kill me," I interjected brightly. "Did you find out anything this morning?"

"Not much. They're printing your car now, maybe we'll get lucky. The real problem is how to keep you safe."

"Who knows that I was working with Mike now?"

"Too many. My boss, a few Marshals and some key members of the State Police. We've put you on the confidential informant list, so that restricts access. But, if we're dealing with a dirty cop, my bet is on someone high up. Someone with access to both Nevada and Illinois sources, someone with influence who could buy silence." Colby looked grim. This was his world and someone was messing with it. This did not make him happy.

"What do we do?" I asked.

"First and foremost I protect you. You are now my full-time job."

Oh yay, I thought and wondered how I was going to explain the tall, black bodyguard to my co-workers.

"Then I'm going to have to figure out who murdered Mike. That's our best shot at unraveling this mess."

"We," I said firmly. "We are going to figure out who killed Mike. Don't think for one moment I'm going to sit on the sidelines."

"Never crossed my mind," he said with resignation as my intercom buzzed.

Dee announced I had a visitor. I quickly looked at my calendar to make sure I hadn't missed an appointment in all the chaos. Nope, my day was a blank slate. I looked at Colby, shrugged my shoulders and headed to the main office. I gestured for him to wait when he looked like he would follow.

At Dee's desk stood a graceful older gentleman, dressed in a tweed three-piece suit. He reached out and shook my hand while introducing himself as Dr. Brady Forsyth. He explained that he was in charge of the volunteer program at the historical society and he was looking for my help.

"Dear, I hear you are an artist." That took me by surprise. It wasn't something I advertised these days. "We are having the grand reopening of the Merriam-Forsyth mansion next month. It is part of my heritage and my family donated it to the city last year. It has been completely restored to its turn of the century glory." He spoke with great pride and dramatic flourish. "The event will be a costume ball with reenactors for all the key players. We would love it if you would consider playing the part of my great-aunt Jean Merriam. She was my maiden aunt, a renowned artist and she traveled the world. We would really like someone who could convincingly put brush to canvas."

A spinster aunt, that sounded about right. "I don't know what to say, Dr. Forsyth. It sounds like an amazing opportunity and I'm flattered, but..." I didn't get to finish.

"Wonderful, wonderful. I'll have Mary contact you directly. She's organizing the event. There will, of course, be costume fittings and we have the make-up artist from the college recreating period hairdos for the night. We'll get you all the details." He finished breathlessly, took both my hands and held them tight as he kissed me lightly on the cheek. I guess since I was going to be playing his maiden aunt, we were old friends now. Before I could say a word in protest, he was gone. I looked at Dee and shook my head.

"Well, that was unexpected."

"You do seem to get around," she replied with all the warmth of a penguin's ass.

"I wonder how he knew I was an artist?" I said more to myself than to Dee, since it was clear we weren't going to be buddies anytime soon.

I couldn't figure her out. I guess she'd been the only woman here for so long, my presence was intrusive. I recently found out she trained under Nick's mother, who had run the place with an iron hand. Dee was very protective of the rules set forth by Mother Butterfield, maybe she saw herself becoming the next Mrs. Butterfield. I had no idea why anyone would think of Nick as marriage material, but I had bigger problems about which to worry. If I had my way, Dee would have her territory back, sooner rather than later.

I headed to my office to finish being interrogated by Colby. Seriously, if he wasn't so hot and kissed as he did, I wouldn't put up with his scolding. Oh, who was I kidding? His overprotectiveness only made him more desirable. It was all I could do not to strip him naked in my office and take him on the inlay top of my Art Nouveau desk.

I watched his eyes flash as he finished his lecture on my safety being his priority. Then he sat near my desk, texting on his phone, while I wrapped up my work. An hour later, after his phone had beeped for what seemed like the hundredth time, I'd done as much as I could. I turned away from my computer and asked him if there was anything new to report.

"No. They're running the vehicle and plates against any known associates of either Shiedeger or the people he was meeting with in Las Vegas. Nothing yet. But it could take a while since all we have is the partial plate." He leaned back in the chair, looking as exhausted as I felt.

"I'm done in. Can we grab something to eat and then go back to my apartment and brainstorm?" I asked as I shut down my computer. I picked up my bag, made sure my phone was tucked in it and headed down the hall to let Dee know I was taking off for the rest of the day. Colby followed and I gave him the side-eye. He ignored me. Nick, Jacob and Dee were all in the main office now. Good, I'd only have to lie once. "Hey boss," I said to Nick, "this is Deputy U.S. Marshal Jameson. He's investigating that shooting from this weekend." I could feel, more than see, Colby tense behind me, wondering what that hell I was doing. "He and I went to high school together, isn't that just the craziest coincidence? If there's nothing too urgent going on, I thought I'd take the afternoon off and show him around the city," I lied.

Nick reached out and shook Colby's hand. "Absolutely. A Marshal, huh, I bet that's exciting. Just awful about that other Marshal, have you figured out who did it?" Nick asked nervously. You'd think he had something to hide. Oh, yeah, that's right, he did, an entire grow operation in the backyard.

"We're looking at a number of leads," Colby answered vaguely.

Nick nodded and quickly looked over at me. "TJ, we're good here. The only service on the board is Mrs. Jenkins and it'll be a small, family-only memorial in our chapel. You deserve an early afternoon after coming in to help on the Shiedeger service. See you tomorrow." I turned to leave, but Nick continued, "Oh, and I hear that Dr. Forsyth stopped by and you agreed to the reenactment. I knew you'd be perfect for it, that's why I told them about you and that you were an artist."

Well, I'll be damned.

Colby and I said our goodbyes and were about to leave when I remembered something.

SIX

The difference between false memories and true ones is the same as for jewels: it is always the false ones that look the most real, the most brilliant. – Salvador Dalí

"Nick, about the Marshal downstairs."

Nick confirmed that Mike had been placed in his casket and was ready for transport. I explained to him that Colby and I would like to pay our respects. Before our eyes, he fell right into funeral director mode.

"I'm so sorry for your loss," Nick said by rote. "Please let me know if you need anything. Marshal Fraser's death was a great loss to the community." There was no emotion behind his words and before we could reply, he was gone. Off to check on his herb garden, I suppose.

As Colby and I walked down the stairs to the room where we began our day together, Colby was having difficulty suppressing a smile. I couldn't look at him, because I was about to burst out laughing, which was absolutely inappropriate given the situation. Exhaustion and stress were stripping me of any sense of propriety. I didn't know what Colby's excuse was, as he stifled a laugh and pulled me into the bathroom next to the embalming room. I buried my head in his chest and did my best to muffle my laughter as I completely lost it. Colby laughed quietly and wrapped his arms around me, holding me close.

"He has quite the casket-side manner, doesn't he," Colby whispered in my ear, "all compassion and caring." This only made me laugh harder.

"We are going to hell," I gasped as I tried to regain my composure. Finally, after a few deep breaths, I was ready to see Mike. The laughter proved therapeutic. It steeled me for whatever was going to come next. Colby holding me tight didn't hurt, either.

I opened the door to embalming room two and stepped inside. Mike was smartly dressed in his uniform, looking peaceful. I walked over to the beautifully carved and polished wooden casket. Colby stood close behind me, his arm protectively around my shoulder. It was obvious that the Marshals spared no expense. Enveloped in cream colored silk, Mike's head rested on a matching silk pillow. I reached over and gently brushed my hand over his hair. It looked too perfect, so I mussed it a bit. It wouldn't last. Jacob would do a final inspection before closing the casket and handing it off to the Marshals, who were providing transport. He would compulsively make sure every hair was in place, that his lips were perfectly positioned and his skin smoothed. He couldn't help it. I think it was in the funeral director handbook.

"Do you need a moment alone?" Colby inquired quietly.

I didn't. I had already said my goodbyes, had my moment. In the van, when I felt Mike slip away. That was real, that was undeniable. This was staged. I felt nothing as I stood there. Mike was gone. This was merely the shell he left behind.

"No, I'm good. Do you?" I said as I turned to look at Colby. He shook his head. We left, quietly closing the door behind us and walking silently up the stairs. There was nothing left to say.

In the parking lot, they were loading my car onto a flat-bed for the second time today. My poor baby, all she'd ever done was be zippy and fun to drive. She didn't deserve this.

"Now where are they taking her?" I asked forlornly.

"Her?" Colby laughed. "To the body shop to get the dings repaired. You are riding with me anyway, so the department thought it would be a good time to get the repairs done."

"The Marshals are paying for it?" I hadn't even thought about the repairs. What would I say on my insurance claim, *damaged while being chased by hit and run murder suspects*?

"Yup, I filled out the paperwork myself," he said proudly. "Easier than having to explain to your insurance company that you were fleeing suspected murderers." I laughed aloud at that. He gave me a quizzical look.

"You read minds, too," I replied, which did nothing to erase the question in his eyes. I turned to look at my car, finally taking the time to assess the damage. Her back hatch had more of a dent than I expected. I guess they hit me harder than I remembered. The front bumper was a bit dimpled where I grazed the tree. I sighed deeply. Colby took me by the hand, led me to his truck and helped me into the passenger seat. He climbed into the driver's seat and started up the engine. He began to put it into gear, stopped and looked over at me.

"Does she have a name?" he asked.

"Who?" I asked, relaxing into the big leather seat.

"Your car. Did you name her?"

"Oh, yeah. SuzieV." I could see he was confused. "Suzie. V as in Valadon. She was a French artist in the late 1800's and early 1900's. But, more famously, she was one of Renoir's favorite models. She was the girl in his *Dance at Bougival,* which is one of my favorite paintings. I sat and stared at it for hours at the Museum of Fine Arts in Boston while in grad school. I bought my car in Boston and voilà, she became SuzieV."

He shook his head. I think he was sorry he asked. He put the car in gear and we headed out of the parking lot. I leaned back in the soft leather and looked out the window.

"Are you hungry?" Colby asked once we turned onto Knoxville.

I had to think about it for a second before realizing, that yes, I was hungry. Very hungry. Colby turned into a cute little drive-in diner with a sign that proudly proclaimed *Lou's Drive-In.* We ordered up cheeseburgers, fries, onion rings, chocolate and strawberry shakes and I threw in a Diet Coke just to balance things. An actual, honest to goodness car hop brought our food to us in red and white bags. I would not have been surprised if she had been wearing roller skates. I was safely stashing the bags while Colby paid the bill. When I looked up to see a black Escalade glide by, a man looking at me from the passenger seat.

"Colby! The Escalade," I said as I pointed out the direction it was going. Colby threw the Silverado into reverse and headed out of the parking lot as I quickly settled the drinks into the cup holders. Traffic was heavy and it took him a minute to merge back onto the road. I was scanning the street trying to pinpoint the SUV. "There! Up ahead, just past that next street."

Colby weaved through traffic as I kept an eye on the vehicle. Traffic eased once we drove past Lake Avenue into a more residential area.

"I see them now," Colby said. "I need to hang back, there's not enough traffic to hide in. Grab the binoculars in the glove box and see if you can make out the license plate." I reached into the glove box and pulled out the biggest set of binoculars I had ever seen.

"I'm pretty sure I could see if someone in the SUV was picking lint out of his belly button with these. Are they standard cop issue?" I joked as I hefted them up to my eyes. "Good thing I'm pretty buff, these weigh a ton." I scanned the street until I located the Escalade. "It's them," I said excitedly, "Nevada SPP-072 and they're turning east on the next street."

Colby, keeping his distance, turned right on Glen Avenue. That's when everything went sideways. The street was a quiet residential with no traffic to speak of and it didn't take a genius to realize we had been spotted. The Escalade sped up, blew through two unmarked intersections and disappeared over a small hill. Colby did not alter his speed. I looked over and he was doing exactly the speed limit. I resisted the urge to scream, *They're getting away!* I clenched my teeth, dug my nails into the leather armrest and kept a lookout. As we crested the small hill, I spotted them, which wasn't difficult since we were the only two moving vehicles on the road. Colby had kept us a good quarter mile back. They disappeared around a small curve and I waited tensely until we rounded that curve and could see them again. Colby reached down and plugged the street name into the GPS. A map popped up and Colby dragged the map down to see what was ahead for us. I

kept a sharp eye on the street until I was momentarily
distracted by a spectacle on the left side of the road. My gaze
was drawn to a five-story red tower with a giant, life-like
woodpecker hanging off its side. It stood in the center of a
large parking lot filled with cars. Completely in awe, I almost
missed the mini-van that pulled out from the lot and directly
into our lane.

"Colby!" I yelled. He looked up from the map just in time
to hit the brakes and miss the van. I looked ahead to see the
Escalade blow through the red light at the next intersection.
We had no choice but to stop behind the van and wait at the
light. Once the light turned green, they signaled to turn left
and waited for an oncoming car to pass before making the
turn. I was wound tight. I was barely breathing as the seconds
ticked by and jumped in my seat when Colby reached over
and patted my thigh to reassure me. When we finally made it
through the intersection, there was no sign of the Escalade. I
sat back, dejected. I didn't understand how Colby could sit
there so calmly.

"The road ends at a wooded area. It looks like there are
paths and trails, but no real roads." He continued to drive until
we reached a parking lot at the end of the street. If I wasn't so
preoccupied with finding Scary Dudes, I would have
appreciated the view. The wooded area overlooked the Peoria
River and the parking lot was high enough that we could look
down past the trees at the panoramic view. I scanned for the
Escalade, which was ridiculous, but couldn't help myself.
Frustrated, I turned on Colby.

"You lost them. Why didn't you drive faster?"

"First of all, it may or may not have been the guys who ran
you off the road," he started patiently. "Second, I was not

going to be involved in a high-speed chase through a residential area. Third, aside from running a stale yellow light, they did nothing suspicious." He looked over, leaned in and kissed my forehead. "I'm sure it was them, but we had no backup and no proof. Why don't you break out lunch and we can have a picnic."

I wanted to be mad, but I knew he was right. I also thought it best not to alienate the person guarding my body. Especially when I was hoping he'd be guarding my naked body later on tonight. I pulled the bags off the floor, Colby grabbed the drinks. We got out of the truck and found a picnic table with a great view of the river. I passed out the burgers. Then I flattened the empty bag, dumped the onion rings and fries on it, and placed it between us. We munched away in silence, looking out at the river, watching a barge navigate down the center.

"It's pretty out here," Colby said, breaking the silence.

"It is nice," I said quietly, grabbing an onion ring and dipping it in ketchup. "I also think I've found a new favorite burger place." Colby laughed. I loved the sound.

"It is good, but it may also be that you haven't eaten since last night and you've had a busy day," he reminded me. I decided not to mention the donut. "So, you have your divorce papers signed? What's the next step?"

You mean besides stripping you naked and taking you right here on the picnic table, I thought. "We have some assets we need to divide up," I said instead. "We made some investments together and Peter still needs to pay me for my half of the equity in our house."

"You have a house? Here in Peoria?"

"Yeah, we bought an older fixer-upper and did most of the work ourselves the first six months here," I said sadly. "I moved out when he 'came out.' I wasn't that attached to it and I knew once everything was settled, I'd be moving on. I only came to Peoria because of Peter's job."

"OK. You're not staying in Peoria and your husband is gay? Anything else I should know?" he asked as he popped the last of his burger into his mouth. Oh, that mouth, it was all I could do not to lick the mustard off the corners of his full lips.

"Sorry, I forgot we barely know each other."

"I wouldn't say that," he replied and gave me a long, smoldering look. I grabbed my Diet Coke and took a lengthy sip to cool off.

"I mean, you don't know all the sordid details of my personal life," I finally managed to respond. "Yes, six months after we moved here, my husband told me he was gay, or at least bisexual. And yes, as soon as everything is settled I'm outta here. It's a pretty enough place, but my sole reason for moving here was Peter."

"And you can work at any funeral home, right?" Colby joked.

"Yup. My life's calling," I snarked. "My dream job, well, you know, besides dead people and horny morticians, is to work at an art museum. I've been applying all around the country. I'm sure I'll have to start at an entry level exhibits position, but eventually, I want to do acquisitions and authentication."

"Well, that's not a surprise considering who…" he started and then his cell phone rang. "Jameson," he said as he answered it. He listened for a moment before replying, "Okay, that's good to know. That would be a good idea, and I've got her covered for now....right," and with that, he clicked off.

"Anything important?" I asked hopefully.

"Your car will be ready tomorrow afternoon, patrol officers checked out your apartment and everything was locked up tight, no sign of the Scary Dudes. My guess is they've figured out you're not alone. There are always lots of people around and I plan to keep it that way. I have undercover officers who are going to do drive-bys and we've told the local police we suspect there are fugitives in that area, so they'll step up patrols. Still, I think we should put a deadbolt on your front door. We'll stop at a hardware store on the way home."

We picked up our trash and tossed it. I took a few leftover French fries and left them at the base of a tree for the squirrel that had been eyeing them. He scarcely waited for me to walk away before he was down the side of the tree and stuffing them into his cheeks. I laughed as I watched him pack away his windfall. "I know how you feel, buddy, they were good fries."

Colby put an arm around me and walked me to the truck. He stole a quick kiss before he opened the door and helped me in. I settled into my seat and exhaustion hit, suddenly and with full force. I was a bug, stepped on by a giant shoe. I buckled up as Colby got in and by the time he turned the key, I was sound asleep.

Next thing I knew we were in front of my apartment. Colby was standing next to the open passenger door.

"Wake up sleepyhead," Colby said playfully. He had a plastic Menards Hardware bag in one hand and was gently shaking me awake with the other. As the cobwebs cleared, I realized he had stopped for supplies while I was asleep.

"I hope you have tools because my toolkit consists of a butter knife, coffee mug and assorted natural bristle brushes," I said sleepily. "I left my good stuff with Peter."

"Come on, let's get you upstairs," he said smiling down at me.

I slept soundly and blissfully dreamless for a couple of hours. When I finally dragged myself back downstairs, Colby had finished adding the deadbolt and was sitting in my alcove with his laptop. He fit right in. I mumbled hello on my way to the bathroom where I could run a brush through my bed head. When I came out, he was in the kitchen, putting on a pot of coffee.

"I've been summoned," he began. "They've formed a task force to combine state, local and Marshals to find Mike's killer. They'd like my input. It's in about an hour, think you can be ready?"

"I'm not going," I said flatly.

"I have to go," Colby said, suddenly wary.

I looked him in the eye and repeated, "I'm not going."

Colby didn't say anything for a moment, probably weighing his options before beginning his argument. "Well, you can't stay here by yourself."

"Sure I can. You just bought me a nice, shiny new lock. I'll close all the curtains, lock all the windows and snuggle in to watch some bad television. I'll be fine," I said firmly. Colby started to protest but I cut him off, "I'm staying here. I'm tired and I simply want to be for awhile. You can't tell me I'd be safer with you, because we know that's not true."

I knew I had the upper hand. The last time I went with him to a meeting, I was shot at, Colby standing just feet from me. That was the moment I became convinced cops were involved and my doubts about Colby began to settle in. It was THAT night, the night they killed Mike, the night I almost danced naked in the sheets with Colby. The night I knew my life was never going to be the same.

That night, once Colby and I had put our clothes back on and cooled off, we had jumped in his truck and headed to the district office downtown. Because Peoria is the county seat, the Marshals had an office here. It was in the federal district court building, only five minutes from my apartment. My mind had still been trying to process Colby, half-naked with his hands all over me when we pulled up and parked in front of the offices.

I'd gotten out and stepped around the large concrete pillars that stood guard between the street and the building before Colby could get to my side of the truck. I waited there, since I was unsure of where we were going. It was the middle of the night in Peoria and the whole area was a ghost town. The only sounds were crickets and the air compressors on the buildings. That was until a bullet had whizzed by my head and shattered the window of the car in front of me.

SEVEN

*Life being what it is, one dreams of revenge. – Paul
Gauguin*

Colby had me down low before I knew what had happened. He'd pulled me toward the passenger side of the Silverado, his body pressed against mine, his hand on his gun. Then the sidewalk filled with people, each one holding a weapon, crouching low, coming to our aid, looking to Colby for direction. Colby was pointing his gun in the general area where the shot originated and everyone scanned the area. It was surreal.

The street was eerily quiet, even the crickets were silent. Colby reached up, opened the back door of the truck, and pushed me into it, sitting me on the floor. He used the open door as a shield and stood up for a better vantage point. I was terrified as he stepped away from the safety of the truck and onto the sidewalk, looking up, gun pointed in anticipation. A moment later, certain that the shooter had gone, everyone converged on the sidewalk by the truck. They talked quietly as they looked over at me. Without a doubt, the topic of the meeting had changed after that.

That incident fortified my resolve. I was not leaving this apartment tonight. I was exhausted. My emotions were raw. I could only imagine what would happen in a meeting where the topics of conversation were Mike being a corrupt cop and the attempts on my life. I don't have a reputation for holding my tongue in the best of circumstances and this was the farthest thing from "the best of circumstances."

I stood in my kitchen. It felt warm and safe. The smell of coffee brewing, my grandmother's table, the warm colors, deepened by the early evening sun as it angled in through the leaves of the tree, created an air of comfort. This was where I wanted to spend my evening. I looked over at Colby, large and imposing, vacillating between frustration and concern. I could see him working through the best way to approach me. I would not be swayed.

"I know you have to go. I'm just telling you, I'm not going with you. I'll be fine here," I argued, "You can call me every ten minutes if you need to, but I am not leaving this house tonight."

Colby stood for a moment, visibly torn between understanding and the desire to pick me up and carry me out to the truck. I could see his shoulders tense, his biceps flex and I stood warily, believing that he might actually resort to that tactic. Instead, he reached over to the coffee pot, grabbed a mug, and poured a cup of coffee. He handed it to me before pouring himself one and sitting down at the table. He waited until I sat before he spoke.

"I think this is a mistake, but I understand why you want to stay here. And you're right, I did a shitty job of protecting you that night." I started to protest, but he cut me off, "We didn't realize...I didn't realize...that you were the target. I won't make that mistake again. I'm not leaving you here alone," he finished with steel in his voice.

"Then I guess we have a problem," I answered with equal determination.

Colby pulled out his phone and pushed the speed dial. He stood up while it rang and walked into the living room. I couldn't hear what he was saying, but by his tone, he was in cop mode, professional and in charge. I had a vision of an entire battalion of Marshals charging into my apartment and forcibly dragging me to a staff meeting. I began to rethink my position when Colby walked back into the kitchen.

"I've called in a Peoria uniformed officer to sit on your place until I get back. As far as he knows, he's watching over a federal witness and he knows it's his ass if anything happens to you." Colby walked over to me, bent down and kissed me. Softly at first, but it quickly became deep and passionate. His tongue finding its way between my slightly parted lips, tangling with mine. Electric warmth spread through me, hitting all the right spots. When he finally pulled back, I was breathless and more than a bit turned on

"What time did you say your meeting was?" I asked, running my fingers through my curls, trying to regain my composure.

"If you promise not to get shot while I'm gone, we'll revisit this when I return," he teased. "Meanwhile, I need you to remember something. My job is to protect you. That is what I'm going to do, even if it doesn't work into your plans. You got your way tonight, but next time, even if I have to handcuff you, you're staying with me," he finished. There was no hint of flirtation or humor. He was deadly serious.

I swallowed hard and met his eyes. Holy shit, I was completely turned on by the thought of him handcuffing me. I am so going to hell.

I checked the locks on all the windows. I pulled the blinds and closed the curtains as Colby got ready for his meeting. I walked him to the door. He pulled me in for another long kiss before admonishing me to lock the door behind him and then he was gone. The uniformed officer was parked in front of the house and per Colby's instructions, he was to walk the perimeter of the house at irregular intervals. I was not to leave the house for any reason. I was fine with that, besides I had some things to do before Colby returned. The lady parts needed attention if they were going to get some action tonight. All I had to do was not get shot between now and then and all would be good. And by good, I mean fucking awesome because I was going to get laid.

After a hot shower and some personal attention, I felt revived. For the first time since Mike's death, I found myself thinking of something besides the awful events of that night. Now my thoughts were filled with anticipation, being wrapped in Colby's arms, running my hands down his hard body, not stopping until I reached that bit of heaven and had my hand wrapped around it. Stroking it, rubbing my thumb over its velvet tip, making him moan with pleasure. Sex with Colby was a coping mechanism, but I would take it. If indecent thoughts of him could drive away the demons that were haunting me, I could accept that. At least for tonight. Tomorrow it would all start again, I knew that and I'd be ready. If I could just have tonight, I could face tomorrow.

I headed into the kitchen and took a quick inventory. I hadn't done much cooking since Peter and I separated. The grocery store wasn't exactly on the to-do list the last couple of days. I did manage to scare up enough ingredients to make dinner. I pulled chicken breasts out of the freezer and popped them into a bowl of cold water to thaw. I grabbed butter, lemons and carrots out of the refrigerator. The little pantry revealed flour, egg noodles and olive oil. I could work with this.

When Colby came through the door a while later, I was busy pounding the chicken breasts flat and dredging them in flour. He kissed my neck as I added the chicken to the hot frying pan. I turned around and captured his lips with mine, kissing him deeply, so there'd be no doubts about what was for dessert.

"I did not get shot at while you were gone," I said as I turned back to the chicken.

"I'm glad to hear it. What's for dinner?" he replied while snatching a carrot slice and popping it into his mouth.

"Chicken Piccata and honeyed carrots. I have wine chilling in the refrigerator if you want to open it." I added the lemons and lemon juice to the pan, turned down the flame and went to drain the noodles. "Want to hand me two plates, please?"

Colby moved around my kitchen with ease. He'd been on hand ever since that first night, when he brought me home...two days ago...or was it three? I was losing all track of time. He had made himself at home and I was glad. He had been sleeping on the couch, being a complete gentleman, after my feeble explanation of my questionable moral dilemma. That was all going to change. My divorce papers signed, though not yet filed, was a technicality I could live with tonight. Colby would be in my bed. I tossed the noodles with butter and added some to each plate. I topped them with chicken and spooned sauce over everything. I added the carrots to the side, grabbed some fresh lemon slices and placed those on top of each breast. I finished up by sprinkling on some dried parsley flakes. Fresh would have been nice, but this was not the week I was going to cook like Julia.

Colby poured wine into my only two wine glasses. We grabbed our plates and sat down at the long table in the dining area. I'd put placemats down along with utensils and cloth napkins. Eat your heart out Martha. "Did you release my security guard?" I asked before taking a bite of the chicken. It turned out quite tasty.

"This is terrific," Colby said as he swallowed his first bite. "Yes, I released him before I came up. He said it was completely quiet, nothing suspicious."

"Good. Maybe Scary Dudes have realized I'm well protected and they'll give up," I said without any real conviction. Colby reached across the table and took my hand. He turned it over and kissed my palm. Dessert was going to be great.

We ate in silence. I wanted to ask about the meeting, but thought Colby could use a bit of downtime before I pelted him with a barrage of questions. He'd been working non-stop since Mike's murder, he'd earned a few minutes of quiet. When he'd finished the last bite on his plate, he sat back with his wine and looked positively relaxed and satisfied. I smiled and asked him if he'd like more.

"Yes, I would," he replied as he set his glass down. He leaned in and kissed me. "Oh, you meant dinner," he teased as he pulled away and picked up his wine glass again, "no, I'm good. It was delicious."

I pushed away from the table, kissed him lightly and started to clean up. I put the leftovers away and piled the dishes in the sink. I started to run water over them when Colby came up behind me. He wrapped his arms around me, nuzzled my neck and whispered in my ear, "Do we need to do those now?" I didn't reply. I turned, took his hand and led him upstairs. On the way, we passed the desk in the alcove where my signed divorce papers sat, freeing me to do as I pleased.

My desire for Colby was edged with the realization that my life was never going to be the same again. I was effectively packing away my married life and embarking on the road of single, divorced female. I wasn't sure how I felt about that, but I sure as hell wasn't going to let it interfere with getting naked with the strong, dark, green-eyed man dancing up the stairs with me. Whatever emotions threatened to dampen this moment would have to move into the dark corner of my psyche currently housing denial and grief. Eventually, I would have to open up that box, but not until I was sure I was going to live beyond today. Why do today what you might be too dead to do tomorrow?

My room was dark except for the excellent light show from the windows. I was going to add curtains when I first moved in, but the previous tenant had put in wonderful top down/bottom up blinds. I could leave the top third of the windows uncovered and have privacy, yet still let in all the beautiful city and celestial lights. I pulled away from Colby, walked around the room, opened all the windows, letting in the cool evening air. I then pulled all the shades about a quarter of the way down from the top, giving us all the privacy we desired. The room was beautifully lit by moonlight and the blaze of the city lights. As I pulled the last blind down, I looked out and saw the glow of lights from downtown where the courthouse stood. It reminded me that Colby had yet to mention his meeting. I turned, suddenly filled with suspicion and apprehension.

"You didn't say what happened at the meeting tonight. Are you any closer to finding out who did this?"

Colby walked over, wrapped his arms around me and kissed me deeply. He moved his hands down to my bottom, where he cupped my cheeks and pulled me in close. When it was obvious I was not fully committed to this and distracted by the case, he relented. He kissed my forehead and then tucked me under his chin. I rested my head on his chest. I could feel his breathing, the beating of his heart, and the warmth of him around me. "There isn't much to report," he began, "but TJ, it looks like Mike was working off the books. He wasn't the original Marshal on the Shiedeger business. He asked to be added to the case right after Shiedeger headed back here to Peoria. No one knows what he was working on before that, but he flew to Vegas as soon as the gambling was tied back here."

I went rigid. I pulled away from Colby. He didn't resist. I needed to process this information.

"So because of this, they think he was somehow involved in Shiedeger's death or in the gambling situation? It makes no sense," I protested, "why involve me if he was mixed up in something illegal?"

"Don't jump to conclusions, TJ. We aren't. All this is, is more information. Something to follow up on, we don't know where it leads, yet."

I looked into Colby's eyes, trying I guess, to see if he knew more than he was telling me, or if he believed Mike wasn't who I thought he was. All I saw was deep compassion for my pain. Reassured, I melted into his arms. I refused to let my fear and doubts overwhelm me, if only tonight. Tomorrow would be soon enough for all the dominoes to tumble. Mike, Scary Dudes and the desire I couldn't help feeling for Colby. Tonight I wanted, no, needed to feel every inch of Colby, to have him inside me, touching every part of me.

"Is there anything we can do about it tonight?"

"No," he said and drew me in close.

"Well, as long as there isn't anything we can do about it tonight," I teased as I fanned my hands over his powerful chest.

Colby kissed me, first lightly, brushing his lips across mine before deepening the kiss. His tongue teased open my lips and darted in, tangling with mine. I grabbed the front of his shirt and pulled him into me while I teased his tongue with my own. Colby moaned and put his hands underneath my t-shirt. His mouth moved to my neck and shoulder, kissing and nibbling his way down. Then he pulled my shirt up over my head and tossed it onto the chair next to my antique vanity. I watched it land across the arm and saw our reflection in the mirror as Colby moved the straps of my pink lace bra down my arms. He kissed the top of my shoulder and followed the arc of the strap with his mouth, kissing down my arm, kissing the lace outline at the top of my breast. He teased his tongue over and under the lace. I shivered with anticipation as he smoothed his hands over the satin cups before unclipping the small plastic hook between my breasts. The lace and satin fell away. The cool evening air and the prospect of Colby's mouth made my nipples firm and sensitive. He pulled me to the edge of the bed where he sat down and cupped my breasts in his hands, gently rubbing his thumbs across my aching nipples. Fire shot through me, liquefying every muscle in my body. I moaned, deep and low. Colby laughed under his breath as he squeezed my breasts between his hands, before finally taking one in his mouth, sucking hard on the nipple then running his tongue across it quickly. I gasped quietly as pleasure threatened to overtake me. I was burning up. I pulled back a bit, looked down, took his head in my hands and tipped his face up.

"What's so funny, Deputy Marshal?"

He nuzzled himself into the soft space between my breasts, then reached up and kissed me before answering. "I like the sounds you make."

I laughed and pushed him away. He fell back on the bed and pulled me with him. He rolled me on my back and straddled me, continuing to feast. He would lick and suck one nipple, move to the other and then he'd squeeze them together and dart his tongue over both. I arched my back with pleasure, the deep throbbing between my legs making me writhe underneath his weight.

"Fuck me," I pleaded in a whispered gasp.

"Not yet." He moved back to my lips, bruising them with his. I reached down and pulled his shirt over his head. If he wasn't going to give me that hard bulge, I was at least going to feel those well-honed muscles under my hands. He continued kissing me as I ran my hands over his arms, his chest, his abs. Damn. He'd make a washboard look soft. I'd have to hit the gym if I was going to continue down this road. I ran my hands up his back to his shoulders. Seriously, what kind of equipment did they have at the Marshals' gym?

Colby bit down on my nipple, pulling and sucking and my thoughts went back to the only rock hard part of his body I was interested in. I moved my hands down his back, ran them around the waist of his jeans until I found the buckle on his belt. I busied myself with the leather, pulling it from the clasp. The buttons of his jeans were next. I popped them with ease as his hardness pressed against them. Then I had what I wanted. I reached my hand beneath the band on his boxers and took a firm grasp. Colby stopped moving as I ran my thumb gently across the tip and then moved my hand down the shaft and up again.

Two could play at this game.

As Colby kicked off his jeans I kept a greedy grip on him, enjoying the feel as he throbbed and grew the more I stroked. Colby moaned as I cupped him before returning to my rock hard toy. I was so wet, I knew I could slip him in and ride him hard right now. But he had other plans. He slipped my pants off and wasted no time removing my little pink satin panties, escaping from my grasp in the process. I whimpered my displeasure, but before I could protest, he spread my legs and was kissing my thighs. "Oh, my god" was the last thought I had as he moved up my thigh.

His tongue was nearly to the promised land when his phone began to chirp.

Son. Of. A. Bitch.

EIGHT

More of me comes out when I improvise. – Edward Hopper

Colby's phone continued to ring. I looked up at him. The muscles in his arms and chest were taut as he leaned over me, the sweat beginning to glisten on his smooth, dark skin. There was frustration on his face. We both knew he had to answer. He got up and searched for his phone, somewhere in the crumpled pile of clothes at his feet. I started to get up. He shook his head and pointed to the bed. I settled back on my elbows as he answered the persistent ring.

"Jameson," he said tersely and then listened intently for a moment. "Where? That's not far from where we lost it this afternoon." He was listening again and I was sitting up on the bed, looking for my bra. "We'll be there in twenty." He ended the call and dropped the phone in the pocket of his jeans before pulling them on.

"Is it Scary Dudes?" I asked as I hooked my bra and adjusted the straps. I picked up the clothes I had been wearing, tossed them onto the bed and went to the closet to pull out a long-sleeved shirt and pair of jeans. The air had taken on the evening chill of late summer and I didn't know how long we'd be out in it.

"Only the SUV, they found it abandoned in the park." He pulled on his shirt and walked over to me, kissing me lightly on the lips, "Sorry. This," he gestured toward the bed, "is not over."

He could count on that, but right now, I needed to see this SUV. I checked my reflection in the mirror, sighing as I remembered how moments ago, Colby and I were the reflection. I tamed my hair into a ponytail and made sure my makeup didn't give anything away. I headed downstairs with Colby close behind. I grabbed my cell and my bag, before taking my denim jacket out of the closet by the front door. I watched Colby strap on his gun holster, check his weapon and then toss on his leather jacket. I held the door open for him. Then I followed him out, locking both locks before we headed downstairs and into the cool night.

We rode in silence to the park, retracing our route down Glen Avenue, past the well-lit red water tower and into the parking lot at the entrance of the deeply wooded park. There were police cars everywhere. Peoria patrol cars, lights flashing, covered the entrance and parking lot. Colby rolled down his window, identified himself and was waved forward toward a State Police van at the back of the lot. The two officers knew Colby on sight. They stepped up to the window, nodding at me before talking with Colby.

"The SUV is about half mile down that spur," the sandy-haired male officer said, "just follow the road and you'll come up on the others"

"Your boss is there waiting for you," added the no-nonsense red-headed female officer. Colby nodded and thanked them before driving on. I was tense, my whole body vibrating. This was the car that had run me off the road. These men might have killed Mike and shot at me. I didn't know what I was expecting, but I wanted the SUV to give me answers and I didn't want those answers to point to Mike's guilt. Colby reached over and gave my thigh a squeeze. I managed not to jump out of my seat at his touch.

"You okay?"

I sighed and wrapped my hand around his, "Yeah. I want this to be something. I'm tired of being shot at. It's annoying." I reached over in the dark cab and squeezed something that was definitely not his thigh. "I have better things to do with my time."

Colby parked next to an unmarked Suburban. The truck barely stopped before I was out. Colby joined me in front of the Silverado as I surveyed the scene. The air was thick with the smell of pine trees. There was a deep covering of needles on the ground, muffling all sound, making it absurdly quiet despite all the activity. We walked over to the circle of people around the black Escalade, which was now the star of the show. Several spotlights illuminated it and every vehicle in the circle around it had its lights on, creating virtual daylight. People with gloves, bags and clipboards were examining every inch of the ground around it. A dark-haired woman was snapping photos inside the vehicle. It was a dizzying display of teamwork.

I followed Colby as he walked up to his boss, Chief Deputy Marshal Dan Strickland, a tall man with pale skin, grey hair and a U.S. Marshal windbreaker. I had to guess by his complexion that at one time he had been blonde. His features were still striking and he was younger than his grey hair suggested. He smiled when he saw me and there was a suggestion of lines around his dark eyes.

"TJ, thanks for coming out this late," Dan said as he held out his hand. It was warm and strong as I shook it. "Is this the SUV?" he asked as he walked us over to it, parting the officers like Moses in the process.

I knew immediately that it was, but I decided to let Colby take the lead. He walked carefully around the vehicle, noting its condition and the license plate. I wanted to see the front end, to see where it hit my little SuzieV. There it was, the damage to the bumper, just a little dent actually, but it was enough. I resisted the urge to run my finger across the indentation, assuming I'd have twenty officers pulling their weapons on me, saying something dramatic like, *step away from the vehicle, ma'am.* Nobody wanted that.

Colby came around to the front and stood next to me.

"What do you think, Kit-Kat, this the bad guys' ride?"

"Yup. And it's Scary Dudes. Get it straight." I looked up at him and smiled. There was something in his manner, that inner calm he had perfected, that made me believe everything was going to be okay.

"Dan," he called over to his boss, "the lady says that this vehicle belongs to the Scary Dudes who ran her off the road."

"All right, you heard the man, let's get to work," Dan commanded. We walked back over to him. He looked tired. "I'm not sure what we'll get from it, but hopefully something. Why don't you two go on home? There's not much else you can do out here tonight. I'll call you if we find something."

I was grateful. It was getting chilly and I was exhausted. Colby put his arm around me and steered me back toward the truck.

"TJ," Dan called after us, "I'm sorry about all of this. I promise we'll get to the bottom of it."

"Thanks."

I was silent as we turned out of the parking lot and back onto the street heading to my apartment. My mood was dark. First of all, I missed out on my orgasm and now it looked like our best lead was abandoned in the middle of the woods. I was beginning to question what life choices had led me here and what I needed to repent in order to get God back on my side.

"Tell me what you like," Colby asked, interrupting the mental list of transgressions I was compiling. I turned to look at him. His face had the appearance of 'serious police officer' - although there was something else.

"I'm sorry, what I like?" I asked, genuinely puzzled.

"Yeah, what do you like? Do you like it slow and sensual? Do you like to be stripped naked or do your own little striptease? What about positions..."

"Are you kidding me?" I interrupted before he could go any further, "we just lost our only lead and you want to quiz me on my sexual preferences..."

"Oh, sexual preference, I assumed you were into men, but if you like girls, too, I can work with that." His face had lost all of its seriousness, replaced by a smile that lit up the dark cabin.

"No. I like men. Strictly men. No judgments, but I prefer penises," I protested.

"Okay, I got that covered. Tell me what you like," he pressed.

"I can't do *that*," I replied emphatically.

"Why not?"

"I'm not that kind of girl."

"I've kissed you. You are definitely that kind of girl. Now come on, spill." He reached over, placed his hand on my thigh and slowly moved it upward. The warmth gave me a rush to all the good spots. Okay, maybe I could play this game, but the nagging voice in the back of my head was whispering again. How much do I know about this man? *Shut up,* I snapped at it. I'd spent my entire life doing what I was supposed to do and where had it gotten me? Divorced, broke and stuck in Peoria, IL. Not to mention shot at multiple times. I think it was time I tried something different. I licked my lips, closed my eyes and swore to myself as I decided to give it a try.

"I like...."

"TJ, I think there's someone in your apartment."

While I had been debating my ability to talk dirty to an almost stranger, we had arrived back at my place. I cursed my lack of spontaneity and then looked up to my living room window. There was clearly a dim beam of light moving through the room. Colby was on the phone calling for backup. He had turned off the headlights but kept the engine running. My heart was racing. I reached over and Colby took my hand and gave it a reassuring squeeze.

"Backup is on the way. We'll just sit tight." He unholstered his weapon and moved it to his lap, keeping his hand on it. I pulled my legs up and wrapped my arms around my knees to keep myself from shaking. I kept an eye on the window.

The intruder seemed to have moved away from the living room, I could see a dim, pinpoint glow deep in the room. A black car pulled up behind us, its lights off. I assumed this was our backup. Colby's phone vibrated with a text. He texted back, then reached up and flipped the button on the dome light so it wouldn't illuminate the cabin when he opened his door.

"Stay put for a minute," he said before stepping out and talking to the man walking up from the car. A woman joined them a moment later. The three of them chatted briefly before Colby walked over to my door and opened it. I stepped out and Colby introduced Marshals Tina Lupo and Tom Carter. "There's a patrol car in the alley, watching the back entrance. We're going to go in together. You are going to hang back behind us and you DO NOT come into the apartment until I tell you."

I followed the three of them up the narrow stairs. When we reached the landing, I started to give Colby my keys, but he waved me off and gestured for me to go back down the stairs. I went to the landing in front of Mrs. Cavaleri's door and looked up. All three Marshals had their weapons drawn and Colby slowly used his foot to push open my door. No key needed. Colby pulled back and stood, alert, at the side of the door jamb as Tina entered my apartment. Tom followed and then Colby disappeared into the breach. The quiet was unnerving, broken only by a whispered, "Clear."

After what seemed like an eternity, Colby popped his head out the door and told me to come on up. I took the stairs two at a time and when I stepped over the threshold everything went wavy. I took a deep breath and grabbed onto the door frame as I looked around. Every light in my apartment was ablaze. Everything in my living room had been tossed around, tipped over or pulled out. I could tell from the look in Colby's eyes that I could expect the same or worse in every other room. I took a deep breath and stepped inside, trying to comprehend what had happened.

Two hours later, the State Police and Marshals had finished processing the mess. I stayed at the kitchen table while they worked. Someone brought me a large coffee in a cup emblazoned with the Dunkin Donuts logo.

My kitchen looked like it had been attacked by a hyperphagic grizzly. Not content to pull out drawers and empty cupboards, whoever did this emptied the glass canisters where I kept all my dry goods. Cereal, flour, sugar, rice, coffee and spices were spilled all over my pantry shelves and tracked across my kitchen floor, intermingling with the forks, spoons and cookware, strewn about erratically.

This had taken time. Whoever did this must have broken in as soon as Colby and I left. They'd been watching us. My guess was Scary Dudes. They probably abandoned the SUV with this in mind. The weirdest part of the entire evening? There was no one in the apartment when Colby entered it and the patrol car out back didn't see anyone leave. We definitely saw a light in the window. There was no possible way that person was responsible for the destruction before me. So who was he and why was he here? More importantly, where did he go?

Colby came into the kitchen and sat down at the table. He looked tired, worried and angry. He reached over and snagged my coffee cup, taking a long sip. He was stubbled, disheveled, looking dangerous and hot as hell. He set the cup down, caught me looking at him and before I could glance away in embarrassment, gave me a long, smoldering look. It didn't take a psychic to know what he was thinking. Suddenly I wished all the people swarming my apartment would disappear. I wanted to strip this man and feel his strong body against mine, feel him hard inside me. At that moment I didn't care who tossed my apartment, all I cared about was getting the night I deserved.

"They're about done," he said, obviously reading my mind, "then we should get some sleep. We can start clean-up tomorrow." Drat, he clearly wasn't reading my mind. "I'm thinking it was your Scary Dudes who did this."

"Why?" I asked. A question that had been haunting me from the moment I stepped in the door tonight. "What were they looking for, or were they just trying to scare me?"

"I wish I had those answers, Kit-Kat."

"I didn't even know Mike that well."

"I suppose they thought differently since the two of you met for dinner and drinks every night."

I froze. I looked at Colby and all my desire evaporated. "How do you know that?" I asked. "How do you know we met for dinner every night?"

He didn't answer. With every second that ticked by, my chest contracted and my mind raced with terrible scenarios: Colby manipulating me to get information, Colby deliberately losing Scary Dudes, Colby shooting Mike.

"We were watching him."

"You were watching him?" I asked incredulously. "Why? He was working on the gambling case with the State Police, with the Marshals. He had me looking at Shiedeger's connections. That's practically all we talked about." I felt the walls closing in on me. "Colby, was he doing something illegal?"

"Not illegal, exactly," he began before looking around at all the ears in the vicinity, "let's talk about this when we've finished here, okay?"

No, it wasn't okay. "Are they done upstairs?" My heart was racing and I wanted to ravage Colby, and not in the good way.

"I think so, I'll check." He went into the little alcove and had a quick conversation with the technician who was in charge of this portion of the evening. Colby nodded to me when he got confirmation and I escaped upstairs.

The bedroom was as disastrous as the rest, but at least the mattress and box spring, flipped and tossed to one side of the tiny room by the intruders, had been placed back in the bed frame. The remainder of the room was exactly as I'd left it two hours ago when Colby brought me up to see if anything obvious was missing. Now as I looked around, it was the perfect representation of my psyche. A blur of colors, lines and shapes, haphazard, making absolutely no sense, until you looked closer and then everything had a meaning and a place. Jackson Pollack in 3-D. I wasn't sure where to begin.

I walked over to my dresser. Everything that rested on top of it now resided somewhere on the floor mixed with lingerie, sweaters, socks and trash. In their place were the contents from the drawers, hastily tossed panties, my favorite pair of winter socks, a garter and an unopened box of condoms. Drawers were either open and empty or pulled completely out and tossed into the heap on the floor. I took a deep breath, closed my eyes and tried to remember exactly what the dresser looked like a few hours ago.

The only way I knew to get through this was to become the artist, to let everything slip away, all that mattered was the empty canvas before me. Thoughts of Colby and Mike and Scary Dudes melted away as I meticulously recreated my dresser. When I opened my eyes, I had a clear image with which to work. I set about the task. Slowly I began to restore order. By the time Colby joined me, the dresser was a masterpiece and I had moved on to the closet.

"Impressive," Colby said when he walked in. I was in the closet, my back to him. I didn't bother to turn around. He sat on the still unmade bed. "Everyone is gone, they didn't find anything. Both locks were picked, looks like they wore gloves and came in the way they went out The back door was locked."

"They were gone long before we got back," I ventured, "so what was that light we saw? It had to be someone else and how did they disappear?"

"I don't know. Mrs. Cavaleri isn't home. We had the landlord let us in to make sure. Maybe they slipped in there and then disappeared while we were up here, before we had enough manpower to cover everything. That's what I would do."

That made me stop rearranging the clothes and turn around. I looked at Colby sitting on my bed, the bed that merely hours ago held so much passion, and realized I had scant knowledge of him. Little about Mike, either. I'd been reckless, under the spell of hormones and stress. That had to stop. At least until we knew what else was going on or who else was going to try to kill me.

"What about Mike? What haven't you told me?" I asked, afraid of the answer. Up to this point, without further explanation, I assumed Mike was under suspicion because Shiedeger was murdered on his watch.

"Mike was working off the books and he was working with you. Then people started dying." Colby began. I'm reasonably certain my heart stopped beating at that point, so I almost missed it when he added, "That tends to raise suspicions."

Once again, the room began to spin. "What do you mean, working with me? I was at the funeral home. The funeral home was on call when Shiedeger died. It was pure chance he ended up there. He said I was the safest contact." I wanted to sit down, but I didn't want to sit next to Colby on the bed, in case my hormones made a sneak attack. I walked over to the upholstered chair and pushed the clothes I'd been sorting onto the floor. I sat down, knowing what was coming next would be worse.

"Mike wasn't part of the Shiedeger case. He only showed up in Peoria after Shiedeger turned up dead and at Butterfield. He was assigned to the task force working with your father when he disappeared. No one in my office believed it was a coincidence when he started working with you."

"Wait, Mike is...was my age, how could he have been working with my dad?"

"Well, your father has been a key asset for years, until he disappeared about eighteen months ago."

"My father is dead," I said emphatically, "he died when I was three."

Colby was still for a moment and with his next words, my whole world went into slow motion. "Your father, Thomas Joseph Wilde, is not dead.

NINE

I think that if you shake the tree, you ought to be around when the fruit falls to pick it up. – Mary Cassatt

I was underwater. There had to be some mistake. Everything took on a fantastical, swirling quality, as if the entire room was painted with van Gogh's brush.

Colby continued on, unaware that all the oxygen had left the room. "As far as we know, he's still alive. For years, he was in WITSEC…witness protection. As time went by, he became an asset. He'd help on the occasional forgery and counterfeit case until the Marshals finally brought him on as a full-time consultant. Eighteen months ago, he simply vanished. We don't know if it was because of the case he was working on or if maybe his identity had been exposed. Counterfeit money and treasury bills provide a lot of temptation."

I stood up and began to pace. "My dad is dead," I repeated. "My mom took me to his graveside every Father's Day of my childhood. You're mistaken. You are all mistaken."

Realization hit Colby's eyes. He stood up and came to me, I waved him off and continued to pace. When I looked at him again, he looked sick, his face drained of blood, his green eyes stricken.

"You didn't know? Mike didn't tell you? No one told you?"

"No, I didn't know!" I shouted at him. "Mike told me he needed my help tracking whoever came and went at the funeral home, asked me to snoop through paperwork. He had me wear an earpiece and camera at the memorial service. Why would he do that if he was interested in my dad?" I was on the verge of hysteria. "All he cared about was Shiedeger. That's it. It was Shiedeger. He was here for Shiedeger."

Nothing felt real. My whole life was a lie. My dad was alive…or maybe now he was dead and all those intervening years when he was alive meant nothing. Nausea overwhelmed me. There was no way I would make it downstairs to the bathroom so I grabbed my trashcan and threw up. When I was done, I threw up again. Then I took the trashcan downstairs and locked myself in the bathroom.

The cold tile floor felt good, felt real, felt solid. Maybe if I sat here for a while my world would stop spinning. Then I would once again know what was true and what was some lie told to me by people I cared about.

When I finally found the strength to stand, I cleaned up and exited the bathroom. Colby was in the kitchen, sweeping up the floor. He started to speak. I raised my hand to stop him and dragged myself upstairs. He had the bed all made. I hoped he had enough sense to know he wasn't going to sleep in it. I stripped off my clothes, dug through the mess on the floor next to the chair and found a t-shirt. I threw it on and crawled into bed. I didn't think I would be able to sleep, my mind racing, but once my head hit the pillow, exhaustion swept over me.

I slept until sunlight and the cacophony of bird chatter woke me. I reached out to check my clock, only to have my hand sweep over an empty nightstand. Before my eyes were fully open, dread filled me as yesterday's events came flooding back. A knot formed in my stomach and my head began to ache. I got out of bed, ignoring my instinct to crawl under the covers and never emerge. I recognized the only way to cope was to take charge and face things head-on. I dug through my clothes and found what appeared to be an entire outfit. I found my robe and some clean lingerie, at least I hoped they were clean, but I couldn't find the shoes I wanted. Oh well, this was a start. I threw my robe on, gathered my things and headed to shower. Colby was sleeping on the couch and I was grateful I didn't have to face him. As soon as I could stand under a hot stream of water and clear my head, things were going to change.

When I walked into the kitchen thirty minutes later, I was clean, dressed and ready for work, if I could find the shoes that went with this outfit. Screw it, if I had to, I'd wear mismatched running shoes to work. Colby was making coffee. He looked like his Silverado had driven over him a couple of times. Good. Someone should feel as awful as I did. I couldn't think of a better candidate. He looked up, gauged my mood and then retreated to the refrigerator for milk. Cop instincts.

"I'm going to work," I stated. This was not going to be a negotiation. "I understand you feel you need to watch over me. You can do it from outside the building. You will not disrupt my office in any manner. Are we understood?"

His look was noncommittal, but he didn't argue.

"I will take care of the apartment when I get home this evening."

"TJ," he started, cautiously, "we can get some help in here to put things back together, you don't need to do it all your..."

"No," I cut him off sharply, "I do not want anyone touching my things. No one. Do you understand? No one." And with that, I went upstairs. I charged into my bedroom closet and by sheer will, found the shoes I wanted. Even my closet knew not to mess with me this morning. I went downstairs, grabbed my bag and keys. Colby was waiting for me at the door. I was going to tell him to go fuck himself. I'd drive myself to work, then I remembered I didn't have a car.

"And I want my car back here by the end of the day," I said, then walked out the door and down the stairs not caring if he was following or not.

The drive to work made the funeral home feel like a rave by comparison. Not a word was spoken between us and I looked straight ahead the entire route. I would have looked out my side window, but watching the buildings whiz by made me queasy and I didn't want a repeat of last night. The ten-minute trek felt more like an hour and when Colby pulled into the parking lot, I bolted out of the car. I paused only long enough to lean into the truck and warn him.

"You are not to come into my office today. I am perfectly safe inside. You'll have to be content to keep watch out here." I turned on my stylish heel, walked up the front steps and through the hundred-year-old doors. Once inside I made a beeline for my office. Harsh whispers, which sounded like thunder in the tomb-like building, were coming from one of the viewing rooms. I sighed, tossed my purse on my desk and went in search of the newest funeral home crisis.

I reached the door to viewing room three, otherwise known as the Oak Room. Each state room had a dignified name, so visitors and families didn't feel like they were cattle assigned to a numbered paddock. The Oak Room, when needed, opened up into the Lincoln Room to make one large room for informal services or large viewings. Otherwise, the Oak Room was an intimate space, decorated in greens and of course, oak, where families could say their final goodbyes. Music was quietly piped into all the rooms, or a family could use the small stereo system in each room to play the deceased's favorite tunes.

Right now though, the only sounds coming from this viewing room were the harsh voices I had followed like breadcrumbs. The door was slightly ajar, so I peeked through the space between the door and the jamb. I was surprised to see Nick and Dee in the midst of a heated argument. Dee looked pissed. I couldn't imagine what Nick had done this time, but I knew this couldn't go on. They were arguing in front of Mr. Dunham, and while in his condition it didn't much matter, his family could arrive at any moment for today's festivities. Mourning and polite platitudes were on the schedule, not Maury Povich. I took a deep breath and stepped into the line of fire.

"Hello," I said quietly, "is everything all right?" They both froze. I saw fear dart across Nick's face. Dee faced away from me, staring at the large arrangement of lilies on the sideboard. Oookay, maybe this wasn't what I thought it was, maybe something besides funeral home shenanigans were going on here. "I'm sorry, I didn't mean to interrupt. It was a little loud by the front doors. I didn't think you'd want families to overhear you."

Dee turned sharply and redirected her fury at me. "Why don't you mind your own goddamn business?" she hissed and then stormed out, leaving a sheepish Nick standing there, looking at his feet. He didn't say anything, only shuffled uncomfortably. Finally, he looked up at me and shrugged.

"I'll be in my office if you need me," was all he said before slinking out the door.

What the hell? Mild-mannered Dee, whom I never heard raise her voice the entire time I'd worked here, suddenly developed a spine and was using it to beat Nick until he seemed actually…ashamed? Maybe cowed was a better word. Shame would be a big leap for him. I walked over to Mr. Durham. He looked peaceful. I reached down and straightened his tie a bit. I was becoming comfortable with the dead when they were embalmed, dressed and casketed. It was all so neat and tidy, so unlike my life. I paid my respects, signed his guestbook and went to my office.

I dug into my messages first. There were two requests for Nick to speak, one with the Chamber of Commerce and the other at the American Legion. This was good. It meant my strategy was working. Get Nick out into the community where his goodtime Charlie persona was appreciated. He sucked at business and he wasn't a great funeral director, but everyone has a talent. Nick excelled at the handshaking and schmoozing. My job was to put it to good use. I wrote down the details and set out to track down the boss. Chances were he wasn't in his office, but I'd start there anyway.

Nick's office was on the second floor near the front of the old mansion. It was as close to a corner office as one could get in an old house. It had large windows facing north and east, giving him a view of the river through the old trees that surrounded the property. It was well-appointed with dark wood and leather, designed by Alton, Jr. and unchanged by the current resident. Why would he change it, he was rarely in it. True to form, the office was empty.

My next best guess was the basement. Ugh. How I hated going down there. It was creepy. There were all manner of dark, dank spaces filled with overstock caskets, urns and god-knows-what-else. I opened the door at the top of the stairs. The lights were on, this was a good indication Nick might be down there...or Freddy Krueger. Some days I rooted for Freddy. I crept down the stairs because the eerie vibe mandated a slow and stealthy pace. As I descended, the dank mold smell overwhelmed me as my eyes adjusted to the low light. As if the basement wasn't creepy enough, none of the light bulbs were over forty watts, keeping it cave-like. Cool, damp and dimly lit, yup, the perfect place to keep your casket stock...or your crazy serial killer uncle.

As I walked down the hall there was a steady, scrape-plunk-scrape-plunk sound coming from the room at the end of the hall. I surmised that room used to be a coal room, where coal was delivered and stored in the early 1900s. It had a short door, even at five-six, I had to duck under to enter, and an oddly boarded up area against the outside wall. They used the room now to store cremains no one claimed. Hard to believe, I know. You go to all the trouble to have Great-Aunt Betty cremated and then never think to pick her up. There were cremains in this room that dated back to the 1950s.

The scrape-plunk-scrape-plunk continued and I had no idea what it was. Undaunted, I turned the glass knob on the door and had to pull hard to get it to open. Every door and drawer in the basement stuck due to the dampness. The door scraped across the floor as it opened and I was startled to see Jacob, jacket off, tie loosened and shirt collar unbuttoned.

"Jacob! Wasn't expecting you," I said a bit breathlessly after my tug of war with the door. "What in the world are you doing?"

Jacob sighed and leaned against one of the dusty shelves. "Would you believe someone came by to collect the cremains of their great-great-grandfather? Records show he was cremated in 1967. I've been searching for twenty minutes and I haven't found him yet. There's no rhyme or reason to anything here."

"How many containers are in here?"

"About two hundred," he said with resignation, "I'm not even through half of them yet." He reached for another container and scraped it across the shelf as he pulled it from the back toward the dim light. He checked the nameplate on the bottom and with a plunk, set it on the floor. Cremation containers surrounded him, looking like little ducks gathered at his feet. "I don't know what they are going to tell his family if he's not here. What are you doing down here? I didn't think anyone came down here voluntarily." He laughed as he reached for another container.

"I'm trying to find Nick. You haven't seen him, have you?" I asked hopefully.

"He gave me this assignment and then headed to the garage. Did you try his cell?"

"He left it on his desk," I said and Jacob gave me a knowing nod before going back to his endeavor. "Well, good luck."

Back upstairs, I debated asking Dee if she knew where I could find Nick but decided against it. Something was going on there and I wanted nothing to do with it. I had enough drama in my life without worrying about those two. I went back to my office, picked up the phone and dialed the extension for the garage. Jim picked up on the third ring.

"Hey TJ, whatcha need?" he asked when he picked up.

"What, I can't just call the garage to say good morning?" I said and he laughed. "Actually I was wondering if Nick was out there." I had my fingers crossed because my next option was the gatehouse, which meant I wouldn't see him for the rest of the day.

"Yup, he's here, hang on." Jim put the phone down. I could hear muffled voices and then Nick was on the line.

"Hi TJ, what's up?"

"I need to discuss a few speaking requests if you have the time," I said as I rolled my eyes. I could not demand that the boss to get his skinny ass to my office so I could get some work done. It tended to shorten one's employment.

"Sure, I'm about done here. Meet me in the kitchen in ten," he said and then hung up.

"Okay, sure, that sounds great. How's your morning going TJ? Oh fine, I recently found out my long dead father might be alive and my apartment looks like it was attacked by wolverines, but other than that, I'm just dandy," I said to no one. I looked out the window toward the parking lot. Colby was across the street, standing next to his truck. He was talking on his cell phone and surveying the area. I missed him.

Ten minutes later, I went up to the kitchen. Nick was pouring two cups of coffee and had pulled stale donuts out of the box, leftover from our staff meeting. He looked over at me and gestured with a donut. Realizing I skipped breakfast and I was lightheaded from hunger, I nodded yes. He popped both donuts in the microwave and hit the button. Seconds later, they came out warm and almost fresh. I sat at the table and Nick brought over the mugs and the donuts, setting one of each in front of me.

"Hey sorry about the ruckus this morning," he started as he sat down. "I guess it was a bit unprofessional." I tried not to choke on my donut. First Dee raised her voice and now Nick was worried about being unprofessional. It must be opposite day at the mortuary and no one told me.

"I don't think anyone heard anything, so no harm" I replied to reassure him. He nodded, content with this.

"You have speaking requests for me? Good ones I hope. I hate going to the old folks' home and giving talks. I feel like the grim reaper."

"No, no, but I can see how that might..." I didn't get to finish because there was a blood-curdling scream from downstairs.

Nick and I ran down the stairs and toward the screams. I was terrified that Scary Dudes had somehow gotten past Colby and were now assaulting Dee, but the screams had turned into yelling and cursing. By the time we reached the Oak Room, it sounded like a melee had broken out. We rounded the corner and stood at the entrance to the room. Two middle-aged women, Mrs. Dunham, the widow, and Ms. Jennings, the deceased's sister, if I remembered correctly, were going at each other like WWE wrestlers. The rest of the guests were trying to pull them apart. Ms. Jennings was screaming that Mrs. Dunham had killed her brother. It seemed to center on her nagging, her bad cooking and Bunco nights. Nick waded in and tried to bring order to the chaos. Dee finally showed up.

"I'd better get Jacob and Jim," was all she said before walking away.

Suddenly, a large arrangement of calla lilies in a tall crystal vase crashed to the floor. Everyone went silent, looking at the Dalí-like tableau on the floor of broken glass, water and decapitated lilies. Then the screaming started again, with Mrs. Dunham accusing Ms. Jennings of ruining a two hundred dollar flower arrangement and insinuating it was on purpose. Ms. Jennings screamed back that her brother hated calla lilies and a good wife would know that. Nick looked over at me, shook his head and then waded back in, trying to calm everyone. Jacob and Jim finally appeared and did their best to help separate everyone and restore order. I wish I could say all of this was a unique workday experience. It wasn't. I walked back to my office and closed the door.

A few minutes later, Nick opened my door and leaned in.

"Crisis averted. Go ahead and book those requests. The only night I'm not free is Friday, my band is playing at Jimmy's Bar," he said before ducking back out and shutting the door. I worked in relative quiet for another hour, then there was a knock on my door and it opened.

"I come in peace," Colby said, holding up a bag from Sarah's Deli, down the street. He must have had it delivered because I couldn't imagine him leaving his post. I was torn between hunger, desire and the need to punish someone for everything that had happened. Hunger won out.

"Come on in. But that better be a turkey club and chips in that bag."

He put the bag on my desk. He opened it, pulled out a sandwich, unwrapped it and revealed that is was indeed a turkey club.

"We need to talk," he said as he pulled the other chair up to my desk and sat down.

"Yes, we do."

TEN

What is important is to spread confusion, not eliminate it. – Salvador Dalí

I dug into my sandwich and watched Colby warily. I had so many questions I wanted to ask him, about my father, about Mike, but I wasn't ready yet. I felt fragile. One more blow and I would splinter into a million pieces with no confidence I could be put back together. Divorce, murder, assaults, Mike's web of lies and now the impossible possibility my father could be alive. *Alive.* That thought simultaneously thrilled and angered me. It was so overwhelming I couldn't spend too much time thinking about it without losing my equilibrium. No, it would be a while before I could delve deeper into this with Colby.

I should call my mom, but what would I say? "Hey mom, did you know dad was alive all this time?" Either I was going to give her the shock of her life or I was going to be pissed as hell. Neither prospect was one I was eager to contend with, at least not today. I would have to know more, Colby would have to give me the details, to prepare me for that conversation.

"Can we talk?" Colby asked as he nicked a potato chip from my bag.

"Depends," I answered cautiously. I took another bite of my sandwich to give him time to bring up whatever was obviously on his mind. He fiddled with my stapler, opening and closing it as he tried to find his way into the conversation.

"TJ," he began in a very serious tone, "I didn't know..."

"I can't talk about that yet," I cut him off sharply in a tone that left no doubts. He looked at me, obviously pained by my pain.

"Okay. Look, up to this point, I've considered us a team. Working together to find Mike's killer and working together to keep you safe. You're smart, quick on your feet and you kind of think like a cop. It worked."

"I feel a big but coming."

"But...when it comes down to it, I'm a cop. I'm a Deputy U.S. Marshal and my job is to protect you. You are a witness to the murder of a Marshal. My job, whether you like it or not, is to protect you with my life. And I will do that, with or without your cooperation."

I chewed on my sandwich and let the silence stretch between us. I felt the schism I wasn't sure we'd ever be able to bridge. Finally, I said, "Well, you've made your position clear. I have to get back to work. Thanks for the sandwich." I pulled out a pile of meaningless papers from my standing file. I pretended to concentrate on them while I munched on the remaining potato chips, ignoring the tall, dark and very sexy man sitting to my right. I hoped he was as frustrated as I was. After a few more moments of silence, he stood up to leave.

"I will be waiting to take you home at five," and with that, he left. I took my first real breath since he knocked on my office door. I was a whirling tsunami of emotions, barely able to identify or sort them, but one emotion was edging out all the rest. My desire for Colby had not abated. I wanted him. What's more, what scared the shit out of me, was I wanted more than his hard, hot body. We had a natural rhythm together, as if we'd known each other for a lifetime. Silence with him was not silent. It was filled with comfort and desire. Conversations together were like picking up in the middle of one we'd been having for years. Sitting next to him in the Silverado felt right, as if I belonged. Having him sitting at my breakfast table made me wonder how I ever had coffee without him. It may have only been days since we met, but I could not deny the draw. As much as I argued with myself that it wasn't real.

I pulled out my notes on Nick's speaking engagements. I needed to stay busy because thoughts of Colby were not productive. Regardless of my feelings for him, my life was in chaos and I needed to fix that first. I made phone calls confirming dates and times and then added the information to the calendar we all shared. Since Nick was ridiculously bad about checking the calendar, I printed out all the information and buzzed his office. No answer. I called Dee, asking her if she knew where Nick might be.

"I have no idea," was her curt response before disconnecting.

I'd have to go looking for him. Again. I found him with Jacob in the casket room. This was where all the casket styles were on display, along with several big books of special order options that could be shipped in within a day. I never understood this, why one wood box mattered over another. Especially if one was heading to the crematory. Seemed like the waste of a good tree. I knew Nick's interest in the different designs and styles had to do with dollar signs. I entered the big room that was the mansion's sitting room, complete with fireplace and hearth at one end. Decorated, convincingly, in the style of a family living room, if you ignored the caskets carefully arranged throughout the space and lining samples hung on racks in one corner, next to the fancier urns. Nick was explaining to Jacob the importance of up-selling the bereaved. I refrained from rolling my eyes.

"Nick, sorry to interrupt, but when you have a chance, can we go over your schedule for the week?"

"I think we're done here. I believe Jacob has the idea," Nick said as he walked over to me. Behind him, Jacob rolled his eyes so hard, it must've hurt. I suppressed a smile. Nick ushered me out the door, taking the papers I'd printed and looking over them. "Let's go outside and get some fresh air," he continued as he walked toward the back door. I followed him, always eager to escape the hushed tones and oppressive smell of cut flowers that filled the funeral home daily.

In the backyard, out of sight of any guest, was an area created for the employees. It was set off from the parking lot and alley by two walls of twelve-foot tall lilac bushes, perfectly trimmed. There were two patio tables and eight chairs, a child's picnic table and a small fountain surrounded by a pretty flowerbed. It was peaceful and beautiful. I'm sure it was all the idea of Nick's mother when she was the manager. I couldn't imagine any of the current staff being this creative. If I had still been painting, I would have set an easel up and tried to capture it.

Nick and I settled at one of the patio tables. He looked over the schedule I set up for him and nodded. "This looks good. I really like these talks, TJ. I think I'm good at them. Better than I am at the whole, 'support the grieving family,' aspect of it. I'm glad you thought of this."

I was caught off-guard by his candor and apparent self-awareness. I scrambled to catch up. "You are really good at it. Every time you do one of these I get a call back telling me how much they enjoyed it," I said sincerely. It had taken me some time to find a way to use Nick in the best way for both him and the funeral home. I felt I'd really accomplished something when I came up with a creative way to utilize his abilities.

"You have brought a good energy here," he said, "and I know you were planning on leaving after your divorce was final, but I want you to know that we'd all be happy if you decided to stay."

I waited for a lascivious remark to follow this declaration. When it didn't happen, I once again felt like I was in bizarro-land. Alice walked through the looking-glass. Soon the playing cards would march across the lawn.

"Thanks, Nick, that means a lot." And it did. "I'll keep it in mind."

"You wouldn't want to come listen to one of my talks?" he asked, holding up the papers. "I would appreciate your input."

I was trying to beat down my suspicion that listening to one of his talks was going to end up with an invitation to something more, when a man dressed in black, wearing dark sunglasses and a black White Sox cap burst from the bushes, pointing a gun at us. Nick stood up and uttered an expletive. I would have screamed, but I guess I was becoming accustomed to being threatened. Instead, I stood up and asked him what the hell he wanted. He aimed directly at me and pulled the trigger as Nick pushed me to the ground. The sound was deafening. He didn't get a second shot off. Colby was around the corner and yelling for him to drop his weapon and get down. I tried to push Nick off me so I could see what Colby was doing. Nick didn't budge and I feared he'd been shot.

"Nick," I whispered harshly in his ear, "are you hurt? Did you get hit?"

He rolled off me, copping a feel on the way. "No, I was enjoying the moment. What the hell just happened?"

"I don't know," I lied. "Attempted robbery?"

"Was that your Marshal friend? Lucky he came along when he did," Nick stood up and helped me do the same, "looks as if he chased the guy off."

I scanned the yard as Colby came over to us and before I could ask, he shook his head.

"He ducked into the bushes and disappeared," Colby said as he helped me up. "Are you two okay?" I nodded as Nick straightened his jacket and swept the grass off his pants.

"That was amazing what you did, Nick, protecting me like that," I said genuinely.

"Well, I couldn't let something happen to you after I'd just convinced you to stay with us," he said with a laugh. I wondered how long it would take for the glib to wear off and the shock of what happened to set in. He looked at Colby and said, "Do we have to report this? It would be really bad for business to have police crawling all over the place."

He thought this had to do with his side business, nothing more. A robbery gone wrong, someone coming after his stash and the last thing he wanted was the police poking around, for fear they'd stumble on the gatehouse. Alice steps back through the looking-glass and all the world made sense again.

"I think I can file a report and keep it quiet. Since you're both all right and he didn't cause any damage." Nick seemed satisfied with this, thanked Colby again and went inside.

After he had gone, Colby sat me down at the patio table and asked me if I was really okay. I assured him I was.

"What happened to the Man in Black?" I asked, not sure how he could have gotten away with Colby that close.

"There's a little path in between two of the bushes, leads right into the alley. He was gone before I could get a shot off."

"Dammit. We cannot catch a break. Are you really not going to report this?"

"I'm going to tell Dan. If he feels the need to report it, that's up to him. Since I didn't fire my weapon, we have options. Think you can cut out early, now that your boss felt you up?"

"Caught that did you? I suppose it was only fair since he did kind of save me from being shot."

"Uh-huh," was all Colby said before escorting me to my office and helping me gather my things. I buzzed Nick and told him I was leaving early. He seemed eager to have Marshal Jameson leave the building, and with that, Colby and I left for my apartment.

Colby insisted on walking ahead of me as we climbed the three flights of stairs to my door. With all that had happened today, I'd almost forgotten that my apartment looked like I had my housekeeping done by angry monkeys. However, reality came crashing in as Colby held the door and I crossed the threshold.

Magic fairies had not reorganized the piles on the floor. I tossed my purse and my bags into the fray. What was one more item more or less? I walked into the kitchen, which was more depressing than the living room and dining area combined. I'd have to start there. Otherwise, I would be adding ants and rats to my list of troubles. Fuck it, I thought, and went upstairs to change my clothes. When I returned to the kitchen, I picked up the broom off the floor in front of the stove and dug through a pile of dishtowels, rags and placemats to find my dustpan. I started with sweeping anything unsalvageable to the far corner. I then went back and began to put my little pantry back together. Colby came in and asked if he could help. I resisted the urge to snap at him, wanting to lash out at someone. I was tired, tense, overwhelmed…and hungry.

"Pizza and beer."

"What?" he asked cautiously, afraid, I'm sure, of doing or saying anything that would push me further into the abyss.

"I would like pizza and beer…for dinner. Do you think you could arrange that?" I tried to sound friendly, but the best I could do was not bitchy. At least I hoped it wasn't bitchy. He left the kitchen. I assumed to hunt down dinner. I went back to fixing the only thing in my life I was able to, my kitchen. I filled the sink with hot water and squirted in dish soap. I picked up utensils from the counters and the floor and placed them in the sink. Colby came back and leaned against the refrigerator.

"Pizza and beer will be here in twenty," he said.

"Pepperoni?"

"Pepperoni, extra cheese, craft beer."

"Thanks," was all I could manage because anything else and I would have come undone. This man knew my pizza order. For some reason, as I stood in a kitchen that could have received federal disaster aid, that was the kindness that would be my undoing. We exchanged a long look, filled with everything we couldn't yet say. Finally, Colby walked over to the sink.

"Let me wash these," he insisted as he plunged his hands into the suds. I didn't object. We worked in comfortable silence for a long while. By the time my doorbell rang, we'd managed to have the kitchen almost back to normal. There was still a pile of pots and pans to clean and the linens needed to be laundered, nevertheless, the proverbial light at the end of the tunnel was near. Colby went to the door to pay for dinner, with his hand on his gun, I noticed. I grabbed napkins, two plates and picked my way across the dining area floor to the table. The good news was, the tabletop was cleared. The bad news, of course, was that everything was on the floor. I sat down and waited for my pizza.

Thirty minutes and four slices of pizza later, I was ready to face the kitchen again. Colby started in on the pots and pans while I put away the plates and bowls from the dish drainer. His phone rang and I handed him a towel to dry his hands so he could answer. It was a brief conversation. He hung up and slipped the phone into his pocket.

"That was Dan, he's downstairs. I'm going to go talk with him about what happened today," he said. He walked to the back door and made sure it was secured. "Will you be okay by yourself for a few minutes?"

I suppressed the smart-ass remark about taking care of myself since I was out of Colby's sight for barely a moment this afternoon and someone came after me. I understood and shared his concern. I nodded and he left. I let the water out of the sink, wiped everything down and then put on a pot of coffee. I would have preferred more alcohol, but it was going to be a long night. I walked past the dining room, resolutely ignoring it, and made my little alcove the next priority. I opened the small window at the bottom of the stairs to let a cool breeze in. It felt good.

I realized the whole apartment was hot and stuffy. Being on the third floor of a stone building, I never hesitated to leave the abundant windows open to get a cross breeze during the hot, muggy Illinois summer. Hundred-year-old buildings generally don't have central air and scaling thirty feet of rough-hewn stone to climb through an open window seemed like a lot of work for any criminal. However, we had closed and locked every one of them after the break-in. Now as I walked around and reopened them, the cool breeze invigorated me.

I went back to the alcove with my coffee poured over ice and a renewed sense of purpose. Someone had picked up my easel and put my painting back on it. It wasn't one in progress, instead, a favorite I kept propped on the easel. It justified having the easel set up in the corner of my tiny office. In the back of my mind, I suppose I hoped it would inspire. Most days it merely mocked. I straightened the easel out and adjusted the painting. Then I knelt on the floor and began to sort through the tubes of paints and assorted brushes strewn about the floor. Luckily, Scary Dudes weren't feeling vindictive enough to open the tubes and empty them all over. Acrylics are a bitch to get out of hardwood. My brushes didn't fare as well. Several had been stepped on either during the crime or subsequent investigation and snapped in half. I salvaged what I could and tossed the rest. I would have been more upset, but whether snapped in half or intact, I wasn't using them.

I went over to my desk and began to sift through the flotsam and jetsam on the floor beside it. As it is with desks, the drawers collected a large quantity of miscellaneous junk, all of which was now on my floor. I wasn't sure how to begin. My hunch was most of this could be tossed and not much missed. I pulled out the top two drawers and set them down next to me. I picked up the pencil tray and put it into one drawer, in the other, I placed two narrow baskets that had held various office supplies. With these as my guides, I began to sort items into each drawer. I picked up an empty file folder that sat atop the receipts, statements and bills it had contained and my heart skipped a beat. My hand shook as I reached down and moved papers out of the way. I couldn't believe what I was seeing. There it was....Mike's keychain.

ELEVEN

In painting you must give the idea of the true by means of the false. – Edgar Degas

I picked it up with shaking hand. It was a black and silver carabiner, scuffed and worn. No flash drive, but instead a single brass colored key. It wasn't a house key or car key. It had a long slender body with only two teeth and an oblong, flat head. I recognized that key. I got up, clutching the keychain, afraid it would evaporate before my eyes. I couldn't believe it was here, yet the disappointment that the flash drive was still missing tempered any excitement. I went into the living room and grabbed my purse, dug out my keys and sorted through the jumbled assortment. Hot damn, there it was. My safe deposit key hung from the chain, hastily clipped there a few weeks ago with the intention of stopping by the bank to take care of some final divorce loose ends. I checked the number on my key and the one on the key hanging from Mike's carabiner. The numbers matched. It was my second key. The one meant for Peter on our joint box, the one he never used, the one I tucked away once it became clear we were parting ways. My heart began to race. A tantalizing idea was forming in my sleep-deprived brain. I could only hope my hunch was right. I pulled the key off. At that moment, I heard Colby coming up the stairs. I slipped the carabiner and both keys into my jeans pocket and turned toward the door as it opened. With that simple act, I knew I changed everything.

"TJ," Colby called out as he closed the front door behind him. I came through the dining room, justifying to myself what I'd done as I walked into the living room.

"What did Dan have to say?" I asked casually, hoping his cop instincts would not kick in. At least until I had time to follow my hunch.

"He was not happy that his only witness, and I quote, 'in the custody of one of his best Deputies,' was the subject of an assault."

"Oh, please, like it's the first time," I said without thinking. "I mean," I backtracked, "Scary Dudes are obviously motivated and not deterred by a badge."

"Nice save. You're right though, a badge does not deter them and that's what concerns me the most. Dan said there is a security camera on one of the buildings at the end of the alley and he's pulling it. We might get lucky, but with the way things are going, I doubt it."

"Even if he shows up on them, it won't give you much. Guy in dark sunglasses and a White Sox cap. Didn't even have the decency to be a Cubs fan."

I didn't know if it was guilt or the events of the day, but once again, exhaustion swept over me. I couldn't face anymore cleaning, so I took a quick shower while Colby sat at the kitchen table and worked on his computer. In the shower, I made my plan. Thinking about the key, hidden away in the pocket of my jeans crumpled on the bathroom floor, kept me from thinking about the hard-bodied man sitting merely feet away from the bathroom door. I toweled off, pulled on my sweat shorts and oversized tee. I picked up my clothes and opened the bathroom door. Steam poured out and the cool air from the opened windows felt good on my damp skin. I stepped into the kitchen to say a quick goodnight to the sexy, dark man, sipping tea at my table.

"I'm headed upstairs," I said as he looked up from the computer screen, "I opened every window in the apartment while you were gone to cool things down. I didn't know if I should close and lock them all - if that would be safer."

"Probably a good idea, but I can take care of it. Get some rest."

With that, I headed upstairs to climb into bed with my secret and my virtue intact. Before I did, I buried the spare key deep in a rolled up sock and tucked it into the bottom of my laundry hamper. I had my key for tomorrow, but in case something happened, Colby might find it later and put the pieces together.

I awoke early, the sun was peeking over the horizon and the birds were going nuts. End of summer jamboree. I wanted to turn over and pull the covers up over my head, but then I remembered I had a plan for the day. This could be the beginning of the end of my nightmare. I lay back, watching the light play on the ceiling, listening to the birds as I went over the plan again, step by step. Everything depended on being able to ditch Colby for a few hours. It was not going to be easy. One whiff of anything suspicious and his cop instincts would kick in. I'd be lucky if he didn't handcuff me to the grab bar in his truck. No, I'd have to play it cool and the best way I knew to accomplish that was to channel the "you lied to me about everything" energy. My guess is he'd want to put as much distance between us as possible rather than face that all day. In addition, I would need my car.

When I entered the kitchen and poured myself coffee, I was dressed and ready for work. Colby looked up from his phone and gave me a quizzical look, but said nothing. I rustled through the refrigerator for milk and something to eat. Leftover pizza and a single apple stared back at me. Other than a few condiments, the shelves were bare, not even a drop of milk for my coffee. I knew the pantry was neat as a pin, but equally bare.

"I think we should make a grocery run after work tonight. I don't think I can face takeout again. And I definitely need milk for my coffee."

"Okay, we can do that," Colby said cautiously. Dammit, my energy was too frenetic. I was having a difficult time tamping down my anticipation. If I wasn't careful, he was going to know something was up. Time to channel my inner ice queen.

"Any idea when my car will be available?" I asked with an edge to my voice.

"The techs are finished with it, so I suppose it could be brought back," he said, before adding, "not that you're going to need it until everything is settled."

"I'm aware," I snapped at him, "that I'm under police protection and have my own personal babysitter. I simply thought it would be nice to actually have my car back. She's part of the family."

"I'll check on it and see what I can do." I'm fairly certain he suppressed an eye roll.

"Good," I said as I bit viciously into the apple. "I'm ready to head to the funeral home when you are." I turned and walked forcefully out of the kitchen and into the alcove to retrieve my bag from the desk. I patted the pocket that contained the key before hoisting the bag to my shoulder. I walked into the living room where I stood impatiently by the couch, waiting for my ride.

It was a cool, quiet drive to Butterfield. Fall was doing its best to push summer out the door. A few trees were turning gold. How had that happened? How had summer slipped away without my notice? Where had the warm nights of sitting out on the brewpub patio, sipping beer and eating nachos gone? I closed my eyes and tried to push past the thought that everything was slipping away, that memories of Mike would fade as summer turned to fall and fall to winter, that my marriage would soon be nothing more than a few pages in a wedding book and a yellowed dress.

Colby reached over and touched my hand and I was so deep in dark thoughts, I flinched. It was reflex, but still, he pulled away as if he realized he could no longer comfort me, only remind me of all the pain I couldn't escape. I felt terrible because even though I wanted to reach out to him, I couldn't. I needed to disengage from him today to implement my plan. More importantly, because I was still in shock over his betrayal, I needed space to think. Intentional or not, he'd kept too much about Mike from me, while I was raw and open with him, bared and vulnerable. My desire for him was not just sexual, but also for him to be the one I could rely on, to be my rock. It was unfair and childish, I knew, but my whole world was on the spin cycle and there was nothing to grab hold of to steady myself. I needed Colby to be the one thing I could count on. Ridiculous considering I hardly knew him. But, there it was. I took a deep breath and exhaled slowly. Now was not the time to unravel. Now was the moment I needed resolve and a spine of steel.

When we reached the funeral home, I turned to Colby and said, "I'd prefer it if you stayed outside today. I don't need my day disrupted and besides, it's getting difficult to explain you."

"Yesterday I left you alone and some guy tried to shoot you and your boss groped you. Maybe outside isn't the best plan."

"It will have to be," I said curtly before exiting the truck and walking to the front door without looking back. My insides felt like a cyclone was raging – channeling one's inner bitch was not for the faint of heart. I dropped my bag onto my desk before walking out to the reception area where Nick, Dee and Jacob were conferring on the day's viewings and services. "Good morning, everyone," I said with more cheer than I felt.

"Good morning," Nick said brightly, obviously feeling we had bonded over our near-death experience yesterday. I rewarded him with a dazzling smile. Flirting was part of the plan. "Your Marshal friend dropped you off again I see."

"My car is in for repairs, so he's been kind enough to drive me to work." Good, Nick had been paying attention that was going to help. "When you have a moment, boss, can we talk over some things? And I have a favor to ask."

"Sure, as soon as we get everything squared away here, I'm all yours."

We lined out the day and then I headed back to my office as Nick went to check on the honored guest of the morning's service. When he was satisfied the makeup was perfect, the clothes straight and every hair in place, he came to my office where I charmed him into letting me borrow the town car after the service to run a personal errand. He was happy to oblige and even offered to drive. I was tempted to let him because it would probably be easier to sneak past Colby if I had a driver. But, it was much too dangerous. I was a hazard to anyone in my vicinity, illustrated by yesterday's shooting.

My plan was simple and reckless. Colby was once again parked across the street, watching my office. Every fifteen or twenty minutes, he walked around the property, checking for Scary Dudes and probably to stretch his legs. Respecting my wishes, he didn't so much as climb the front steps. After the service, I would wait until he finished walking the grounds and then I would make my escape. From his vantage, he couldn't see the garages in back. I would slip out the back door and leave via the alley behind the funeral home. The bank was across town, but unless someone went outside to Colby's truck and ratted me out, he shouldn't even know I was gone.

The morning service was small. The solarium on the north side of the mansion had been converted into a small chapel for just such a service. Once all the guests had arrived, I was able to return to my office and catch up on work. There were calls to make and emails to read, plus a new ad to approve for the *Journal*-Star. It needed to be tasteful, but eye-catching, as it sat opposite the obituaries each day. Not an easy balance to reach, but as I reviewed the proof sheet, I felt confident they had achieved the goal. Still, the ninety-minute service dragged on and I was grateful the reception was to be at the family home. I popped back into the chapel at the end of the service as a show of support.

Butterfield had a strict policy of unity with each family. The entire staff signed guest books and when a memorial or funeral was held on site, everyone was to be there, at least at the beginning and end of the event. I offered my condolences as the family made their way from the chapel to the front entrance. They departed with Grandpa safely tucked away under his daughter's arm, in a brass urn. His name beautifully engraved on the brushed silver band that artfully wrapped around it.

After Nick and Jacob escorted the family to their vehicles, Nick dropped the town car keys on my desk. Freedom! I picked up my bag, held it low to my thigh while I left the office, in case Colby had those big binoculars out and was keeping a closer eye on me than I wanted at the moment. Safely in the long hallway that led to the back door, I hiked the bag to my shoulder, patting the pocket with the key as I did. I looked out the window on the door before I ventured out, keeping an eye out for both Colby and the Scary Dudes. It appeared clear, but I still found myself looking over my shoulder as I walked into the garage. Too late I realized I should have found an excuse to have Nick accompany me to the car. I stepped into the dimly lit garage and almost slammed my bag into Jim's head when he said hello.

"Sorry, Jim," I said sheepishly, grateful I didn't scream when he came out from behind the limo.

"You okay? You seem a bit jumpy."

No shit. "Yeah, I didn't realize anyone else was out here. My car's in the shop and Nick was kind enough to let me take the town car to run a quick errand," I said as I opened driver side door and slipped in. "I promise not to get it dirty." Or blood splattered, I thought with a grimace. Jim backed all the cars into the garage, so all I had to do was pull out and head down the alley. I held my breath until I turned onto Knoxville.

Once I was sure Colby wasn't chasing after me and my cell phone didn't ring with a call from him asking me what the hell I was doing, I assumed part one of my plan had worked.

I headed toward my bank, which I had chosen because it was minutes from my old house, not, unfortunately, conveniently located next to my office. I drove south on Knoxville, being careful not to let my nerves transfer to the gas pedal. The last thing I needed was a ticket in the company car. Not to mention, I suspected every Peoria cop knew who I was by now and had been instructed to report directly to Colby if anything happened to me. I jumped on I-74, jumped off at exit 93 and headed downtown. I turned onto Washington and wound my way around to Adams, turning into the parking lot for my bank. By the time I put the car into park, I was shaking in anticipation of what I might find. I took a few deep breaths and was careful to look around to make sure there weren't any surprises waiting for me when I got out of the car. I tucked my keys deep in the pocket of my slacks. I was taking no chances. I got out of the car and walked into the bank. It was cool and quiet, which made my beating heart sound like a timpani in my chest.

Get it together, I thought. The last thing a bank teller wants to see is a nervous, sweaty customer walking toward them. I paused a moment before the big double glass doors, catching a glimpse of my reflection. Good lord, I was going to need a spa day when this was all done, no amount of makeup could cover up the stress and lack of sleep.

The scariest thought jittered across my brain. Would it ever be over? What were the odds of my life actually looking normal again? What was normal? What I knew to be true six months ago had disappeared like a dream at dawn. I was no longer a wife, no longer a family. I was single and alone in the world. Panic welled up. I took a deep breath and cleared my mind. The only way I was going to find out what my future could be was to move forward and see what Mike thought important enough to hide in my safe deposit box. I swung open the door, crossed the threshold into the vestibule and without hesitation, through the second set of double doors into the bank lobby.

Banks creeped me out. They are as quiet as the funeral home without the overpowering floral fragrance. The tellers are always so serious and the recent trend of greeting me by my name was disquieting. I couldn't help but suspect they were scanning my data as I walked across the thick carpet to their window. I expected them to greet me with some solemn news. "Hello again Ms. Wilde, we regret to inform you your bank account balance is minus ten dollars." Or, "Ms. Wilde, pleasure to see you again, don't you think you should be saving more?" Well, hell, I'd faced bigger demons than this. Until they tried to run me down or shoot at me, I could brave them. I stepped up to the first smiling teller and told him what I needed.

Brad stood with me in the vault and waited until I put my key into the slot on my safe deposit box, then he did the same. He handed me the box and took me to a little room. He helped me settle and then closed the door behind him as he left. The box felt light when I pulled it down. Whatever Mike had put in there, it wasn't gold bars or a 9mm. When I signed the card to the box, I noted the signature before mine, a neatly scrawled Peter Mason. NOT Peter's signature. His resembled a weird P with an indiscernible squiggly line following it. It looked like nothing in the current English alphabet. Since he'd never signed for the box before, the tellers had no reason to doubt Mike's version. A key and a signature were all I needed to get in, but they did check my signature against the one I had used to open the box originally.

Now the box sat there, beckoning me to open it. My hands shook as I pulled it toward me and went to lift the top. What if this turned out to be nothing? What if after I opened it, we were no closer to solving the question of who killed Shiedeger or Mike? Worse, what if what Mike put in here incriminated him? Proved he was a dirty cop? Then of course, if it was the answer to everything, this could all be over and Colby and I could go back to our separate lives, which was equally forbidding. Without a doubt, I was a ridiculous mess. Ruthlessly, I yanked the top back to reveal the contents. Jackpot.

TWELVE

*I've been absolutely terrified every moment of my life –
and I've never let it keep me from doing a single thing I
wanted to do. – Georgia O'Keeffe*

There it was. Perched on top of the few items I kept in the box was the flash drive I remembered seeing on the keychain. It was black and folded in on itself like a pocketknife. I set my purse on the table and pulled out my tablet. It had a USB port and I hoped I could use it to see what was on the drive. I turned the tablet on, pulled out the flash drive and opened it up. I slipped it into the port and waited. A moment later a menu popped up and I opened up the document files. It took what seemed like an eon to open. When it finally did, what spilled onto the screen was nothing more than strings of numbers in neat columns. It made absolutely no sense to me. That was what I had feared, it meant I would have to confide in someone and show them the data. Of course, that someone would have to be Colby.

I saved the files onto my tablet. It was risky, carrying around information that in all probability had resulted in Mike's murder, but I needed Colby to see it. Sooner, rather than later, and in case the bank closed before we could get back, at least we had a copy. The flash drive was staying in the safe deposit box. I started to tuck it underneath the papers and treasures in the box when I noticed an envelope. I turned it over and it took my breath away. I pulled out the leather chair next to the table and slowly sat down. It was a plain white business envelope. Colby's name was neatly written across the front in the same handwriting that had signed the safe deposit card. My hand trembled as I turned it over to find it sealed.

What the hell? Of all the Marshals in Peoria, in Illinois, Mike decided to leave an envelope addressed to Colby in *my* box? I wanted to open it, to rip through the mystery. I needed to find out once and for all who Colby really was and what he knew about all of this. What he wasn't telling me. But, I couldn't do it. Once I opened it, there was no going back, no saying, *Hey, I know you saved my life a couple of times there, putting yourself between me and flying bullets, but sorry, that's not enough. I opened this here envelope to see if I could trust you or not.* Maybe Colby couldn't be trusted, but I damn well could be. This mess hadn't taken me that far down the rabbit hole. It would gnaw at me, but it would stay sealed, at least for the moment.

I dropped it back in the box, along with the flash drive. Until I knew whom to trust, these would stay here. When I got back to the funeral home, I would write up a document for Nick to tuck away. If something happened to me, someone would need to know where to find this information. I closed the box, tucked my tablet into my purse and rang the buzzer for the teller.

Driving back to the funeral home I tried to run through a scenario with Colby that didn't end with a disapproving look and a long lecture on ditching my personal protection when people where routinely gunning for me. There wasn't one, so I was going to have to take the handsome, well-muscled and fully armed Marshal by the horns. It wasn't going to be pretty. I did not believe that finding the flash drive was going to temper his annoyance. I'd kept the information from him and then went out on my own to retrieve it. He wasn't stupid. He'd know that had I been able to decipher the information on the drive, he'd still be in the dark. Maybe I could flash my breasts to distract him.

Then there was the envelope. I regretted leaving it behind. I should have at least opened it. Was it proof that Colby and Mike had been working together all along? Had Colby been lying to me since the moment he showed up at the van? Was Colby's presence in my life a ploy to watch my every move? To ascertain what I really knew about all of this, about Mike's investigation, about Shiedeger, and whatever the hell any of it had to do with my dad?

The trip back to Butterfield was too short. My head was full of 'what ifs' and none of the 'ifs' led to anything good. None of them led to me wrapped up in Colby's arms in a tangle of sheets.

I pulled up to the garage, where Jim met me and offered to put the car in the garage. I presumed it was more about protecting the paint than chivalry, but either way, I was grateful. If I tried to back it into the garage in my current state, there was no guarantee I wouldn't end up driving it right through the back wall. I debated between walking back to my office, or out front, where Colby was parked across the street. I decided I needed more time to plan my approach, so I went inside. I stopped at Dee's desk and asked her if anyone had stopped in or called me while I was away. She pulled out three pink slips of paper and handed them to me. "Jacob wants to talk to you," was all she said.

They developed Prozac for people like her. Shame I couldn't spike her tea with it. I walked down the hall, stepped into my office and closed the door. I sat down and looked across the street to Colby's truck. It appeared it hadn't moved since I left, but I was sure he'd walked around the building once or twice in my absence. I looked through the messages, nothing urgent. I picked up the phone and speed-dialed Jacob's cell. This was the easiest way to locate him since I had no wish to ask Dee if he was in his office or not. We connected on the second ring.

"Oh, good, you're here," he said when he picked up. "I was hoping you could help me with this afternoon's service. Nick had to run to a meeting and Dee has a couple coming in to do some preplanning."

"I'm happy to, but I'm not really dressed for the occasion," I said, thinking of Dee's flight attendant attire. "I don't even have a jacket with me."

"That's okay. This is going to be very informal. Graveside. I need an extra hand in case Grandma or someone else needs help getting from the limo to the grave."

"What time do we need to leave?" I asked, thinking Colby was going to hate this.

"How does now sound?"

"I'll meet you in the garage," I said and hung up. I reached in my bag and pulled out my cell. I dialed Colby, he answered on the first ring.

"Everything okay?" he sounded tense.

"Well, no one has shot at me yet, but the day's still young," I said, attempting humor while gauging his mood. He didn't laugh. I began to wonder if he noticed my absence, though I suspected there would be more yelling if he had. "There's been a change in plans this afternoon and I have to work a graveside service. I'll be in the limo with Jacob. You can follow us. It will be a very brief service." There was silence on the line. I wondered if we'd lost the connection. I couldn't be that lucky.

"This isn't a good idea," he said flatly. I was definitely missing something.

"Well, first of all, this is MY JOB and somebody has to pay my rent. And secondly, there's no one else around today to help out." Fuck him. He wants to play pissed off bodyguard, fine. If anyone should be pissed off, it's me. I'm the one who has been played by not one Marshal, but two. Both of whom I trusted with my life, both of whom had no problem lying to me. I should have opened that envelope then I could find out what other lies were out there. Colby interrupted my mental tantrum.

"Keep your cell open while you're in the limo. I'll be close enough at the cemetery to intervene if anything looks suspicious."

"Okay, I'm headed to the garage now, so you should head that way." I hit the speaker button and turned the volume down. I slipped the still connected phone into the outside pocket of my bag. I hoped that would work and he would be able to hear everything. I was nervous. Not for myself, but for the people I might be putting in danger just by riding in a limo with them. It was unavoidable though; there was no way to wrangle out of the service without raising suspicions and risking my job. Once again, I walked down the path to the garage. Jim had the limo and the hearse out and they were blinding. A car never left for a service looking anything but showroom quality. Jim was meticulous. Jacob and Jim were coming down the path with the casket on rollers. I opened the back of the hearse for them and they slipped the ornate wooden box with pewter handles into the compartment. It wasn't the most expensive casket available, but it was pretty darn close. I had to wonder why such a showy box when they were having a family-only graveside service. If there was one truth I had learned in my short time here, people do incomprehensible things when it comes to death and funerals. Jim shut the door on the hearse and at that moment something occurred to me.

"Jacob, who is driving the hearse to the cemetery?" I asked warily. For an answer, he held out the keys. "I am not driving a dead body around the city," I said a bit loudly. I looked around to make sure there were no family members lurking. "Come on, you said you just needed help with the family."

Jacob smiled. "He is family."

"Bastard," I said as I grabbed the keys from him. "Fine, but if I have nightmares tonight, I'm calling you at 3 a.m."

"I'm on call. I'll most likely be up." He was enjoying this. Funeral director humor, make the rookie escort the deceased around town.

You would think with everything else going on, playing delivery girl for the dead wouldn't be that big of a deal. But I couldn't help it. Driving a hearse with a dead guy in a casket had horror movie written all over it. I knew I was going to look in the rearview mirror and he'd be climbing out of the coffin and saying "brains" or something equally terrifying.

Sure, guys with guns were shooting at me at random moments and I had a man die in my arms, but that had nothing on supernatural happenings. The dead rising, ghosts wandering the halls, or the devil reanimating a lifeless corpse and making it do his bidding, these things were the stuff of irrational, heart-stopping fear. I gave Jacob my best, you-owe-me face and took the keys. I would be the lead vehicle, so I climbed behind the wheel, adjusted the seat and mirrors, and then started the hearse. I swear I heard Colby chuckling on the cell. Afraid the casket would shift, I drove slowly to the front parking lot where the family had gathered. I definitely did not want to jostle the dead, lest he be annoyed and rise to criticize my driving.

"Dammit woman, I'm trying to rest in peace here."

Jacob followed with the limo. I watched as he opened the doors and helped the immediate family inside. He then explained to the remaining family that they should put their lights on and follow behind the limo. He returned to the limo and gave me the signal to begin the procession. I pulled out and drove toward McClure Avenue. Luckily, the cemetery was almost a straight shot east. There weren't many chances to screw up, simply follow McClure to Prospect and into the cemetery. Fewer chances I might take a wrong turn and give the deceased a scenic excursion as we headed toward the river. I could envision Jacob trying to explain why the hearse he was following was touring the city before interment. As was the custom, it was a slow cortege, as we paraded toward the final resting place. The normal three-minute drive would take us about ten. We didn't want to lose anyone along the way. At least it was a pretty drive through tree-lined residential areas, past the zoo, the botanical gardens and ending up along the river's edge.

I distracted myself with the Craftsman bungalows that lined this stretch of McClure, trying to ignore any thoughts of my passenger. I felt bad that I hadn't had time to learn his name. I eased my way up to a four-way stop. I stopped, looked both ways at the empty streets and then behind me to see how my gaggle of goslings was doing. I appeared to still have everyone. I pulled slowly into the intersection when a silver sedan came barreling toward me from the left at a high rate of speed. I slammed on my brakes and the casket smacked into my seat as I avoided the collision. "Son of a bitch," I swore as the car screamed past me, through the intersection and down the street without so much as braking. It turned right three streets down and that was the last I saw of it.

"TJ! TJ! Are you okay?" Colby said, muffled by my purse. I slowly pulled through the intersection and continued down McClure. I dug my phone out of the pocket it was crammed in and set it on the seat beside me. I took a deep breath as Colby implored me to answer him.

"I'm okay," I said, still a bit breathless. "Did you see where they went? Are you going to follow them?"

"I couldn't get a good look," he began before I interrupted him.

"They turned right, three streets up. You should go after them," I said slightly frantic. I was tired of being chased, shot at and otherwise having my life disrupted by these lunatics.

"TJ," Colby started, his voice calmer now that he was reassured I was uninjured, "it could be an ordinary reckless driver. They are long gone by now, and besides, I'm not leaving you alone."

"Alone? I have a dead guy trying to ram his way into the driver's seat and a processional of aged mourners following me. I'm hardly alone," I said, exasperated and freaked out by the proximity of the damn casket. I heard Colby chuckle.

"Regardless, you are my main concern. Besides, I have to make sure you get the dead guy to the cemetery in one piece. I thought for a minute there you were going to lead a hot pursuit in a hearse."

"I thought about it, but I assumed that taking a loaded hearse on a joy ride around Peoria and ending up on the front page of the *Journal-Star* wouldn't be the best career move." My phone buzzed with an incoming call. "Hey that's Jacob, I've got to answer it." I hit accept, putting Colby on hold before he could object. "Hey boss," I said in the general direction of the phone.

"Are you okay? That was a close call," Jacob asked, sounding concerned. "Is Mr. Baize all right?"

Oh, Mr. Baize, so my passenger had a name now. Too bad I couldn't use that information to ask him to back the hell up. I looked over my shoulder at the coffin now inches from my head, "He's fine. He slid pretty hard into my seat. I think he might want to drive. We're not opening the casket before burial, so if he shifted it shouldn't be an issue, right?"

There was a long pause before Jacob answered and I suddenly had a nightmarish vision of him having me on speakerphone in the limo and frantically trying to turn it off. I was so fired.

"I don't think the family even noticed the close call. I was far enough back I didn't have to brake hard. I'm glad you're okay. When we get to the cemetery, take the first right and wind around until you see the awning," he reminded me before clicking off. I breathed a sigh, looks like I might still have a job after all. I glanced at the phone and Colby was still connected. Good, I hadn't hung up on him.

The remainder of the ride to the cemetery was uneventful. It was a beautiful, late summer day. There was a cool breeze coming off the river, so the chance of any of the grieved fainting and falling into the freshly dug grave was limited. I parked the hearse on the lane next to the awning and gravesite. I waited inside until the limo arrived and parked. I got out and helped Jacob escort everyone out of the limo and lead them to the graveside. The other cars parked where they could. As the mourners exited and walked over, Jacob and one of the cemetery attendants removed the casket from the hearse, placed it on the rolling cart and rolled it to the grave. There it was placed on the winch above the opening. I looked around to make sure everyone had a seat and that there were no stragglers that needed help to the area. Then I looked to see where Colby had stationed himself.

He had parked one lane over, got out of the truck and to the casual observer, looked as if he were visiting a grave. He was looking at the random headstone and had his cell phone in his hand, dropped to his side, where he waggled it back and forth. Too late, I realized I'd left my purse and phone in the hearse. I shrugged my shoulder in his direction. He had a visual of me, which would have to be enough. The minister began speaking, so Jacob and I wandered back to the lane and stood by the limo.

"That was a close call. Good thing you were paying attention," he whispered as we tried to position ourselves so the sun wasn't blinding us. Without the breeze from the river, it would have been scorching hot. Summer was not leaving without a fight.

"Sorry I jostled Mr. Baize." I really was sorry and I was trying to be serious, but I saw the corners of Jacob's mouth twitch and I knew he was trying hard not to laugh. "What?" I leaned in close and whispered. Jacob put his lips close to my ear, still trying hard not to smile or laugh, both taboo in front of mourners.

"It's okay. He was a sonofabitch."

Small towns, you couldn't get away with anything. I looked over at Colby, who was giving me a funny look.

THIRTEEN

A young woman has young claws, well sharpened. If she has character, that is. And if she hasn't so much the worse for you. – Henri Matisse

I looked over Jacob's shoulder as he recounted Mr. Baize's misdeeds. Colby alternated between gazing down at the headstone and over at me with a look best described as suspicious. Could he be jealous? No, not my big, bad Marshal. He carried a gun and probably knew ten different ways to take down a suspect without ever unholstering it. Nevertheless, the thought cheered me.

The minister droned on for much too long. The mourners concurred and began to shuffle and stir. A few got up from their chairs to step to the back of the awning, ready to make a quick exit once the service concluded. Jacob took note of the situation and moved toward the casket as a signal to the minister that it was time to wrap up. It didn't take much for the minister to shift gears. He asked if anyone had something they wanted to say about the deceased, which I thought was a bit misguided, taking into account Jacob's narrative. Thankfully, no one decided this was their one last opportunity to air Mr. Baize's dirty laundry. The service concluded

144 · ANNIE DEMORANVILLE

without any bloodshed. Jacob and I helped the family back to
the limousine. Once they were underway and the other cars
followed, I walked over to the hearse and waited for Colby to
join me.

He walked back to his truck and had to drive down two
separate lanes to get to me. I imagined this made him tense.
Sure, I could have met him halfway, but I was still pissed at
his earlier attitude and the fact he didn't give chase to my
suspected assassins. Truthfully, I wanted to put off the
inevitable questioning on the off chance he noticed my earlier
absence. He parked behind the hearse and slid out of the truck
like a bronc rider dismounting his mighty steed. Oh, that man
was fine in his tight jeans and his untucked shirt. Untucked
not so much as a fashion statement, but to hide the bulge of
his gun. His sleeves were rolled up, revealing his powerful
arms. He walked over to me, in a manner that was much too
casual. He was suspicious, I was sure of it. I braced myself for
the interrogation. Instead, he leaned against the hearse and
looked out at the cemetery.

"Did you know," he began, "that Shiedeger had a little
black book of information in his possession when he was
killed?" He paused for effect, "Neither did the Marshals"

"No. Wait, what? You mean there's been a book with
possible suspects and motive sitting in evidence all this time
and no one has been following up on it?" I was astonished by
this revelation. "What, were they all too busy ruining Mike's
reputation?" Shiedeger had been dead almost two weeks and
this was the first anyone had mentioned a black book.

"First of all, everyone wants to find Mike's killer as much
as you do," he began.

"I doubt that," I muttered angrily. He ignored me and continued.

"The book was in some sort of code. It took a while to decipher it. It wasn't all that sophisticated, but it was definitely Shiedeger's own creation," he paused, pulled his sunglasses off his head and slipped them over his eyes, "I was wondering if you had any interest in exploring a few leads that came to light. This morning."

And there it was. He knew I was gone. He must have received the information while I was out wandering the city and came looking for me.

"Why don't we get this coffin wagon back to the funeral home and then take a ride over to the River Dogs stadium. Unless of course, you have too much work to catch up on, I mean the service kept you away from your desk all afternoon."

I decided it was best to ignore the elephant in the graveyard. "Let's go roust us some bad guys," I replied, getting into the hearse. It was turning into an interesting day, first the flash drive and now a little black book. I pulled my phone out of my bag and dialed Colby's number. "Hey," I said when he answered, "did they ever get anything off the black SUV?" I drove slowly down the dirt lane toward the cemetery exit. Colby was close behind.

"It was conveniently reported stolen the day before we found it. Nevada police are questioning the owner very thoroughly. They want to know why it took him more than a week to notice it was missing."

I edged the hearse away from the stop sign and turned left onto Prospect Road, when a car sped out from a side street, aimed straight for me. I tore at the wheel, hit the gas and barely avoided the collision. The hearse lumbered and veered across the road. The tires met gravel and then grass. I slammed on the brakes, finally coming to a lurching stop inches from a telephone pole, so close I could smell the creosote. My phone flew off the passenger seat, landing on the floor. My bag followed, settling on top of it and spreading its contents everywhere. I caught my breath and attempted to stop the involuntary trembling. I looked behind me to see Colby in full pursuit.

Sitting there alone, suddenly I feared this might be a diversion and the real threat was waiting for my bodyguard to be distracted. I hit the automatic locks and rolled up my window. I jammed the hearse into reverse and hit the gas. The heavy wagon lumbered back onto the pavement. Back on the street, I threw it into drive and mashed my foot to the floor, hoping to catch up to Colby and my assailants. I didn't get a good look, but from what I did see, it sure looked like the same vehicle from earlier today. My mind was racing. Unfortunately, my mighty steed was not. Being a hearse, it wasn't exactly built for speed, so it chugged its way from zero to thirty-five in about a minute and a half.

The road ahead was curvy and heavily wooded, with too many residential side streets and no sign of Colby. I should have retrieved my phone off the floor before I drove after him, but the adrenaline of almost being broadsided twice in one day clouded my brain. I continued to drive down Prospect, hoping to catch a glimpse of them, but there were too many additional roads where they could have made their escape. I drove until I reached McClure. I pulled into a gas station on the corner and retrieved my phone. There were two missed calls, both from Colby. I hit redial.

"Did you catch them? I asked when he came on the line.

"Where are you?" He asked sharply.

"I'm at the gas station on the corner of McClure and Prospect. I tried to follow you, but by the time I got turned around…"

"Stay there," he demanded as he cut me off. "I'm about four blocks away."

"Well I wasn't planning on taking a scenic tour of Peoria in a hearse," I replied sarcastically. I didn't have to ask again about my almost hit and run driver, I could tell from his foul mood he'd lost them. Which meant that sitting out in the open, even on this busy street, could be dangerous. Whoever was coming after me had proven a crowd was not a deterrent. If pulling a gun on me in broad daylight in front of witnesses gave them no pause, a busy intersection on a summer afternoon offered no safety.

"TJ," Colby interrupted my thoughts. Good thing because anxiety was setting in. "I'm a couple minutes out. I lost the car, but I managed to get the plates. They were stolen off of a vehicle this morning."

"So we've got nothing, once again." I was fighting down the panic of being caught indefinitely in this freakish loop. Something was nagging at me, though. No one knew I was going to be driving the hearse, except Jacob and Colby. Absolutely no one, which meant this was either some weird random attack on a funeral procession or, well the other thought was too horrible to contemplate. I took a deep breath to steel myself because I was going to have to ask Colby. I had no choice. I needed to know and I was going to have to listen carefully to his response and trust my instincts. "Colby," I began, unsure I would find the words, "no one knew I was driving the hearse. Jacob sprung it on me in the garage and that's when I told you."

There was a long pause, in which I died several times, before Colby answered. "I know and I don't like what that means. I'm behind you now." I looked up into my rearview mirror and saw him pull up. "Let's get you and the hearse back to the funeral home in one piece and then we'll talk about all of this."

I pulled out onto McClure and pointed the hearse toward the funeral home. Colby followed closely behind and only veered off when I pulled into the back parking lot and drove to the garage. Jacob and Jim were waiting for me with curious looks. I had no idea how I was going to explain the gap between when they drove off and when I finally arrived. I suspected, *hey, I ran your hearse off the road and then went on a high-speed chase* wasn't an appropriate excuse. I pulled the hearse up to the open garage door, put it in park, turned off the motor, gathered my things and exited.

"Where ya been?" Jacob asked pleasantly. Why should I be surprised, Jacob did everything pleasantly.

"I took one last look around the chairs and gravesite to make sure nothing had been left behind. Then when I started to drive out of the cemetery, I took a wrong turn and ended up looping around several lanes before I found my way out to the road again," I lied, rather convincingly I thought. "I think I saw most of the cemetery by the time I managed to exit."

They laughed and then Jim slid into the hearse. He adjusted the seat and drove down the drive, turned around and expertly backed it into the garage. As everything seemed to be in order, I excused myself and went inside.

I stopped at Dee's desk and asked her if I had any messages or if Nick needed to see me. She didn't even look up from her filing when she replied. Since it was only three o'clock, I didn't tell her I was going to be leaving in a moment. I assumed she didn't give a damn. I stopped in my office, checked my email, shut down my computer and slunk out the back door. I figured less chance of Dee judging me if she didn't witness my early departure. I called Colby and asked him to pick me up in the back parking lot. I was anxious to hear more about these leads we were following. Did he think they were substantial or if this was how it was going to be, chasing down every lead no matter how insignificant?

Tedium. That's what Mike had said to me that first night. The first rule of investigation was tedium. And with that, I was lost in the thought, remembering our dinner, how excited I was to be helping him, to be part of his investigation. But, it was all a lie, wasn't it? Everything, the investigation, my participation, Mike's reason for being in Peoria, none of it was real. Except for Mike's murder, that was real. Mike dying in my arms – that was real. If the rest was a lie, he had paid the ultimate price for it.

"TJ," Colby startled me as he rolled down the passenger window and called my name. I had no idea how long he'd been there. "Are you okay?" he asked as I climbed into the truck and buckled myself in.

"Sure," I replied, not at all convincingly, "tell me about these leads."

Colby didn't press me, instead, he told me of the morning's developments. Seems Shiedeger's little black book was discovered by the Peoria police when they executed a search warrant at his office. After his death, it had been dumped into a box with all the other evidence collected that day. It wasn't until after Mike was killed, that anyone bothered to even look at the boxes. Once they realized what they had, the Peoria cops turned it all over to the Marshals. It took a few days to break the coded entries. According to Colby, it wasn't very sophisticated and once they deciphered a key, it was easy to interpret.

It was a gambling ledger filled with names, dates, wagers and payouts. Shiedeger kept hundreds of thousands of dollars in illegal gambling transactions in a simple black leather bound journal. Moreover, it contained the names of every person over the past year who had bet on the River Dogs games, among other things. There were some prominent Illinois names listed and it wasn't difficult to imagine there were quite a few people who would do anything to keep all of this from becoming public knowledge. The ledger was exactly what law enforcement would need to clinch their racketeering case and from there, money laundering wouldn't be a stretch. At least that part of the story Mike told me had some truth to it.

"So why are we going to the stadium?" I asked after digesting most of what he'd found out.

"No one outside the Marshals knows we've deciphered the ledger. I thought it might be fun to ask a few questions at the management level and see who lies to us the most."

"You have an odd definition of the word fun, but I agree this could be interesting. Do you think Shiedeger would have turned on his associates if the Marshals had arrested him?"

"Probably."

That raised a few questions. Like, could someone in the Peoria Police Department have been paid off to silence

Shiedeger and Mike? What about the Marshals? According to Mike, the whole case was exploding into an interstate crime. Could someone have persuaded a Marshal to betray his own? I didn't ask Colby any of these questions. They came perilously close to topics I wasn't ready to discuss: betrayal and the badge. Besides, we had arrived. Colby parked near the entrance of the front office.

"The team is technically owned by a corporation," he explained, "but intel says there are four members who actually control things and they use the stadium as their personal clubhouse. Shiedeger was one of them. Rumor has it the other three are here today."

"Is there a plan?"

"We're going to go in, ask some pointed questions and see if anyone flinches."

"That's not much of a plan."

He shrugged. "We don't have a lot to go on here. Nothing so far links anything Shiedeger did to the rest of the management team. They've made no wagers, at least on record, and nothing in the black book implicates anyone within the River Dogs organization, except for Shiedeger. Everyone had hopes that once he was arrested on federal charges, he'd flip on his accomplices."

"He's the only one you have connected to illegal activity?"

"Yup. Once he was murdered, everything the task force had gathered became pretty thin."

"So," I said slowly as it began to sink in, "the list of people who would benefit from Shiedeger's demise could be long."

"That's the presumption."

There was a light in the back of my mind that was starting to glow, casting shadows on most of my assumptions up to this juncture. "The pieces that don't fit into that scenario are Mike's murder and the attempts on my life." I held up my hand preemptively, "And don't tell me that Mike was somehow involved. Nothing...and you know it....nothing supports that theory. He may have lied to me, but he wanted information on my father and this gambling mess provided him the opportunity to get to me, nothing more." I'd stopped walking. I needed Colby to be on my side, on Mike's side, to believe in his innocence. And for him to come over to my side, I was going to have to trust him with the information in the safe deposit box. It would either clear Mike completely or implicate him. Whichever way it fell, Colby needed to know.

Colby stood beside me, not questioning why I had suddenly stopped, waiting instead for me to find the words. I looked up at him, still searching for the way to explain what I'd done today.

"You okay there Kit-Kat?" he finally asked.

"I need to tell you something, but I think we should question the bad guys first." I was asking for permission, looking for any indication he trusted me, even though my trust in him was fragile.

"Bad guys first. Confession and absolution later. Got it." He put a reassuring arm around me and then dropped down to hold my hand. We walked with renewed purpose to the stadium doors.

I was stalling, but I needed the time to collect my thoughts. I also wondered if chasing these leads would help brighten that light bulb in my brain. Maybe shed some light on that nagging feeling I had that we were missing something very important. Unfortunately, I was going to be disappointed and those shadows would only deepen by the time we left.

Colby introduced himself to the woman who sat in a large reception area outside the offices. He explained he was here to speak with the partners. He was charming and polite, but she was having none of it. She buzzed the president's office and he came out to greet us. He was polite and professional but insisted any questions go through the corporation's attorney. Colby nodded his understanding and thanked him for his time. We started to leave, but then Colby stopped and turned back to both of them.

"You should know, Mr. Shiedeger left behind a coded little black book filled with all his extracurricular activities. A brilliant tech decoded it this morning. It made for interesting reading. You might want to make sure your attorney is on speed dial. Thank you again for your time. Have a good day." With that, he guided me out the big double doors in the lobby. I couldn't help but notice the absolute silence that followed us through the door.

We pushed out into the brilliant late afternoon sun and for a moment, I was blinded. I put my hand up to my eyes to block the light and thought I saw the car that had run me off the road, driving out of the far side of the lot. It was too far away to be sure, so I didn't mention it. Damn them for swapping out that conspicuous SUV for a more modest and unremarkable sedan. They were one step ahead of us and it was pissing me off.

"That was a letdown," I said without much emotion.

"Sometimes it's more about planting a seed and seeing what grows. I let them know we were close and I also made sure they knew you were protected." I started to protest. I doubted anyone in that office even knew my name. Colby stopped me and put his arm around me. "I agree, there was no recognition, no one appeared to care that you were there. I wanted to cover all the bases. Now, what did you want to tell me?"

FOURTEEN

We live in a rainbow of chaos. – Paul Cézanne

We settled into the truck and I pulled out my tablet and the carabiner, now with only an empty ring on it. Colby looked puzzled at first, but then recognition flooded his face as he realized that it was THE keychain.

"You found it."

"Yes."

"Where?"

"When I was cleaning up the mess from my desk. It was buried under a lot of other drawer junk."

"There's no key, no flash drive."

"Well, not exactly. See, when I found it, it had a key on it. It was the spare key to my safe deposit box." I paused, knowing that I was at the point of no return, but still distrustful. I looked over at Colby. Every fiber of my being said I should trust him. Still, a car tried to ram the hearse I was driving today, twice. Very few people knew I was behind the wheel. One of them was sitting next to me.

Colby waited patiently as I did the mental gymnastics. Finally, I decided for better or worse, this was the man I would have to trust until I had serious proof to the contrary.

Or he shot me. I suppose that would be pretty conclusive evidence of treachery. I took a deep breath and continued. "I went to the bank this morning," I paused for possible yelling, when there wasn't any, I felt it safe to continue, "Mike hid the flash drive in there."

"Where is it now?" Colby asked sharply. I studied him before answering, trying to determine if he was annoyed, excited or behaving suspiciously. He had his cop face on, so who the hell knew. I would not want to play poker with this man.

"It's still in the box. I thought it was the safest place."

"Smart girl," he said with genuine praise. I beamed inside. On the outside, I was channeling my own version of cop face. "Let me guess, you have your tablet out because you downloaded a copy of the drive to it." I nodded, he looked over the steering wheel, out the window for a moment before continuing, "I suppose it didn't occur to you that people have been dying for that information."

"I thought about it and decided it was a risk I was willing to take if it meant finding Mike's killer." Now it was Colby who nodded, ever so slightly.

"So, don't keep me in suspense. What's this all about?"

"I have no idea." I turned on my tablet and touched the folder where I had stashed the download. I opened the downloaded file and passed the tablet to Colby. "Make any sense to you?"

He looked over the information, swiping through all the pages, shaking his head with each swipe. He swiped back to several pages and then forward again. I had hoped that meant he saw something that made some sense, but that would have meant our luck had changed. It hadn't. He looked up from the tablet, "It's cryptic, but there is a pattern here, it may take some time to see it."

"We're not turning it over to anyone," I said. My tone brooked no argument. I was conflicted about trusting Colby, but I knew for certain, there was no one else I would trust with this information.

"No, we are not. Not yet anyway," he stated quietly, surprising me. He paused and looked out the window again. I held my breath because I knew what he was going to say. Something he had been working all afternoon to come to terms with, but something I'd assumed for some time. "TJ, I don't think Mike was corrupt in any way, but I think he suspected someone else was, someone in the Marshals or connected directly to us." He was still looking out the window as he spoke those damning words. I could tell it broke his heart to say them out loud.

"There is something else." I turned my tablet off and stole a look at the Silverado's clock, it was four forty-five. The bank would be closed before we could get there. I chided myself for the delay, wondering if the envelope held the key that would unlock the code to the information on the flash drive. "Mike left something for you, an envelope. I left it in the safe deposit box. The bank closes at five. I'm sorry I waited so long to tell you all of this."

"TJ, you've been lied to, shot at, run off the road – twice, and your apartment ransacked. The fact you needed some time to decide whom to trust is understandable. Whatever is in the safe deposit box will be there tomorrow."

I looked over at him, all my doubts and anger evaporated. He understood that I was struggling, knew what a leap I was taking to trust him. "How do you feel about making a grocery run and then I'll make us dinner?" I asked, faith renewed and eager to spend an evening alone with him.

"How about we go to the grocery store and I make *you* dinner," was his reply. I smiled all the way to the store.

We carried six bags stuffed with kitchen staples and the ingredients for the night's dinner up the stairs and into the kitchen. I busied myself with putting away items while Colby started on dinner preparations. Tall, lusty, handsome, cooks and carries a big gun. Yup, he was damn near perfect. Colby pulled out two rib-eyes, a bag of small red potatoes, fresh green beans and a flash drive. He handed the flash drive to me.

"I want you to download the information onto this and then delete it from your tablet. I'm not taking any chances. Something is going on that I don't understand and I don't like it. I don't want you carrying that information around and I definitely don't want it on a wireless device that could easily be hacked."

Jeez, I hadn't even considered that. Another thought skittered across my brain. "Colby, do you think someone could have bugged my phone...my apartment? Is that how they appear to know every move we make?"

Colby pulled a small device from his pocket and held it up. "No, I've swept your apartment and checked your phone, more than once. Nothing," he replied, discouraged.

What he left unsaid was that if I wasn't bugged or otherwise monitored, it had to be someone very close. Likely, someone Colby trusted. I did as he asked and transferred the information to the flash drive, moved it to my recycle folder and then deleted it completely. Colby was scrubbing the potatoes and putting them on a rack to dry.

"I deleted it. I know it's still possible to recover it, but I guess that will have to do." Colby dried his hands, took the tablet from me and spent a couple of minutes configuring it.

"Now it will be more difficult." I didn't ask him what he did, I was just grateful he didn't reformat the whole damn thing.

"Do you need a sous chef?" I asked as he started scrubbing potatoes again.

"No, this is a pretty simple guy meal, it won't take long. You could open the wine, though."

After I opened the wine, I went about finishing up with the disaster cleanup. The alcove looked better than the pre-toss period, and if I had to be honest, the post-toss era was looking remarkably tidier than before throughout the apartment. I headed into the dining area. It was so sparsely furnished to begin with, it was easy to bring back to order.

I dumped all the napkins, placemats and my two "company" tablecloths into the washing machine and started it up. We'd have to be satisfied with paper napkins tonight. I wiped down two of the wood-slat placemats and arranged them on the table, grabbed two butter knives, forks and steak knives from the kitchen and placed them on the mats. I added the wine glasses. I filled two other glasses with ice, water and wedges of lemon and took them to the table.

Meanwhile, the kitchen was filling with delicious smells and sounds – butter, garlic, rosemary, accented by the sizzling of steaks in my cast iron skillet. Colby stepped away from the stove to grab my smaller skillet and I snuck a peek in the oven. There were the most unusual looking potatoes I'd ever seen.

"Hey, what did you do with the potatoes?" I asked.

"Those are called 'smashed potatoes' and wait until you taste them," he said with a touch of pride.

"Entice a lot of women with your smashed potatoes, do you?" He bent down and kissed my forehead.

"A few. Now get out of the kitchen while I finish up. Dinner in about fifteen minutes."

I did as I was told. I went to the alcove and pulled my divorce papers from the vertical file on my desk. There was an instruction sheet attached to the front. I'd been so busy since I picked them up from Peter I wasn't sure what to do next. The instructions were fairly simple, I needed to mail them in or drop them off at the courthouse. I tucked them into my work bag and made a mental note to put them in the mail tomorrow.

That reminded me, I would have to let the office know I'd be in late, given that the bank didn't open until eight thirty. I pulled my cell phone out of my purse and dialed the backline to leave a message. If I dialed into the mainline, the answering service would have picked up and solemnly asked me if I'd lost a loved one. Let's not even go there, I thought. I could have called Nick directly, but since he wasn't on call tonight, he would be rehearsing with his guys for their gig at Jimmy's Bar. I left a brief message, knowing it would start Dee's morning off on the right foul foot she seemed to so enjoy.

"Come and get it," Colby called from the kitchen and my only thought was how much I wanted to get it and come, right then and there. *Well, don't let the threat of imminent death impede my orgasm*, that's what I say. I stepped into the kitchen and Colby handed me a warmed plate and then placed a sizzling rib-eye on it. "Help yourself to the potatoes and green beans," he said and stepped aside so I could fill my plate. The potatoes looked amazing. Crisp and golden, split open, revealing a creamy center and lying in a puddle of butter and rosemary sprigs. I piled several on my plate, moved to the small skillet, added perfectly cooked green beans and carried it all to the table. I went back to grab the wine and impulsively reached up and kissed Colby's cheek. He looked down at me, grabbed my arm and pulled me in for a deep, warm kiss – filled with all the longing we were feeling. When he let me go, we were both breathless. I tucked my head onto his chest.

"Sorry," was all he said.

"Don't be," I replied and moved away to get the wine.

The food was delectable and we ate in comfortable silence, grateful for a bit of normalcy. Mr. and Ms. Ordinary Citizens, sitting down to a home-cooked dinner, soon to retire to the bedroom for some not so ordinary sex. I could not quiet my mind, though, and it whirled with questions. Who in Colby's universe could be so deeply involved in all of this they would kill to protect themselves? Was my father involved or was Mike inadvertently caught up in this situation while searching for him? More importantly, what was the information on the flash drive and how were we going to decrypt it?

"TJ," Colby interrupted my thoughts, "I think I see smoke rising from your overworked brain."

I shook my head, "Just trying to put the puzzle pieces together. It still feels like we're missing most of them."

"We are. Nothing that I had assumed appears relevant. I don't even know if any of this has anything at all to do with Shiedeger or the illicit gambling. Mike's death, the attempts on your life, if they were about the information on the flash drive, we won't have real answers until we unravel that piece." He looked pained. "The list of people who knew our moves has narrowed considerably. The attempts on your life and ransacking your apartment were too coincidental. I was suspicious of peripheral personnel. So, I tightened up the line of communications. Obviously, I needed to look a little closer to home." He was angry. He picked up his wine and took a long sip. This was messing with his cop world.

"On the plus side, these potatoes are amazing," I said, holding up a fork filled with the buttery goodness, trying to lighten the mood. I made a small production out of scooping the fork full of potatoes into my mouth and savoring as I ate, complete with eyes closed and a muffled "mmmm" and a heavy sigh as I removed the now empty fork. I looked over at Colby to see if he was sufficiently distracted and amused with my performance. He sat perfectly still, the wine glass paused halfway to his lips, his eyes dilated into two dark circles. He inhaled deeply and without taking his eyes from mine, took another long sip of his wine.

"Thank you. I'll trade you my secret recipe. Later." He said, putting his glass down and forking up a scoop of potatoes.

"Trade what?" I asked, putting down my fork and reaching for my wine glass.

"I'll think of something," he teased as he ate the mound of potatoes on his fork, never taking his eyes from mine.

I was never going to look at potatoes the same way again.

Once we had finished eating, we cleared the table and piled the dishes beside the sink. Despite the earlier flirtations, Colby did not seem to be in any hurry to make good on his trade. He ran water in the sink and put the dishes to soak while he began to put away the leftovers. I sat on the edge of my grandmother's table, thinking very un-grandmotherly thoughts. I would have to take things into my own hands, so to speak.

"Colby," I said, pausing until he turned around. His eyes met mine. My pulse quickened. "I think the dishes can wait."

He dried his hands on the towel hanging from the oven door, his eyes never leaving mine. They were dark and liquid with desire, making my pulse race as he moved toward me. He parted my knees with his legs and stepped possessively between them, sliding his hands behind me, down my waist, to my hips, pulling me into him. His eyes moved to my lips and I inhaled deeply, taking in his scent, warm and masculine. Then he leaned in and caught my bottom lip with his lips, gently kissing it. He paused there for a moment before hungrily covering my mouth with his. He leaned into the table until there was no space between his hips and mine, bending me back into his arms as he devoured my mouth, parting my lips with his tongue, darting it in and out with a sensuous rhythm. I moaned with pleasure, wrapping my legs tightly around his hips and rubbing against his growing desire. He kissed a trail from my mouth to my neck and then buried his head into my shoulder, nuzzling it before pulling back.

"Hey, come back here," I protested as he stood up, pulling his warmth away. But he didn't. Instead, he reached up and ran his hands down my arms and grabbed my hands, stepping back, but keeping his fingers interlaced with mine.

"TJ, I want you more than I've wanted anyone. I want to be deep inside you..."

"I hear a big but coming," I interrupted as the heat of a moment ago was replaced by the cold chill of rejection.

"But," he said, without irony, "right now, I am all that stands between you and a killer. Someone who knows intimate details about you and this case, I can't allow myself to be distracted from that. For better or worse, my job is to protect you and that has to come first."

I pulled away from him and moved my arms behind me, leaning back and resting my weight on my elbows as I gazed at him, wondering what had just happened. Had I come on to this hunky Marshal, putting aside all my doubts and suspicions, only to be rebuffed? Colby stepped back a bit more as silence stretched between us. I slid down from the table, walked over to the sink and pushed my hands deep into the hot sudsy water. I grabbed a plate, washed it and then ran it under cool water to rinse it before placing it in the dish drainer. The cool water felt good on my heated skin and I wished I could submerge my whole body into it. Colby moved beside me, grabbed the towel and started to dry the freshly washed plate.

We finished the dishes in silence. As I wiped down the stove, I finally spoke. "The bank opens at eight thirty tomorrow. I put your bedding in the trunk next to the couch. See you in the morning." I walked out of the kitchen to get ready for bed. A little bit later, I was sprawled across my still made bed in the dark, looking up at the stars and getting a good sulk going.

My alarm went off at six thirty. I reached over to shut it off after having tossed and turned the night away. I got up, grabbed my robe and headed downstairs to make coffee and take a shower. I didn't bother to make my bed. I had never unmade it. I found Colby at the kitchen table, reading the news on my tablet with a mug of coffee beside him.

"Morning. How'd you sleep?"

"Lousy. People keep trying to kill me and I don't even have sex to distract me." I said as I poured a mug of coffee.

"Yeah, sorry about that," he said and then gave me that killer smile that made his eyes twinkle.

Bastard. I took my mug and went to take a cold shower.

Later in the truck, as we drove to the bank, Colby's phone chirped with a text. He reached over for the phone, pressed his thumb to it to unlock it, and then handed it to me. "See what that says, will you?"

"What if it's from your wife and your middle son, Theodore, needs medical attention?" I teased as I reached for the phone.

"My wife," he deadpanned, looking directly at me for a moment, "would never let me name our child Theodore."

"Good to know," I said and lifted my hand to shade the screen so I could read the text. "Screen is a bit dark don't you think. Or do you have super night vision?"

"I think that's Batman," he corrected me before adding, "I keep it low so the bad guys can't see me at a nighttime stakeout. Tap it twice and it will get brighter."

I did that and the message became readable. "Huh," I said and then read it again.

"Are you going to read it to me any time soon?"

I looked at the screen. "There's a lead in the Shiedeger killing."

FIFTEEN

It is the eye of ignorance that assigns a fixed and unchangeable color to every object; beware of this stumbling block. – Paul Gauguin

I stared at the phone screen. I read the text again, I guess, hoping that more information would magically appear.

"TJ, am I going to have to pull the truck over to find out what the text says?" Colby's voice managed to sound both exasperated and concerned.

"It's from Dan. There's a lead in the Shiedeger killing," I said flatly, still staring, hoping more was coming.

"And...?"

I handed the phone back to him. "And nothing. That is all it said. Will you call in?"

Colby didn't reply. Instead, he pulled into the parking lot of what looked like a church. He put the truck in park and cut the engine. He turned to me, he had his cop face on, but it wasn't enough to cover the concern in his eyes. He picked up his phone, turned it over and pulled out the battery.

"Hand me your phone." I handed him my phone and he did the same thing. "Do you have your tablet with you?" I nodded and pulled it out of my bag. "Power it off." I powered it off and placed it back in my bag. "TJ, I don't want to frighten you…"

"Too late," I interjected.

He continued as if I hadn't spoken, "I am not calling in…"

"I gathered that," I interjected again, trying to lighten the mood. He looked at me. I shrugged and gave him my best, "what" look.

"I think, until we know what's really going on here, no one should know where we are and what we are doing."

"You think they're tracking our phones?"

"Tracking our phones would be the lesser of the nightmare scenarios running through my mind all last night."

"If you had sex you would have slept like a baby." I was not going to let that go and sarcasm kept me from spiraling into a state of panic. That wouldn't do anyone any good. That would lead me down the dark and thorny path of *I'm such a horrible person, people are trying to kill me, they're ransacking my apartment and my husband prefers men.* Unfortunately, there was no time for such self-pity and the little corner of my brain where I was storing all the bad thoughts was becoming frightfully overcrowded. It wasn't going to take much for them to all come spilling out. Colby's rejection was threatening to be the straw that would unleash it all.

"I am sorry about that, honestly. Unfortunately, life and death situations are not great aphrodisiacs. Despite what you may have seen in movies." He waited to see if I had a smartass remark queued up. When I didn't, he continued, "I think until we have more information, I trust you, you trust me and everyone else is suspect. Can you handle that? I know it's asking an awful lot right now, with everything that's already happened. If I have to, there are people outside the Marshals, outside the State Police, that I can trust, if it comes to that."

And there it was, what we'd both been thinking for days now, but were afraid to speak out loud. Someone Colby knew and trusted could possibly be at the center of this. Someone with a gun and a badge. Someone who took an oath to protect and serve, and it wasn't Mike. I was going to have to trust a man I had barely known for a few days with my life because he was the only one who could protect me if what we suspected was true.

"I know I'm asking a lot, asking you to trust me, trust my instincts, but I think this is the only way to keep you safe. At least until we figure out what Mike was trying to tell me."

"I trust you, I do. Just don't get shot or dead, okay?" He reached over and placed his hand over mine. I let myself have a moment of panic, of gut-wrenching fear, until Colby turned the ignition over and pulled out of the parking lot. Then I took a deep breath and focused on our current goal, retrieving the envelope in the safe deposit box. A few minutes later, we parked in the bank lot. I watched as Colby took an extra moment to assess his surroundings before exiting the truck.

"Stay put." I did as I was told. He walked around the truck, opened my door and took my hand. Every muscle in his body was coiled, on alert for anything out of the ordinary. He stood close to the door as he helped me out and then pulled me close to him before he shut it and beeped the alarm.

"Colby," I said quietly, so as not to spook him, "is there something you're not telling me? Something about the text?" We walked toward the big glass double door entrance.

"Last night, I did a final check in with Dan, let him know we might have a lead and we were going to follow up on it first thing today." He paused at the entrance. "The timing of the text felt too convenient, or maybe I'm paranoid. Something doesn't feel right and it seemed a good time for an overabundance of caution." He opened the door and waited until I crossed the threshold, then followed me in. "Cop instincts," he said as we passed through the second set of glass doors.

I signed in and we followed the teller into the vault. I put my key in and she followed, turning them both and pulling the box out. Colby took it from her and we followed her to the little room. She opened the door, ushered us in and closed it behind her as she left us alone. I opened the box and pulled out the envelope with Colby's name neatly written across the stark white surface. I handed it to him.

"How well did you know Mike?" I asked as Colby took the envelope and examined it.

"I met him once or twice, fairly routine. Last time I remember, I was in Dan's office when he came in. We did little more than exchange a hello."

"So why leave an envelope for you in my safe deposit box?"

"The only way we're going to know that is by opening it," he said as he carefully peeled back the gummed section of the envelope. He was going so slowly, it was all I could do not to grab it out of his hands and rip it open. I knew he was treating this as potential evidence, proceeding deliberately and with purpose. I suppose it was fortunate he didn't break out the latex gloves and swab for DNA before opening it. After two geological eons, he had the flap completely loosened and pulled up. He widened the opening and examined the contents, holding the envelope up into the light and tipping it one way and then another, until he finally pulled the folded paper out. He turned it over in his hands, again looking at all sides before carefully unfolding it and revealing the handwritten note. He read it silently, and either he was the world's slowest reader or he read it several times before setting it down next to the box.

I folded my arms across my chest and gave him my best, "Well?" stare. He shook his head and shrugged his shoulders. "TJ, I have no idea what this means." He handed the note to me. I unfolded it and read:

> Colby, I want you to know I enjoyed the pizza and beer. That was one of the best brews I've ever experienced. Do you think you could send a six pack to my office in time for my next birthday celebration? Thanks, partner.

I looked at Colby, handed the paper back to him, completely discouraged. Any hope I had for answers were dashed.

"Is that it? Maybe he wrote more in invisible ink or something" I was reaching, but I couldn't believe he took the time to jot down a Miss Manners thank you note. It had to mean something.

"Do you have any idea what he's talking about?" Colby asked.

"How do I know what beer you guys drink in your spare time?" I snapped.

"TJ, we never had pizza and beer. He's trying to tell me something. Tell us something. That's why it's in your safe deposit box and not in my desk or slipped in my truck." He carefully folded the note and tucked it back into the envelope. He pulled out the flash drive and examined it. "Are you sure you copied everything off of this?"

"I think so. I mean everything that would copy to my tablet. It didn't look like there was anything else on it."

"I think you're right to leave it in the safe deposit box. If everything else we have turns out to be nothing, we can retrieve it and try it on the office computers, see if it gives up any additional files." He dropped it back in the box and closed the lid. "I'd like to keep the letter in here, too, but I think we should work from the original," he looked down and grinned at me, "you know, in case we need to take lemon juice and a blow dryer to it to reveal the secret code."

"Smart-ass," I said and smiled for the first time that morning. We packed up everything and buzzed the buzzer.

Back out in the bright late summer sunlight, we returned to the truck. Colby maneuvered out into traffic and headed down Main Street toward the courthouse.

"Where are we going?" I asked, since I had assumed he was going to take me to my office.

"I want to be near the office when we turn our phones back on. That should confuse the shit out of anyone tracking us." He continued down Main until Adams, where he turned and parked near the courthouse square, about a block from the Marshals' office in the Federal building. He reached into his pocket and pulled out his phone, popped in the battery, powered it on and I did the same with mine. Both our phones blew up with texts and voicemail message alerts. I looked over at him.

"I think something might be going on," I said.

I typed in my code, slid open my phone and started with my text messages. Nick reminded me that I was going to help him prep for his meeting tonight. Dee telling me that if I was going to bother to show up today, I should remember I promised to talk with the historical society about scheduling a fitting for my costume. The voicemail was from my mother wanting to know if I'd forgotten her number. It had been so long since she'd heard from me. She left me the number, just in case. Mom humor. I saved her message, looked up from my phone and over at Colby. "Uh-oh," I said when I saw his face.

"The text from Dan this morning was legitimate. They had a lead on Shiedeger's murder. They found his killer."

"You're kidding. Where? Is he in custody? Did Dan say if it's the same person who killed Mike?" I couldn't believe this. Here we were trying to decipher cryptic files and notes, while everyone else was tracking down the actual killer.

"He's dead, TJ."

All the air went out of the cab of the truck and the street started to swim in front of me. I powered down the window for fresh air as Colby dialed Dan. It was a brief, tense conversation. At least the side I heard. Colby ended the call, started up the truck and pulled into traffic. I was full of questions and I wanted answers before we arrived wherever we were going.

"What did Dan say?" I asked, feeling a bit guilty he'd spent the morning on our unspoken Marshal-most-likely-to-be-dirty list. "How do they know he was Shiedeger's killer? Who shot him?"

"The local cops shot him last night after a lengthy standoff at the suspect's home. They went there on a tip that he might be involved with Shiedeger and it sounds like all hell broke loose."

"Why didn't Dan call you in on this last night?"

"They didn't put all the pieces together until it was all over."

"I don't know, that all sounds awfully convenient."

"TJ, you have a suspicious mind." He meant it to be funny, but neither of us laughed. "Dan gave me a brief explanation. He seemed...unhappy...that I was unreachable this morning. I think he may be under the impression we were...otherwise engaged."

Great, total strangers thought I was getting more sex than I was actually enjoying. Colby pulled into the parking garage and maneuvered the truck into a Marshal Only space. We got out and walked toward the entrance. Thankfully no one shot at us this time. Shiedeger's murder may have just been solved and possibly Mike's, too. And all I could think was, in a moment I was going to have to face a man who thinks his deputy was AWOL this morning because I was distracting him with my lady parts. However, that wasn't why I was going to hell. I was going to hell because I really wished that were true.

The U.S. Marshal office was located in the Federal Building. The building was listed on the National Register of Historic Places. Designed in the Art Moderne style, it was built in 1938 and was filled with beautiful features of the period. My first two visits, I was a bit preoccupied and wasn't able to take in the details. Today, my first time in the building during daylight hours, I was awed by the terrazzo floor, marble walls, and the decoratively painted ceiling, gleaming in the sunlight pouring in from the ten-foot tall windows. Despite the tone of today's trip, I paused to breathe it in. Colby squeezed my hand and smiled.

"It's so beautiful."

"Yes, it is," he replied, looking directly into my eyes. I felt myself blush and he laughed as he walked me to the elevator.

We walked into the bullpen, which was organized chaos. Colby exchanged a few words with several Marshals as we made our way to Dan's office. There was a palpable excitement in the air. The adrenaline was understandably running high. This could be the break they needed to solve the murder of a fellow deputy. I had only been a part of this environment for a short time, but the sense of fellowship between these men and women was undeniable. Mike's death hit them hard.

The night Mike had died in my arms I sat in this office, answering questions over and over, when the most amazing thing happened. One by one, as they discovered who I was, found out what had happened, each Marshal came up to me and thanked me. On some level, I was now one of them. It had been too overwhelming for me to take it all in then, but today as I looked around, I could feel it. They would look up as Colby walked by, catch my eye and nod. I was part of the team. It was heartbreaking to think one of them might be compromised. As we reached Dan's door and he waved us in, I found myself praying that everything Colby and I had suspected was wrong and that what Dan was going to tell us would answer everything.

"Close the door," Dan said as we crossed the threshold. I reached around and pushed the door shut. It was a heavy wooden door, surrounded by wide wood trim. It felt serious and official, like the door to the Chief's office should feel. Dan indicated to the two chairs across from his desk, "Have a seat." Colby didn't move. I followed his lead and stood next to him. Dan sat on the edge of the desk. I wasn't sure why Colby was being so guarded, so I watched and waited. "I was surprised it took you so long to respond to my messages this morning," Dan began.

"I had trouble with my phone. I've replaced the battery, so it won't happen again," Colby lied. He had his cop face on and I was certain he could have passed a lie detector test with the cool tone in his voice. Something to tuck away for future reference. "What exactly do we know at this point?"

"Local LEOs responded to a 911 call last night at a bar over on Water Street. Seems the deceased did a bit of drinking and then started bragging that he shot Shiedeger because he believed he was working with the Feds," he paused and picked up a piece of paper on his desk. "He said, and I quote, 'I shot that motherfucker before he could rat out the whole damn organization.' There were quite a few friends of Shiedeger's in the bar and things took a turn for the ugly. The deceased decided it was best to call it a night and he went home. That's when one of the patrons made the anonymous 911 call. Officers went to the suspect's house to question him. He barricaded himself inside and began shooting. Officers returned fire and when the smoke cleared, he was dead. There was a preliminary match with one of his weapons to the one that killed Shiedeger. Between the barroom confession and the weapon, everyone is considering this murder solved."

I looked over at Colby. I wanted to ask about Mike, but I knew from experience his murder was a delicate topic. I decided to let Colby inquire about that aspect. His demeanor had not changed and I had to admire his professionalism in the face of everything. The only reason I wasn't completely losing it and demanding to know why they would kill the only person who might know what the hell was going on, was because I was surrounded by people with handcuffs.

"Are we any closer to knowing what this organization is or who else might be involved?" Dan shook his head. Colby continued, "And what about Mike, did you find a weapon that matched the one," he glanced at me, "that was used in his murder?"

"They're still searching the deceased's home and business. But, my guess is, we'll find a connection between him and Marshal Fraser. One way or another, someone tipped him off about the investigation."

It was all I could do not to pick up the wood and brass nameplate on his desk and beat him with it. But, again, I was aware I was surrounded by people with handcuffs and loaded guns. I turned away and walked to the windows that framed the big wooden door. I looked out into the bullpen and I fought back tears. Nothing Chief Strickland had to say after that was of any interest to me. He and Colby continued to discuss the case, but it was barely a low hum accompanying the movie that was playing in my head. I replayed everything that had happened over the last few days. None of it could be explained by a drunk dying in a hail of bullets last night. My thoughts were interrupted by Colby's voice, no longer even and professional.

"Why the hell would you discontinue TJ's protection?"

SIXTEEN

Creativity takes courage. – Henri Matisse

I turned around to see Colby move toward Dan, his cop face gone, replaced by that flash of anger I had seen once before.

"Why would you discontinue TJ's security detail when there have been multiple attempts on her life?"

"With Shiedeger's killer dead, the Marshals Service believes the threat to Ms. Wilde-Mason is over. I'm sure she'll be glad to return to her normal life without an armed guard." Dan looked over at me, expecting me to agree, I suppose. I remained noncommittal and looked to Colby for our next move.

"You think some drunk in a bar is responsible for trying to run TJ off the road three separate times, shooting at her in front of our offices and ransacking her apartment?" Colby asked, trying for professional, but coming off slightly pissed.

Dan stood quietly for a moment. He picked up a solid walnut paperweight with a brass Marshal badge mounted on its face. He turned it over in his hands and placed it back in its exact spot. "The PPD is doing a thorough investigation. It's their jurisdiction now. I can talk to them about extra patrols for her apartment."

"She's the sole witness in the murder of a Deputy Marshal." Colby's voice was tinged with anger and suspicion, but still, he remained professional.

"By her own admission, she didn't see anything. If the locals come up with more information, we can bring her in for another interview. Right now, we believe we have Marshal Fraser's case resolved."

Colby was quiet for a moment, then he turned to look at me. I knew that look. It was the same look he had when he pulled the batteries from our phones. He turned back to Dan.

"I need to get TJ to her office and arrange for her car to be returned to her. I'd like to request the remainder of the day off to take care of things that I couldn't while I was working her detail." The discussing me as if I wasn't in the room was beginning to get on my nerves.

"Fine. Take today. I'll have a new assignment for you tomorrow."

With that, we were done, not even so much as a "thank you for all your help, TJ" from the bastard. I didn't know what was going on, but Chief Dan now jumped back to the top of my suspect list. Colby pulled the heavy door open and I could see his muscles tense against his sleeve. I was sure it wasn't because of the weight of the door. I crossed over the threshold and almost ran into a heavyset, older man. "Oh, sorry," I said as I stepped back into Colby's chest. Balding, with a slight paunch, he clearly did not have a membership at the Marshals' buff gym.

"I'm sorry ma'am," he said as he stepped back. He then looked up over me, at Colby. "Haven't seen you around much this week, Jameson. Chief got you on a hot assignment?"

"Morning, Clarkson." Colby ignored his inquiry. He was committed to remaining on lockdown. "This is TJ Wilde, TJ, Deputy U.S. Marshal Kyle Clarkson. He is the senior Deputy here and our liaison with the State Police." I nodded toward him as a hello.

"TJ Wilde? Wilde-Mason? The brave young woman who was with Marshal Fraser when he was shot? It's an honor to meet you." He stretched out his hand to shake mine. I leaned on Colby for support as reminders of that night always made me shaky. I took his hand and shook it gingerly. I wanted nothing more than to leave this place and scream at the heavens, or at least sit down at my desk and do something, anything that felt routine. Colby, as usual, read my mind.

"I have to get TJ to work, Clarkson. When I get back, I'd like to hear your thoughts on the recent developments on Marshal Fraser's murder."

"I look forward to it." With that, we changed places with him. Colby and I moved away from the Chief's door and into the bullpen and Clarkson slipped into the Chief's office, closing the door behind him.

Colby moved us quickly through the room and out to the hallway, avoiding any more questions. Once we were back in the parking garage, he slowed his pace and took my hand. "Are you okay?"

"You mean am I okay with your asshat of a boss thinking that some guy who was dumb enough to get drunk in a bar and confess to his many crimes was the mastermind behind everything that has been happening, including murdering Mike? What do you think?"

He smiled and squeezed my hand before opening the passenger door for me. I settled myself into the now familiar and protective leather while Colby walked around and climbed in the driver's side. "I'm going to drop you off at your office. I think it goes without saying, you are to stay put. I'll spend the morning wrapping up some loose ends and making a plan that does not include leaving you vulnerable to whoever is out there making attempts on your life." He started the truck, backed out and exited the garage. "Then we'll get to the bottom of the information on that flash drive."

I began to feel better. I never thought Colby would stand by while Dan dismantled my protection, but it was reassuring to hear him say it aloud. We'd make a plan, take it to Dan and make sure I was safe. Then we could continue looking for Mike's killer. By the time we reached the parking lot of the funeral home, I was feeling downright cheerful. With Shiedeger and his killer out of the picture, the focus narrowed. With the flash drive in our possession, I was sure we were nearing a resolution. Colby parked the truck near the front door, killed the engine and turned to me. "Think you can find your way in on your own?" he asked with a grin. I rolled my eyes and opened my door. "Give me a wave from your window when you get in there," he added seriously. My protector.

"I will. When do you think you'll be back?" I asked as I gathered my things. He took my hand and rubbed his fingers over mine tenderly.

"Afraid you might have to put in a full day's work?" He pulled my hand to his mouth and kissed my fingers. My stomach did flip-flops and I looked into his viridescent eyes. Desire mixed with fear. "We are going to figure this all out, I promise."

He was worried. I'm not sure he believed what he was declaring, but he wanted me to believe it. He didn't want me to worry. I nodded and reached for the door handle. "I know we will. See you later this afternoon," and with that, I stepped down and walked up the stairs to the front door. Colby waited until I was safely in my office and I waved the "all clear" to him from the big window over my desk. He started the truck engine and drove out of the parking lot.

I stood in my office, tamping down the fear of being alone and vulnerable. The quickest way to squelch that was to dive into my day. It was nine fifteen. I was only forty-five minutes late. I doubted Nick even noticed I was gone. Dee would be another story. It would probably be best to walk to her desk, let her know I was here and retrieve any messages, rather than buzz her. Instead, I powered up my computer and checked my voicemail. Chicken. While my computer downloaded my emails, I decided to brave the dragon.

Walking down the window-lined hallway, I reflected on how beautiful it was here with the abundance of natural light in the offices and public spaces. The viewing rooms were generally windowless, but the high, ornate ceilings kept them from feeling claustrophobic. It was a pleasant place to work, well, except for the dead people and all the grieving families. No job was perfect.

Dee was sitting at her desk, deep in conversation on the phone, so I waited at the door. She was talking with one of the local clergy, scheduling a service. It sounded like it would have been easier to schedule the President and the Queen for tea, as Dee juggled various family needs against the clergy's obligations. Finally, they found a common time. Dee wrote it down with a triumphant flourish, thanked the minister, hung up the phone and turned to me. Her entire demeanor changed. Gone was the pleasant, professional flight attendant, replaced by a look of contempt and impatience.

"Good morning, Dee. That sounded like quite the negotiation." Nothing. This was some of my best pleasant morning conversation. Okay, I'd just get down to it then. "I wanted to check in, see if you had any messages for me, or if Nick was looking for me." She turned back to her computer, all but ignoring me.

"No," was all she said and she said nothing more.

I should have taken the hint and left, but I was feeling feisty after my morning with the Chief, so I decided to poke the bear. "I left a message that I would be late this morning. Did you get it? I needed to stop at the bank to pick up some documents so I could mail in my divorce papers. The bank didn't open until eight and it was all the way across town, so I didn't think I could get here on time." She sighed and opened up a file on her computer. I was obviously her burden to bear. "Anyway, I wanted to make sure you got the message." I waited a moment, expecting what, I don't know, and then left with Dee's deafening silence following me down the hall.

Back in my office, I tried and failed to focus on the growing pile of work in front of me. There was a request from the local paper for an interview about the changing face of funeral services. The reporter's email stated he wanted to focus on the growing trend of highly personalized funerals and the increase in cremation and green burials. I would have to call him to get a sense of his true intent. Was he being honest or was this a way to do a hit piece on the recent acquisitions? I wasn't going to let Nick be ambushed and would probably sit in on the interview to make sure everyone played nice. Peoria was a small town and I never knew who was related to whom or what politics needed to be played, so I approached any press with an abundance of caution. I felt it was better to have Nick, Jacob and Tom out in the community doing good works than giving interviews or glad-handing local politicians. I sorted through what I could, prioritizing what absolutely needed to be addressed today. My office phone buzzed, once again jarring in the tomb-like silence. I took a breath and answered it. Nick needed me upstairs in the kitchen for a quick staff meeting.

I grabbed my notebook, tucked my cell phone into my pocket and made my way to the kitchen. Jacob was seated at the table with a fresh cup of coffee, looking over some papers. Nick was standing near the window, talking on his cell. I poured myself a cup of coffee as Dee entered and silently sat down, looking cold and unapproachable. So maybe I wasn't the only one on her list today. I sat next to Jacob. Nick hung up the phone and walked over to the coffee pot to top off his mug. He turned around and leaned against the counter.

"Last night we caught a coroner call," Nick began, "Jacob picked up Dale Himmel, the owner of the Sports Stop, the sports memorabilia store over by the stadium."

I tried to concentrate on what Nick was saying, but with the mention of the stadium, my thoughts drifted to my current situation, so I almost gasped when I caught the last bit of what Nick was saying.

"...it will be an immediate cremation because the bullet wounds are extensive and the autopsy didn't help matters."

"I'm sorry, Nick," I interrupted, "bullet wounds?" I could feel more than see Dee rolling her eyes in disgust at my inattentiveness.

"Yes, TJ, that is usually what happens when you die in a hail of police bullets," he smiled at me, clearly feeling our shared close call had created a mutual intimacy. "This could be a very hairy memorial service, especially since we also handled Shiedeger's service. I suggested to the family they might want to go elsewhere, but they want to stay here, since we buried their grandmother last year. Due to the nature of the death, understandably the family wants it to be small and private. But…"

"…it's a small town," Nick and I said in unison. We nodded at each other, knowing I'd have my work cut out for me dealing with the press inquiries.

"We need to be on lockdown with this," Nick continued. "No information goes out. If anyone calls asking if the deceased is here, we have the family's permission to say that we have no information on him. Can you handle that Dee?" It was an innocent question but she responded with an unmistakable *fuck you* glare. He ignored it as he finished with, "No matter what he's accused of, we treat the family like any other family. We make them feel safe here. That's our job. Jacob, give us the details you have so far."

"Mr. Himmel, age fifty-seven, lifelong resident of Peoria. He was on the board for the River Dogs and ran a local sports memorabilia shop."

Jacob went through the family's wishes, which were rather simple and we mapped out a plan. The meeting broke up and I went back down to my office to rearrange my priorities.

Nothing like a shoot-out to completely reorder my day. Though I was grateful I wasn't the target this time.

I sat down and called Colby. I thought he would be interested in the development. It wasn't a surprise we'd get the call. Because of the merger, Butterfield comes up in coroner rotation more nights than not since the other two funeral homes operate as their own entities. That meant in any given month, Butterfield had three weeks on the rotation. Coroner rotation was originally established so that local law enforcement and medical facilities wouldn't favor one funeral home over another with an unexpected death. Funeral homes alternated weeks when they were on coroner call, thus assuring fairness. At least, that was until the Butterfield family started buying up the competition and successfully argued that because each location operated under its own LLC, the rotation should remain unchanged.

This meant that in the roulette wheel of death, odds were in favor of him landing at the same funeral home as his victim. A private service would fuel the chaos, as people tried ingenious ways to pry information out of the staff. Old family "friends" would call wanting contact information for the family, concerned "clients" and "customers" would want to extend their condolences while quizzing Dee on any details she might have on the death, investigation or funeral arrangements. They would have no luck, but that wouldn't stop them from trying.

I hit redial on my cell and Colby picked up on the first ring.

"What's wrong?" he asked.

"A little jumpy?" I replied, before filling him in on the news. "I thought you might like to know."

"Too bad the service is going to be private. It might be interesting to see who turned up. Although it looks less and less likely that Shiedeger's death has anything to do with Mike's murder."

"Agreed, I can't help but think though, that when we untangle all of this, he'll be wrapped in there somehow." I was still holding out hope, I suppose, that not everything Mike told me was a lie. "How are your errands coming along?" I asked, not wanting to follow that thread any further.

"Good. I should be back there before lunch. What can I bring you?"

What could he bring me? Peace. Safety. Hot sex. Unfortunately, none of those were available at Subway, so I settled for turkey on whole wheat.

My next call was to the reporter from the *Journal-Star*. I needed to put him off for a day or two so the interview didn't shift from a human interest piece to an investigative report on how we handle criminals and murderers. As I pulled up his email to retrieve his phone number, the phone rang again, fracturing my already brittle nerves. I picked up the receiver and pressed the blinking light.

"Butterfield Funeral Home, this is TJ," I said a bit too brightly as the adrenaline flooded my system.

"Hello," responded an older woman, "this is Mary Johnstone, from the Peoria Historical Society. I'm doing your fitting and I wanted to confirm our appointment on Monday afternoon at two.

Fuck. Fuck, fuck, fuck. I completely forgot. There was no way out of this and Colby wasn't going to be happy, then again Monday was a long way off. A lot could happen, like death. "Of course, Mrs. Johnstone, I'm looking forward to it. Do I need to bring anything?"

"Please call me Mary, dear, we'll have everything, including period undergarments. See you at two," she said crisply and disconnected.

Great, it wasn't enough I was being shot at regularly, now I had to wear someone else's panties. I picked the phone up and looked for the volume button. I turned it down to almost mute. One more phone call and they'd have to peel me off the ceiling. I called the reporter, then I busied myself until Colby texted me he was on his way with lunch. I told him to meet me out back in the courtyard. I ran up to the kitchen, grabbed a couple of plates, knives, and a handful of napkins for our impromptu picnic.

When I stepped into the yard, Colby was already there pulling food out of the bags and arranging lunch on the table. Sandwiches, chips and cookies sat next to two large drinks. I added my contribution and sat down, anxious to hear what he had done with his morning.

The day was perfect, warm and sunny, the slightest of breezes blowing through the tall hedge. I took a moment to breathe it in, the pretty garden and a sexy man bringing me lunch. I could almost believe that someday soon, my life would return to normal. I reached over to grab my sandwich and unwrap it. Colby opened another bag and pulled out two boxes.

"I bought you a present."

SEVENTEEN

My curves are not crazy. – Henri Matisse

Colby slid one of the boxes over to me. It was a pre-paid cell phone. "Burner phones for both of us," he responded to my quizzical look.

And just like that, the beautiful day and fantasy picnic with the sexy man were washed away by the reality of what we were about to do. Go underground. There wasn't an alternative, yet it still required a leap of faith. My hands shook as I opened the box and unpacked the phone. My mind raced, trying to trace back how I arrived at this moment. Once we went off the grid, everything would change.

"Earth to TJ," Colby gently prodded. I looked over at him and smiled weakly as I powered the phone on. The battery was fully charged and Colby's number already programmed in. "I paid extra for the charged batteries," he joked.

"We are really going to do this?" I asked, knowing the answer but needing to hear Colby plead the case.

"I need people to stop trying to kill you long enough for me to put the puzzle pieces together. I have personal time available, so I can drop off the radar for a few days."

"But I don't," I interrupted.

"I know. I believe having you stick to your schedule can work to our advantage. We don't want anyone to get too suspicious. I think Dan and anyone who might be involved will assume I'm taking time off to keep an eye on you. However, if we both disappear, that might tip our hand. Even with the burner phones, I want you to use your personal cell phone for work calls. But I want it to stay at the office, not on your person."

"I'm going to be tied to the office for the next few days. This memorial service is going to generate a bushel full of calls, I'm certain." I thought about Mr. Himmel downstairs. I had been so caught up in the shock of Shiedeger's killer also being dead, I hadn't even inquired about his name in Dan's office. I didn't feel much guilt about that lapse. It was more astonishment that this had become my life.

We finished lunch and I went back into the office to chip away at the work piling up on my desk. I wrote out a statement for anyone who called inquiring about Mr. Himmel and gave it to Nick. He approved it and I emailed copies to all the staff. I knew it would piss Dee off, but I was beyond caring. On my list of things to give a shit about, she didn't even make the front page.

Colby came into my office and I was about to send him away when I looked at my computer clock. It was five-fifteen. I had no idea where the afternoon had escaped to, but I was very glad to see it end with a tall, dark, and seriously sexy man at my door. I smiled, turned off my computer and powered off my cell phone. I tucked it into my desk drawer before I followed him out to the truck.

"So, how was your day, dear?" Colby teased once we were underway.

"Well, so far, no one has shot at me, so I'm calling it a win," I replied. "How about you, hone in on any suspects yet?"

"Interesting you should ask. I believe I may have made some progress on Mike's cryptic clues."

"What?" I said, practically squealing, "And you didn't open with that?"

Colby grinned as he turned onto the interstate leading to my house. "Don't get too excited, but I kept going over the message in the envelope. Since the message didn't relate to any experience I had with Mike, I wondered what part was actually factual. The numbers – six-pack and his birthday. I think it's the numbers. We only need to decipher what they mean."

I nodded. If I had to guess, those numbers were going to be the key to unlocking the list on the flash drive. We had a long way to go, but we were making progress. We knew that Shiedeger's killer was not likely to be Mike's murderer. We had a flash drive full of clues and I was confident we would be able to interpret the information given enough time. I doubted Mike would make it too difficult. I also believed, as we delved deeper into the information, I'd know something that would be crucial. Something he told me in a quiet moment. Something I would remember in an odd flash, just as I remembered the drive on his keychain.

The late summer air was warm and the locusts were in full song as we pulled up to the grand lady on the corner. I looked up at her rough-hewn stone and felt like I was really coming home. For the first time in days, I had a moment of hopefulness, a sense that there was a light at the end of this tunnel. Colby parked at the curb and turned off the truck. I hopped down from the cab and he met me on the sidewalk. He beeped the alarm and we walked up the stone steps, through the big grey wooden door and up the three flights to my door. It was ajar. I swore under my breath as Colby unholstered his gun and motioned for me to stay behind him. He slowly pushed the door open and my heart sank. My apartment had been tossed, again.

It took Colby five minutes to clear the apartment before he would let me cross the threshold into the living room. I looked around completely dejected. I didn't understand, I lived a good life. I went to college, got a degree, held down a good job, married, paid my taxes, and remained faithful to my husband. Okay, at this moment in time, I was lusting after a hunky lawman. But still, in the balance of things, I'd always done what was expected, the right thing. Yet, very bad things kept happening to me. Maybe I needed a priest. Or an exorcist. I sighed, put the cushions back on the couch and sat down.

"Which one of us is ordering the pizza?" I asked and Colby looked down at me with concern. He didn't say anything and instead ordered pizza. Then he went to look at the front door locks. I got up and wandered around the apartment to assess the damage. Cushions tossed, drawers opened and rustled through. All the cupboard doors in the kitchen were wide open, chairs tipped over. The few items on the kitchen table were on the floor. I walked to the office, everything on my desk was on the floor, the drawers opened and things were shoved aside, but still in the drawers. I climbed the stairs to my room. The bed pillows were on the floor, the closet door was opened and a few items of clothing were tossed on the floor, but it was as if they'd lost interest by the time they reached the room. My dresser was relatively untouched. Panicked, I checked in the hamper. The safe deposit key was still securely wrapped in my sock.

I sat on the edge of the perfectly made bed. Something was amiss. Whoever did this wasn't looking for anything. Instead, they were looking to distract us from something. I just didn't know what. I went downstairs. Colby was sitting at the kitchen table, a flash drive plugged into his computer. He looked up as I entered the room and closed the laptop. He pulled out a chair and I sat next to him.

"This isn't right," I started and Colby nodded, but let me continue. "This isn't like the last time. It was half-hearted at best. What did they want?"

"I don't know. The back door lock was picked. They let themselves in and then left out the front door. They barely touched anything in the apartment."

"It's a distraction. But from what?" I asked, genuinely puzzled. It wasn't even an effective scare tactic. Colby suddenly stood up, realization hitting him. He pulled the little gizmo out of his pocket and began to scan the rooms. I stayed in the kitchen and let him work. I heard a "fuck" come from the living room and went to see what he had found. I had a hunch what it was. As I entered the living room, he was standing near my couch. He put his finger to his lips when he saw me.

"Sorry, stubbed my toe," he said as I stood near him. He lifted the end table up with one hand. I tried not to swoon as I watched his bicep ripple under the strain. He flipped it over with his other hand and showed me a tiny square box, not much bigger than a penny. He set the table upside down on the couch and motioned me to follow him. He swept every corner of the small apartment and found two more boxes.

Colby grabbed his laptop, dragged me into the bathroom, turned on the faucet in the bathtub and played music on his laptop. "Those are sound activated listening devices. They turn on only when they detect speech." I nodded stupidly. I suspected that these were not available to the local bookie at *Spies R Us*. He continued in a low voice, "I don't think we should remove them yet. I need to come up with a plan."

He sat on the toilet seat and I sat on the clawfoot tub, balancing carefully on the narrow edge, waiting, resolving not to succumb to panic. If Colby would only lean forward and balance his elbow on his knee and his chin on the back of his hand, he would look exactly like Rodin's The Thinker, bathroom version. I chuckled to myself. That would make him The Stinker. He looked over at me and I couldn't meet his eyes. I started to laugh, he smiled and I laughed even harder. I couldn't stop. The absurdity that was my life was too much to bear. Colby stood up, grabbed my hand and pulled me into him. I could feel him laughing quietly as I buried my head into his chest, feeling it rise and fall in a syncopated rhythm, punctuated by staccato movements as he laughed. We continued to laugh for a few minutes, Colby wrapping his arms tight around me until he unexpectedly pulled me back and kissed me. It was a warm, passionate kiss that started out slow, but quickly deepened as his tongue explored mine. I grabbed his shirt and pulled him in close to me. Finally, he pulled back and I struggled to catch my breath.

"What are we going to do," I asked, not sure if I meant about the kiss or the bugs.

"I think the best thing to do, for now, is to move the device that is in the bedroom down here and spend the evening upstairs, devising a plan, see if we can decipher more of Mike's message."

This seemed a reasonable idea, so I went into the kitchen to gather items for dinner, while Colby relocated the bug down to my office. He then placed the portable radio I kept in the bathroom – what can I say, I like to sing in the shower – next to my desk and turned a talk radio station on low. The doorbell rang. Colby instinctively went for his gun.

"It's probably the pizza." I stood up to answer the door. Colby put his hand on my shoulder and motioned for me to stay. He walked to the living room, gun at his side, ready for trouble. I hoped he had put the gun away before he opened the door. Otherwise, we might have trouble getting delivery in the future. The future. I wondered what that was going to be for me, and for Colby and me. I listened for gunshots, since there were none, I assumed the pizza and beer had arrived. I walked over to the cupboard and pulled down plates and mugs. Just because we were hiding didn't mean we couldn't enjoy the finer things. I wish I'd thought to put the mugs in the freezer. I grabbed napkins from the pantry and headed to the bedroom.

Upstairs, I changed out of my work clothes and set up a floor picnic. I put down a tablecloth, set out the plates, mugs, extra cheese and napkins. Colby popped in carrying a large pizza box and a six-pack of soda. I frowned.

"I thought we should keep our heads clear," he answered my unspoken rebuke with a grin.

"My apartment has been trashed, again. I think alcohol is a perfectly acceptable response."

"Noted," he replied as he put the pizza on the tablecloth and settled on the floor, "but I think we should focus on how to make that stop happening. Then we can drink."

I looked at the extra large pizza box. "Decided on the family size?"

"Leftovers."

"Also good in case you had to shoot the delivery boy and Antonio's refused to deliver here again."

I served up the pizza, while Colby poured drinks. I leaned back against the bed and took a bite of my slice, waiting to hear what Colby was about to propose. If it was for us to go deeper underground, I was against it. I was ready to bring these people out into the open, even if it meant using me as bait. I was tired of all of this death and destruction. Colby grabbed his pizza and settled across from me.

"I reached out today to D.C.," he began. "I spoke with my old boss. I worked with him for years, trained under him actually, before I transferred to the central district of Illinois." He paused, waiting to see if I was going to react. I remained impassive. He knew the inner workings of the Marshals Service. I had no choice but to defer to him on this. "I needed to make sure that in case something happened, someone was aware of circumstances. I gave him as little information as possible, not even my burner number." I nodded. Cryptic notes were clearly not the most effective way to communicate. Colby took another bite and chewed slowly. I suspected he was trying to find a way to break more bad news. Instead, he surprised me with, "Can you shoot a handgun?"

"I've never shot one," I replied, wondering where this was going.

"Are you afraid of guns, or against using a weapon?" he asked cautiously.

"Colby, I grew up in West Virginia. All my uncles hunt. I know my way around a shotgun. Never had the opportunity or the need for a handgun, but get me a big stick and I know how to handle it," I replied with a smile. He smiled back. "Get your mind out of the gutter. I have a black belt in Kendo." Checkmate.

"You do? I'm impressed."

"Started when I was in college. After we moved here, I took up kickboxing. Just for fun," I said with a wicked grin.

"TJ Wilde, you are full of surprises," Colby chuckled. He put down his pizza, leaned over my carefully spread out tablecloth and touched my cheek with his hand. Then he pulled me in close and kissed me. It was a sweet, careful kiss, gently caressing my lips, first the bottom lip and then my top lip. He kissed the corner of my mouth, licking away some stray sauce, murmuring his approval as he did. I sat still and savored his touch, but I did not respond, even though I wanted to grab his shirt and pull it off him and take him right in the middle of my pretty blue tablecloth. I was still stung by his previous rejection and I wasn't about to go all in unless I knew he was serious. A moment later any doubts about his intentions were washed away.

Colby parted my lips with his tongue and began to explore my mouth with his, tangling his tongue with mine as he crawled across the floor and pinned me to the edge of the bed. He knocked over my half-filled glass and my only thought was, ginger ale doesn't stain, don't stop. He didn't even notice, intent on mapping my mouth with his lips, his evening stubble scraping across my cheek, his hands holding my face close to his. He continued like this until I was so hot, so filled with desire for him that if he suddenly decided to abort this sexual interlude, I would have no choice but to finish my orgasm myself and I would make him watch. But, he had no intention of stopping. He reached down, cupped my bottom and slid me up onto the bed. He stretched over me, still kissing, but now moving downward past my chin, to my ear and down my neck. His lips grazed the collar of my shirt, his hands moved down my arms and back up again. He nuzzled himself between my breasts, rubbing his cheek against my soft mounds before sucking on my ever hardening nipples through the soft cotton fabric of my t-shirt.

I moaned with pleasure and encouragement. He bit at my nipple and I gasped with desire. That was it. I pushed him away and sat up enough to take off my shirt. Then I pulled him back into me, feeling the warmth of his skin against mine as he began to kiss around the lace edges of my bra. Damn, why didn't I think to take it off when I was changing out of my work clothes? Just one more piece of fabric between me and my desire.

Colby must have had a similar thought because he reached up and slid the straps down my arms and moved the cups just below my erect nipples. He paused for only a moment before taking one in his mouth and suckling it hungrily. I was panting with desire, scratching my nails against the fabric on his back, wishing I could rip open the buttons and wrench off his shirt, but not wanting him to stop, even for a moment. His shirt would come off eventually, but until then, I was content to reach down and pull it up so I could get my hands under it and feel the heat of his skin and the solid muscles across his back. I pulled him in close. He licked and nipped first one nipple and then the other, each time his tongue lapped across one, fire shot through me, making me throb in all the right places. I was hot and wet and ready and I wanted him deep inside me, but he had other plans. He kissed his way down my stomach, his hands moving past the cuff of my shorts and down my legs and back up again. He teased his fingers around the edges of the cloth, pushing it up high on my thighs, fingers teasing ever closer to the holy land. His lips brushed over my navel and down to the waist of my shorts and I shivered with each movement. Then he reached up, unsnapped and slowly unzipped my shorts.

Before I could catch my breath, he had them down around my ankles. His eyes were dilated and looking at me hungrily, as he slipped my shorts off completely. He watched me carefully as he slipped his hand up to my panties and caressed me. I arched my hips up to him, pressing myself against his firm touch. He pressed harder and as I moaned my desire, he bent down and was between my thighs, kissing his way up, his mouth finding the hot damp, thin silk. I writhed with pleasure as he teased the fabric. I was in a fevered state of arousal when he reached under me and pulled them away. Then he covered me with his mouth. The last thought I had was that I hoped the radio downstairs was loud enough to conceal the sounds I was making in the bedroom.

EIGHTEEN

There are unknown forces in nature; when we give ourselves wholly to her, without reserve, she lends them to us; she shows us these forms, which our watching eyes do not see, which our intelligence does not understand or suspect. – Auguste Rodin

Colby teased me with his mouth, his tongue, his fingers and my blood boiled with the fever of arousal. If he had missed a bug, then someone, somewhere, was hearing more than they bargained for as the pleasure of Colby's mouth brought me to my long sought after orgasm. I lay, panting in the middle of the bed as he reached up and over me, pulling a condom out of the nightstand drawer. I started to protest, reaching for him. I wanted him hard and hot inside me, but I also wanted to explore and taste.

"Later," he said in a low growl.

Well, at least I was going to be the one to unleash his weapon. I quickly undid his jeans and murmured my approval as I grasped him and slowly moved my hand up and down his shaft. He slid out of his jeans and into the condom. Wasting no time, he pulled my hips up to his and found his way. He moaned and I gasped at the pleasure. He began to rock gently at first, but at my urging, pumped faster and harder. My hips reached up to meet his every thrust, taking him deeper with each stroke. His every movement took me further from the stress and uncertainty that had enveloped me and closer to another mind melting orgasm. Then before I fell off the cliff again, a small thought crept in, I was falling in love. Before that thought could overwhelm me, my body took over, going taut and then trembling to a climax, rendering my brain useless. I wrapped myself tightly around Colby as he rocked into me harder and harder, until it was his turn to shudder with a moan as he came, pumping and grinding until he was spent.

Then he was lying on top of me, sweaty and breathing hard. He started to roll off, but I caught him and pressed him close to me, comforted by his weight and strength. He pushed up on his elbows and looked at me. He looked as relaxed as I felt.

"Just for the record, I usually last longer," he said with a wry smile. I laughed gently and arched my hips up to his.

"You'll get no complaints from me. But if you'd like a do-over..." I wiggled my hips suggestively against his. He lowered himself and kissed me.

"You are a minx," he said before kissing my neck.

"You only now figured that out? I thought you were an observant law enforcement officer." He replied by covering my mouth with his and I chose to shut up and enjoy the attention. I was so busy enjoying I didn't register the knock at the door until Colby stopped kissing me.

"Shhh," he said in my ear, even though I hadn't said anything. However, I was breathing heavily. I held my breath for a moment and there was another knock on the door.

"Fuck," was all Colby said as he moved away from me. I grabbed him and tried to pull him back.

"They'll go away if we ignore them," I protested.

"Unless they decide no answer means they can break in," he replied with an edge. I sighed and let him go. He sat up, pulled on his jeans, grabbed his gun and headed down the stairs. I searched around for my underwear, found them, slipped them on, then my shorts. I grabbed Colby's shirt and threw it on, buttoning the two middle buttons. I then followed him out of the room.

Downstairs, Colby had already answered the door and I heard a familiar voice. I went into the living room. "Peter, what are you doing here?" I said with barely disguised annoyance. Colby was tucking his gun in the back of his jeans and he turned and gave me a quizzical look. "Colby, this is my ex-husband, Peter Mason. Peter, Colby Jameson."

Peter stammered hello as he realized what he had interrupted. Colby motioned him in and closed the door behind him. I thought it was more strategic than an invitation. Always the cop, always on alert, an open door was difficult to defend.

"I didn't mean to interrupt, I was doing some organizing and found a few things you left and wanted to drop them off." He handed me a canvas bag with the word Boston stenciled below a watercolor of the Boston skyline on it. I couldn't imagine what I left behind. I took it and we all stood there awkwardly. Nothing like a post-coital visit from the ex to put a damper on things.

"Why don't I leave you two to talk," Colby said before beating a hasty retreat to the kitchen. Obviously, he felt the threat had passed. Coward.

206 · ANNIE DEMORANVILLE

"Thank you for these, Peter," I said, not sure why he was here, but confident it had nothing to do with the bag I was holding.

"No problem. I was also wondering if you'd filed the divorce paperwork yet?" he asked, a note of sadness in his voice. I thought of the papers still sitting on my desk, just feet away, and lied.

"Yes, I did. We should have the signed decree in a few weeks." I made a mental note that no matter how many people were shooting at me tomorrow, I was buying a stamp and mailing the damn papers.

More awkward silence. I could hear Colby starting to brew coffee. Outside the late summer sun was giving way to twilight. Apparently, he was planning on a long night. I smiled to myself.

"Well, that's good, I guess," Peter interrupted my thoughts. "I just thought I'd check. So, who is Colby?"

"We work together," I said, not quite a lie, "he came over for dinner." And so much more.

"Then I'll let you get back to…it," Peter said and gave me a knowing smile. I tried not to, but couldn't help it. I blushed. He bent down and kissed my forehead. "Talk to you soon." With that, he was gone. I closed the door behind him and sat down on the couch. I could not catch a break. At the moment I think I have some semblance of control in my life, the façade is shattered.

"You okay in there?" Colby asked affectionately as he peered around the corner. I smiled, got up and walked over to him. He wrapped his arms around me, pulled me into him and held tight. "Nothing like having the ex stop by to make things interesting."

"Yes, because my life evidently lacks interest."

"Come on, I made us coffee." Sounded good, but I thought first I should get dressed or we'd never get any more work done.

Sitting at the big oak table in the kitchen, in silence with Colby, I tried not to think about Peter. I wanted to protect him and throttle him, simultaneously. It dawned on me that our relationship would forever and always be complicated, but it would never be over. We'd always be a part of each other. It made me sad and happy at the same time. I shook my head. I must be hormonal. On the other hand, maybe this was normal when your life was under siege from several different directions and there was a Sexy Lawman at your table and in your bed. I looked over at my Sexy Lawman and smiled. I hadn't had time to enjoy the afterglow, but I could still feel him, still smell him on me. I began to wonder why we were sitting here drinking coffee when we could be back upstairs. He answered my unasked question.

"We need to make a plan," he said quietly before getting up and retrieving the listening devices and a tissue box. He tucked them carefully into the middle of the box, so they were surrounded by layers of tissues. He then took the box into the laundry room, placed it on the washing machine and closed the door behind him as he returned to the kitchen.

"Won't they get suspicious if they don't hear anything?" I asked, not wanting to tip our hand, but also anxious to not trigger another unwanted visit.

"I was thinking about that. If we leave them in the backroom, we can control what they hear. We can even use the back door as a decoy to disguise our comings and goings.'"

"That might work. But not for long." I was skeptical, thinking they might also be watching us, but willing to give it a try. Anything was better than handing them an all-access pass to our private conversations.

"We won't need long. I think we are close to cracking Mike's code and then maybe we can figure out what the hell is happening."

"Or get shot," I said without much emotion, "I mean we are assuming whatever information Mike had is what got him killed, right?"

"Boy, sex makes you fatalistic," Colby teased.

"No, people trying to kill me and randomly trashing my apartment makes me fatalistic. Sex gives me a reason to live. Don't be trying to get out of an encore performance tonight."

Colby closed the distance between us and kissed me, parting my lips with his tongue and deepening the kiss until every cell in my body was electrified. He released my mouth and gave a wicked grin. "Now about that code."

"Devil," I said, but reached for the computer. "Where's the leftover pizza?" I asked, thinking if the Scary Dudes didn't kill me, my dietary selections would.

"I'll get it," he replied and walked into the backroom to assure our dinner plans were noted by persons unknown. I hoped they were sitting in a hot car with only a stale baloney sandwich envying our epicurean choices. While Colby went upstairs to retrieve our floor picnic leftovers, I stared at the scanned copy of Mike's note on Colby's computer screen. I had no idea what it could mean. I picked up the original paper and held it up to the light, hoping to see something I missed. Colby walked back in. "Lots of pizza left, I guess we were hungry for other things. I left the radio playing in the laundry room to give us some privacy." He smiled as he watched me holding up the paper, "Still thinking Mike used invisible ink?"

"Have a better theory?" I handed the paper to him as he sat down next to me.

"I'm convinced he used a simple substitution code and the note is part of the key. We have the numbers. The problem is we're missing the encryption key word. Letters that would then correspond to those numbers."

I looked at him puzzled. He pulled out a piece of paper from his laptop case. He sketched out a table and added the alphabet, one letter to each column in the first row. Then he numbered the columns underneath each letter, one to twenty-six. Next to the table, he wrote the word Peoria. Underneath Peoria, he wrote the six numbers: six, nine, one, four, eight, and five.

"What are those numbers," I asked, catching on to where I thought he was going with the table.

"The numbers from the note. Six, for six-pack, nine, fourteen, eighty-five is…was, Mike's birthday. See, now each of those numbers corresponds to the letters in Peoria. Then we go back to the table and for each of those letters, we substitute the number. P becomes six, which then makes F, sixteen. E becomes nine and the I becomes five, and so on. Then when we open up the file on the flash drive, we substitute all the numbers with the letters from the table."

"That's brilliant. You solved it!" I couldn't believe we were this close.

"I've figured out a possibility. The problem is, we don't know the keyword."

"Do you think it's one of the words in the note?" Even as I said it, it seemed unlikely.

"I don't think he'd put the numbers and the word key together. I've scoured it for clues to something or someone he assumed I would know, but I've come up with nothing. We passed in the halls, spoke a few times, nothing stands out. The most we have in common is you."

Two slices of pizza and a couple of sodas I was wishing were beer later, I picked up the note again. Mike enjoyed the pizza and beer. However, Colby and Mike didn't have pizza and beer together. Mike and I had pizza and beer together. That first night, when I went to be "debriefed" after a day of fruitless inquiry, we shared a pizza. Mike flirting with me, teasing me about my wish for more excitement, smiling at me and warning me I just might get more than I wanted. If I only knew then what I now know, I'd be happy for that quiet day and innocent flirting over dinner.

"TJ? You are somewhere else again." Colby interrupted my contemplation. "Those must be some pretty deep thoughts."

Startled, I looked up. "Pizza and beer, that's what Mike and I had the first night we had dinner together. After I spent the day snooping around for any information on Shiedeger. I think the note might be referring to that."

Colby was quiet. He took my hand. Finally, he said, "Tell me about that dinner."

I inhaled deeply, the memory a sharp knife. It felt a lifetime ago and yet, it wasn't even a month. I remembered how excited I was to be involved with something interesting and working with a man with eyes so blue, you could swim in them. How disappointed I was that I couldn't bring him a juicy piece of information that would break the case wide open. And then there was his laugh as he explained to me the first rule of investigative work...

"Tedium. Tedium!" Colby looked at me as if I'd finally cracked under the pressure. "That night, he...he teased me about my desire for excitement. He told me the first rule of investigations was 'tedium'. It became a little joke between us."

Colby's eyes lit up as he realized what I was saying. He reached for the computer and opened up a file. It was one of Mike's pages, but at the top was a table similar to the one he drew for me. It had three rows, twenty-six columns, the alphabet across the top row, corresponding numbers underneath. The third row was blank, waiting for the substitutions. Below the table were the numbers from Mike's cryptic note: six, nine, one, four, seven, five. Under each number he typed in a letter: T E D I U M. He looked at it for a long moment.

"Do you think that's it?"

"I think so. We won't know for sure until we try and apply it to the numbers Mike left us." Colby's eyes hadn't left the screen. He began typing again.

I stood up to get a better look, resting my hands on his shoulders. They felt strong and warm. I could smell sex and sweat. I felt a familiar pulse run through my body and once again realized I was going to hell for thinking about stripping this man naked instead of solving a murder. For a brief moment, I wondered what was going to happen once we were free of this forced isolation. What was next for us? I quickly pushed that thought aside and forced myself to concentrate on what Colby was doing. He was typing numbers into the third row, based on the numbers that correlated with tedium.

When he was done, he saved the document and copied it to the flash drive. I grabbed my tablet and took the flash drive from him and plugged it in. We had disconnected the Wi-Fi to the apartment and Colby made sure both the computer and tablet were secured so no one could hack in. It wasn't perfect, but we needed to be able to work out this code without looking over our shoulders. I opened the file and looked at the table. Now it was only two rows, one of letters and one of numbers.

"Here's the beauty of a simple substitution code, it's simple." He grinned at me and my heart skipped a beat. It was a beautiful smile, contrasting with his dark skin and finishing up as a sparkle in his eyes. "All we have to do now is substitute the letter for the number in each line. Hopefully when we are done, if we have the correct keyword, these pages of numbers will reveal whatever Mike needed us to see."

I looked at the long list of rows and columns in front of me. "I should probably make us more coffee." I suspected there would be no encore tonight. I went to start the coffee, pulling down the grinder and beans. "How will we know we've got the right keyword?" I poured beans in the grinder, pulled the coffee pot to me and lifted out the old filter and tossed it in the trash. I replaced it with a new one.

"It shouldn't take long. If the first few lines don't form recognizable words, then we'll have to try something else."

I whirred the beans with the grinder and measured out the grounds. I added water and hit the start button. I pressed the bold brew for good measure. I walked back to the table and sat down. "Anything yet?"

"I'm not sure. I'm afraid we may have to play Word Search as we go, there aren't any spaces in the rows."

I studied my screen and picked up my stylus. Colby was working on the first page, so I skipped down to the last page. I began to change out various numbers for letters. I had almost finished the first row when there was a knock at my door. Colby was up with gun drawn before the knocking stopped. I looked over at the clock. It was nine thirty. It felt much later. I stood up and gently grabbed Colby's arm, it was reassuringly firm. The knocking started again. It was a gentle rap, not a strong, firm knock. I thought I recognized it.

"Colby, I think that's Mrs. Cavaleri." He looked at me like I was crazy. I shrugged, "I recognize her knock." We walked into the living room and Colby made me stand to one side of the door, out of firing range I suppose. "Who is it?"

"Oh darling, it's just me, Mrs. Cavaleri. I'm sorry to disturb you," came the sweet reply through the door. I reached over to open it, Colby still cautious, lowered his gun, but kept it at the ready by his side.

"Hi, Mrs. Cavaleri, is everything all right?" I asked as I opened the door all the way, so Colby could see there was no threat. Mrs. Cavaleri was standing there, holding a tiny orange fluff ball.

"I wanted to check with you to see if this was your kitten. He's been sitting outside your door for the last hour." She handed me the kitten, who weighed almost nothing and was clearly more fur than anything else. I couldn't help myself. I held him up to my face and made baby sounds.

"No, he's not mine. Though he is adorable." I reluctantly handed the now purring softness back to her.

"If you want a kitten, I can outfit you with all the essentials, litter box, litter, kitten food." She said hopefully. I looked over at Colby, whose expression clearly said, *we're in the middle of a murder investigation and hiding out from corrupt cops what are we going to do with a kitten?* Sadly, I shook my head.

"My life is a little...complicated right now. Maybe he belongs to Jeff?"

After leaving Mrs. Cavaleri to take care of what was surely going to become her next cat, Colby and I went back to deciphering the numbers before us. Somehow, between the prospect of solving this piece of the mystery and snuggling the little fur-ball, I was feeling cautiously optimistic. I tried to contain it, because people were still trying to kill me and I suspected anything we found hidden in these numbers would only increase the risk. I continued the slow process of decoding my page.

"Well, would you look at this," Colby declared, turning his computer screen to me.

NINETEEN

I live life in the margins of society, and the rules of normal society don't apply to those who live on the fringe. – Tamara de Lempicka

I pulled the computer closer, looking at the letters replacing many of the numbers. At first, it looked like we had the wrong key. Even though they appeared to form words, none were recognizable. Then there it was, column three, row four: **Strickland D**. Colby's boss. Well, at least we knew we had the right key. I slid the computer back to Colby. I was afraid to look at him. I couldn't imagine what it would mean if this confirmed we were dealing with corruption and murder in his own backyard. So far, though, we only had what appeared to be a bunch of names.

"This isn't telling us much, yet," I said as I continued the task of slowly replacing my numbers with letters. My efforts to decode were less than helpful. "Either I'm doing this incorrectly or we need a different key for this page."

"Let me see," Colby said as he took my tablet from me. He studied it for a minute, tapped on the screen a couple of times and showed me the screen. "I think some of the numbers are actually numbers. See the spacing here, like an address or numbering system."

He was right. Once he put the numbers back in, words began to form and the numbers obviously corresponded to the word or name. "You're brilliant. I didn't even see that. Does the Marshals Service have a decryption division? You could be a natural."

I grabbed another slice of pizza and Colby got up to refill his coffee cup. I wanted a beer, but instead went to the refrigerator and poured myself a glass of milk. I sat back down and in between bites, continued the task at hand. Colby was silent and focused. I was nervous and fidgety. It was all I could do to sit still. We were so close and yet the answers still eluded us. Frustration and anxiety were threatening to suffocate me. I pushed on and willed myself to stay focused.

"Well, I'll be damned."

"What, did you discover something good?" I leaned over to see what prompted the invective.

"I appear to be on this list." He moved the computer over so I could see what he'd highlighted with the curser. **Jameson C.** There it was, row seven, column four.

"Then you might as well confess now."

"Okay, I confess. I want to rip all your clothes off and take you right here on your grandmother's table."

"I just might let you." I met his gaze. His eyes were like melted emeralds and I felt the heat rise and my pulse quicken. "But first, tell me why your name is on an encrypted list." He smiled and sighed. I didn't know if it was because he knew naked was still a while away or because he was on the list.

"I have absolutely no idea."

We worked for two more hours until we had all four pages deciphered. I looked over the two pages I had completed and tried to find a pattern. There were two pages filled with two rows of various number and word pairs. 111 Valley. 475 Backstrom. 1237 Palladium. None of it made any sense to either Colby or me. His pages were mostly names. Some he knew, others were a complete mystery.

"I don't know about you, but I'm done." Colby hit the save on his computer and then powered it down. "We need more information for this to coalesce. Let's get some rest and try again tomorrow." I powered down my tablet and handed it to Colby. He took it and the computer upstairs to my closet, which had an old skeleton key lock. Not as secure as a safe deposit box, but it would have to do for tonight. I cleaned up the dinner remnants and set the coffee pot to brew in the morning. Colby came back into the kitchen as I was putting the last plate in the dish drainer. I wiped my hands on the towel by the sink. Colby grabbed the towel and pulled me to him.

Without a word, he backed me to the big oak table and leaned me against it. He parted my legs with his and bent me back, leaning in to kiss me. He covered my mouth and took my lips in his. There was no gentleness, no caressing his lips to mine. Instead, he devoured my mouth hungrily, crushing my lips with his, his hands fisting in my hair, pulling me close while at the same time bending me back hard against the table with his hips.

I met his desire with my own. I grabbed at his shirt, pulling him in close to me. I pushed my hands beneath the fabric and scraped my nails across his chest and back. Colby wrapped his arms around me and pulled me into him, his lips moving over my cheeks and down my neck and back to my lips. We were having a good old-fashioned make-out session. His hardness pressed against me and I could feel my dampness grow as I pulsed with desire. Finally, he released me. I was breathing hard as he grasped my hand. I thought he was going to lead me upstairs. Instead, we went to the backroom. He uncovered the listening devices. He opened and closed the back door.

"That was a long night of nothing. I'm beat, how about you?"

"Ready for bed, that's for sure."

Colby grinned and took me upstairs. The moon flooded my room with light. Colby stood in front of me and stripped off his shirt. His well-sculpted chest glistened with sweat from late summer heat and lust. I walked around the room and opened the double-hung windows at the top and bottom to let the evening air cool down the room. Hot man, check, romantic moonlight, check, cool evening breeze, check, but all I could focus on were the bugs in my laundry room and the cryptic files on my tablet. I looked out the window, wondering if they were out there watching us, knowing our every move, even if they couldn't hear us.

Colby came up behind me, wrapping his arms around me. He didn't say a word, but pulled me in close, resting his head on mine. I took a deep breath and relaxed into him. No matter what was out there, he was here and that was enough. I turned to him and he bent down to kiss me as I unbuttoned his jeans. He pulled my shirt over my head and buried his head in my breasts, rubbing his stubbled cheeks against the exposed skin, then adeptly removing my bra while I fumbled with the last button on his jeans. Before long, we were both naked, illuminated only by moonlight. Colby's hands explored my breasts, my hips, my shoulders and my hair, pressing me against his erection. I had my hands on his firm ass, thinking Michelangelo's David wasn't as well sculpted as my Sexy Lawman.

Colby maneuvered me to the bed and tipped me down until I was sitting on the edge of the bed. He grabbed a pillow, placed it on the floor in front of me and then kneeled down until his face was even with mine. He began kissing me again, his hands cupping my breasts, teasing my nipples. Soon his mouth worked its way down to my breasts where he sucked, pulled and licked at my nipples until they were hard little nibs and I was moaning with pleasure. I ran my hands over his head, feeling the soft, short-cropped hair and then over his shoulders and down his firm arms.

He felt sexy, safe and powerful under my hands. He felt even better in me and I began to wonder what was taking him so long. As if to answer that thought, he pushed me back against the bed and kissed his way down my stomach and to the holy land. With all the stress and tension of the day, it didn't take long before I was moaning a growing chorus of "yes, yes" and feeling pretty damn good.

He began to kiss his way back up to my breasts and move us both to the center of the bed. He was leaning on his arms over me and I reached down and stroked his impossibly large, hard penis. He became still and moaned as I stroked faster from tip to base and back again, rubbing my thumb over the soft velvet tip. I had a firm grip on him, so when I sat up, it was easy to catch him off balance and switch our positions. I straddled him, never letting go of my treasure. I kissed his grinning mouth. Then worked my way down until I was exactly where I wanted to be. I took all of him in my mouth and sucked, licked and teased while my hands kept busy cupping him.

Later, as we were wrapped together, looking up at the moon, we didn't talk. There wasn't a need to – there was comfort and trust, which was much better. We basked in that because everything else around us was chaos and betrayal. We drifted off to sleep. Later, we woke to the moon, lower in the night sky, peeking through the big oak tree, and indulged in another passionate interlude. After that sleep was deep and peaceful for the first time since Mike was killed. I awoke to the symphony of the birds that filled the backyard trees. The sun wasn't quite up, but the sky was hued in pink and blue.

For a moment, I was blissfully happy, feeling the comfort of a strong male presence in my bed. Then, like the sun peeking up over the horizon, anxiety flooded over me. Another day without answers. Another day wondering who was going to try and kill me next. I moved away from Colby, trying not to disturb him. I slipped on my robe and turned back to him. He was awake and gazing at me.

"Don't look at me like that, I have to get ready for work…and you could easily distract me."

"I'm enjoying the view," then he pulled back the covers and invited me to enjoy that view. I smiled and suggestively began to loosen my robe before quickly tightening the belt and moving toward the doorway.

"I'm going to take a quick shower."

"Need some help?"

"Then it wouldn't be a quick shower, would it?

"Oh, I could make it quick."

I smiled, shook my head and left him lying there in all his smoldering glory. Downstairs I hit the brew button on the coffeepot and went to shower. I was slightly disappointed that I was uninterrupted. Then again, the temptation to skip work and stay in bed all day was already high, so it was best I showered alone with my thoughts. I hoped Colby had some ideas of next steps because it wasn't looking good. I thought for sure decrypting the notes on the files would be a watershed moment. Instead, we had more questions than answers. I stepped out of the shower, clean but discouraged. I toweled myself off, wrapped up in my bathrobe and headed to the kitchen. Maybe coffee would change my mood.

I stepped into the kitchen and my spirits were immediately lifted. Not by the smell of heavenly brew, but by the sight of a shirtless Colby at my table, bringing a mug of coffee to his luscious lips. Reminded of all the pleasure they gave. He looked up and smiled at me as I poured myself a cup. I sat beside him. He reached out and wrapped his arm around me, then pulled me in for a deep kiss.

"Good morning," he said as he leaned back in his chair. His computer was open in front of him and I could see he had started in on the puzzle.

"Any progress?"

"No. We need more data and it's not here." He paused for a moment, took a sip of coffee and continued, "I'm going to have to go into the office today and see if I can find more information."

Panic welled up and my heart began to beat rapidly. This was not a good idea. We had no clue who to trust, but I was certain we could not trust the Marshals. At least not in Peoria. "Do you think that's a good idea?"

"No. But I'm out of options. We can't sit around and wait for the next attempt on your life. The longer this goes on, the harder it is to find a killer. I know, I'm a law enforcement professional." His attempt at humor did not lessen my apprehension.

"Can I talk you out of it?"

He sighed. "No. It'll be okay. I promise." He reached over and kissed me lightly on the forehead. "I'll be in and out. I'm going to check files for a few of the names we have and to do that I need access to my computer." My hand shook as I tipped the cup to my lips. He reached over and wrapped his hands around mine. "It is more secure than trying to use my laptop."

Despite my best efforts to stop them, tears welled in my eyes. It was highly probable that something on the flash drive was the reason Mike was murdered. Mike bleeding in my arms...Mike cold and lifeless on the steel table...Mike laughing at dinner... Mike's blue eyes sparkling as he talked of his beloved Marshals Service. It all flashed before me. Now Colby could be next. I'd be all alone. Facing who the hell knows what, on my own. A tear slipped down my cheek and I wiped it away viciously. "Do what you need to, but could you make sure I get my car back today. You know, in case I need to make a quick getaway." I didn't look at him as I got up and went upstairs to get ready for work. It was going to be a bitch trying to put makeup on while crying.

I didn't say much on the drive to Butterfield. Clouds were rolling in and a storm was forecasted by mid-afternoon. It felt ominous. I could not quell the cold fear that gripped me. I'd been shot at, chased and vandalized, but none of that compared to the panic I felt when I thought of something happening to Colby. Colby bleeding out, Colby lifeless in my arms, Colby downstairs in the embalming room.

We pulled into the parking lot and when Colby turned the truck off, I shook my head. "You don't need to walk in with me." I gathered my things and stepped out of the truck. "Call me as soon as you are done." I turned and walked up the steps and through the big oak doors. I didn't look back. I was afraid if I did, I'd burst into tears. That wouldn't help anything.

I dropped my things into my office and continued on to the reception area to check in. Dee wasn't at her desk, so I didn't have to run the gauntlet of disapproval. Instead, I went up to the kitchen, feeling the need for coffee and a stale donut. I was in luck. Someone had decided to replenish our donut supply with a fresh batch. I pulled a small plate out of the cupboard and put a chocolate glazed on it. I poured coffee into my mug, added milk and was about to take plate and mug down to my office when Nick walked in.

"Good morning. I see you found the donuts I brought." Nick smiled as he reached over me and grabbed the carafe to top off his mug, managing to brush against my breast as he did. "I decided I needed a peace offering because I'm going to have to ask everyone to put in some time this weekend. The Himmel funeral has become a circus."

I looked up at the scheduling board and sure enough, the next three days were filled with viewings and services, not just for Mr. Himmel, but other families who probably preferred their experience to be low key. That feat would be difficult to pull off with our current celebrity status. Nothing like murder and mayhem to bring out the mourners. My days were blurring together, so I might as well work the weekend. I sipped my coffee. I had been feeling guilty about the time I had been missing all week and this would give me a chance to make it up. Colby wouldn't be happy, but he would have to understand.

The thought of Colby brought back that sinking feeling. We were playing with gasoline here and we didn't know who was holding the match. What was Colby walking into today? Whoever murdered Mike held the whole deck and we didn't know what game we were playing. Gambling, murder, corruption, or something we were unaware of, and how did my father fit into all of this?

"TJ, where'd you go?" Nick asked with a smile. "Trying to think of a way to get out of weekend duty?"

"No, not at all. I'll be available to help with whatever you need."

"Okay, good. Staff meeting in an hour and we'll go over the game plan."

Back in my office, I booted up my email and sorted through the various papers on my desk. I watched as my mailbox filled with media requests, speaking engagements, a couple of notes from the Historical Society and one subject line that made me stop breathing for a moment. It read, "Happy Father's Day."

I sat down hard. My hand trembled as I grabbed for the mouse and moved the cursor over to the email and double-clicked to open it. Time stood still as I waited the half second for it to open. When it finally filled the screen in front of me, I scanned for a sender, not sure what I was hoping for, but it was simply a generic return address. The body of the message was short and simple: You don't have the whole story. Yet.

"Well, why don't you tell me what the story is, asshole," I cursed under my breath at the screen. When it didn't magically answer me back, I closed the email and moved it into my private file. Colby would want to see it. I looked at the clock on my computer. Colby was probably just arriving at the Marshals office. I dug into my bag and pulled out my burner phone. I made sure it was on and the volume was up. I didn't want to chance missing his call. I was about to put it down when it began to ring and Colby's name popped up on the screen. I fumbled to answer it.

"Colby? Is everything all right?"

TWENTY

Forever will be you and me. – Salvador Dalí

My hand shook as I held the phone. I took a deep breath and listened to Colby's deep voice, hoping he would reassure me that everything was going to be fine.

"I am headed into the lion's den."

"You have to be careful. Especially when you leave there, I keep thinking that is when…when you could be in trouble."

"I will. I promise." He paused for too long and fear began its climb again. "I arranged for your car to be delivered to the apartment this morning." He paused again and I knew he was searching for a way not to scare the crap out of me. I could have told him it was too late for that and to just get on with it, but I let him find his own way. "If something happens to me, and I'm not saying it will, but if it does, I want you to get out of town. Fast. Do you have somewhere you can go?"

"I'd go home, to West Virginia, my mom's house."

"Good, that would work. Use cash, no cards. Use the burner phone and don't tell anyone where you are going. Call your mom from the road, once you are out of Illinois. Got it?"

"You are scaring me."

"This is worst case scenario, TJ. It's only a plan, okay? I'll be fine and with any luck, I'll bring you lunch."

With any luck, I thought. We haven't had any so far, why would today be any different? I took another deep breath and dove back into my emails. That is when I realized I forgot to tell Colby about the mysterious one, presumably from my father. I picked up the phone and was about to hit redial when an ear-piercing scream came from somewhere down the hall. I jumped up and started for the door, assuming some family member just saw their final bill. A flash of Scary Dudes or Black Baseball Cap stopped me in my tracks. Tired of chasing me down, deciding to take advantage of Colby's absence, maybe they had invaded the funeral home. I was contemplating what to do when there was another scream. I grabbed the letter opener on my desk, opened my door and listened. I wasn't sure from which direction the scream had emanated, so I paused until I heard Nick's voice in the main office. With my letter opener poised for optimum defense, I hurried toward the commotion.

The voices became clearer as I moved down the hall. Nick was trying to calm an elderly woman in a bright yellow pantsuit. Dee was standing up and forcibly putting herself between a well dressed middle-aged woman and everyone else. I lowered the letter opener, confident I could take one or both of these ladies without a weapon. I contemplated turning back and returning to my office, but Nick saw me and indicated he could use reinforcements. I waded into the fury.

"YOU CREMATED MY BOY!" screamed Little Old Lady as I opened the door and entered the office. I closed it behind me, in case other guests wandered into the building. Not that the door would do much to contain the sound as she shouted, "HOW COULD YOU DO THAT?" Then she screamed again, a long, high pitched cry. In the small confines of the office, it was an ear-splitting sound. I gritted my teeth as Nick tried to put a hand on her shoulder to calm her. She would have nothing to do with that and was beginning to scream again when she was cut off by Smartly Dressed.

"That son-of-a-bitch does not deserve to be laid out in some expensive coffin for everyone to gawk at! Cheap bastard! And he murdered a man! Do you know how humiliating that is for me?!" She yelled over Dee's shoulder at the old woman.

"YOU HAD NO RIGHT TO CREMATE MY SON."

"Listen, you old bat, he was my sorry-assed husband and if I could cremate him again, I would. Just. To. Piss. YOU. OFF!" She pressed against Dee trying to get to Little Old Lady. To her credit, Little Old Lady made a "come and get me" motion. She was not going to be intimidated by a bleached blonde. "My reputation is ruined now. My business is ruined now. I was one of the top-selling real estate agents in the tri-city area. Who is going to want to buy a house from a murderer's wife, huh? Tell me that you old biddy." No doubt these women were related to our infamous Mr. Himmel.

Old Lady Himmel lunged for Himmel the Younger, but Nick caught her. He looked over at me with what was plainly a "what the fuck am I going to do" expression as he kept the two Mrs. Himmels from killing each other. What could he do? It wasn't as if he could reassemble Mr. Himmel. I momentarily entertained the thought of pretending I witnessed none of this and walking back to my office. But that would have been wrong. So very wrong. Instead, I had to think on my feet.

"I am so sorry to interrupt," I threw caution to the wind, hoping a stranger in the mix would momentarily distract them, "but Nick, I have been fielding calls from the press all morning about Mr. Himmel's funeral arrangements. I could use some guidance on what to tell them." What the heck, it wasn't really a lie, I was sure that the calls would begin soon.

"Tell them nothing. NOTHING, you hear me. Vile creatures have been knocking on my door and calling me since this awful thing happened. Vultures." Mama Himmel pulled a tissue out of her substantial handbag and dabbed her eyes.

"Exactly," Widow Himmel agreed readily, "they can rot in hell before you tell them anything. They can read the obituary like everyone else. If they want to know anything more, you tell them 'no comment.' And that's all you tell them." They still stood on either side of Nick and Dee, but at least they weren't screaming at each other anymore.

"Okay. I will tell them that the family has no comment on anything regarding Mr. Himmel. Thank you, ladies. I am terribly sorry for your loss." From the look on Nick's face, I might have expected a Christmas bonus if I had planned to stay that long. He took advantage of the respite from fighting to redirect the bereaved.

"Why don't we go on into the arrangement room and compose the obituary. We can finalize the memorial service. We will highlight all of the good things he did with the River Dogs and his community service." He continued to talk to them in his soothing funeral director voice as he ushered them out of the office and down the hall. "It would be nice if we could get some photos to display in a video montage…"

Yeah, don't forget to include the YouTube video of the shootout, I thought to myself. "Crisis averted," I said to Dee before returning to my office. She ignored me.

I suspected our morning meeting would be delayed while Nick finished soothing ruffled feathers. I wondered where Jacob could be, Nick usually foisted arrangements on him. What the heck, I didn't want to face what was in my office anyway. Therefore I went on a Jacob hunt instead. I stopped by my office to grab my coffee cup, planning to begin my pursuit in the kitchen. I also grabbed the burner phone and my regular cell. Wouldn't want to be out of touch, in case more family feuds erupted or Colby needed me for backup.

As I walked up to the kitchen, I reproached myself for letting him go alone. Whether Colby liked it or not, we were partners. And from all those cop shows I watched, the one thing I took away was, you always had your partner's back. Jacob wasn't in the kitchen, so I topped off my cup and continued on to the embalming rooms. There wasn't anyone new on the board but that didn't mean there hadn't been an early morning pickup and with all the commotion it hadn't made it up there yet.

Walking down to the prep rooms, I could only think about Colby. I wondered if he would find anything. I wondered if he'd make it out unscathed. And I thought that despite my desire to be his backup, he would never have let me follow him back to his office. I was betting his plan was to let them believe I was now out of the picture. That he had come to agree with Dan's assessment that Himmel killed both Shiedeger and Mike. I knocked lightly on the door to embalming room one and pushed it open. Jacob was there and before I could step into the room, he rushed to the door and pushed me out.

"TJ, you don't want to come in here. Give me a second," he said and closed the door in my face.

What the hell? I've been in the embalming room many times and except for the head-on car accident, which I was careful to avoid, I'd never been pushed out before. I couldn't imagine what Jacob was doing that I couldn't see. He opened the door and stepped out, closing it behind him and answered my question.

"Sorry. I picked up a six-year-old girl who fell out of a tree. I didn't want you to see her without warning."

"Oh, no, how awful," I said, thinking I wanted to go upstairs and slap the bickering Himmels. "Is she going to be able to have a viewing?" I asked, thinking it would compound the tragedy if her family couldn't say goodbye. I'd quickly learned on the job that funerals were for the living. There was a lot of catharsis that goes on in the process.

"She's beautiful. I'll have to use a little hat to cover up where they shaved her head, but she's perfect."

As difficult as some of the things were that Jacob saw in this job, a perfect six-year-old who would never see seven had to be one of the hardest. I was grateful he wanted to spare me that. "When is her service?"

"We're thinking that the viewing will be on Monday and the service on Tuesday afternoon, both at her church. Nick and I thought it would best to keep the family as far from the Himmel chaos as possible." He looked upward and shook his head.

"I'll leave you to her. Can I get you anything? Coffee?" I lifted my cup to him. He shook his head no and we both returned to our work.

Back at my desk, I picked up the burner phone for the tenth time and willed it to ring. When it didn't, I finished up the details for the Himmel guidelines. I looked up to see Nick escorting the Himmel ladies down the front steps. After they were on their way, he came back in and popped his head into my office.

"Thanks for the assist. Some days the dead are the best part of the job. Meeting in ten," and he was gone.

I printed out the notes for the meeting, checked my phone again before slipping it into my pocket and left to join the others in the kitchen. Jacob was pouring coffee when I got there and Dee was sitting in the corner looking bored. I was pleasantly surprised to see Tom Garner standing by the funeral board, though it made total sense since weekends were his beat. I wondered if he felt infringed on with two big Saturday funerals in a row. He was semi-retired and seemed to enjoy the usually quiet weekend duties. He was in charge of the weekend deaths, met with families as needed, and ran any small Saturday services. Mostly he was on call from Friday to Sunday and spent Saturdays in the office listening to whatever local sport was being broadcast.

Nick stuck his head in the door, phone clamped to his ear, listening to someone. He signaled that he would be there in a minute and ducked back out to the hallway. I poured myself a cup of coffee and heard him say, "Dad, I have this covered. If we had turned him away, how would that have looked? I have a staff meeting to lead. Can we talk about this later?" I grabbed a donut and took my seat next to Jacob, realizing for the first time that Nick's job was more difficult than it appeared. I could relate to the parental disapproval. "Sorry about that," Nick began as he poured himself a cup of coffee, "let's gets this going. We have some serious issues to address about the Himmel service."

Turns out, despite our best efforts, the service details were leaked and Nick was planning for the worst-case scenario. We strategized how best to handle the possible crowds and potential conflicts. No one may have been eager to claim Shiedeger's body, but that didn't mean once his murderer was revealed, resentments wouldn't surface. Nick was mapping out the first line of defense when my phone buzzed. My burner phone. I pulled it from my pocket, excused myself and slipped out into the hallway.

"Hello," I whispered as I walked away from prying ears toward Nick's office at the far end of the hall.

"Where do you want me to pick up your lunch?"

My heart beat a little harder and I put my hand up against the door frame to steady myself. I stepped into Nick's office and sat down in the closest chair. "It better be something good, I've worked up quite an appetite while worrying. Everything went okay?"

"Interesting developments, I'll brief you over lunch. See you in an hour." With that, he was gone. I wandered back to the kitchen in a daze. I was relieved he was out of the office, but still worried about what could happen next. We'd stirred up the hornet's nest, I was sure of it.

I mumbled my apologies as I reentered the kitchen. I only half listened as Nick finished up and Tom filled us in on the other events for the weekend. Nick had to ask me twice to brief everyone on my memo and the strategy for handling

media interest. I snapped out of my fog long enough to walk
everyone through the guidelines and answer their questions.
Dee then walked us through the schedule for the next few
days and I drifted away again. Wondering if my apartment
was being ransacked once more, if Colby had unknowingly
come face to face with Mike's killer this morning, if the little
lost kitten had settled in at Mrs. Cavaleri's, but mostly I
wondered about the big, dark, handsome, green-eyed Marshal
in my bed. Of all the challenges facing me, my feelings for
Colby were the most alarming. Crazy, I know, since I was
alternately being chased, shot at and vandalized, but there it
was. I was falling fast and hard. And had no way to put any
distance between us without endangering us both.

I had no business diving headlong into a serious
relationship. I was damaged, vulnerable and on the run. Not to
mention, I had no idea what Colby was thinking. I could be a
situational dalliance. I was driving a hundred miles per hour
into heartbreak and I couldn't stop it, didn't want to stop it. A
sigh escaped me and I looked up at Dee to see if she noticed.
She had.

The meeting finally wrapped and I escaped to my office to
do my part. I pushed open the door to find Colby sitting at my
desk, feet up, surrounded by Chinese food cartons, looking
over a notebook. My stomach did a little flip as I entered, so
grateful to see him. Totally aroused by the tableau. He stood
up, reached behind me and pushed the door closed. He then
took me in his arms and kissed me long and hard. By the time
he released me I was breathless and could give a crap about a
broken heart. I took a step back and put down my papers.

"How was your morning, dear?" I said in my best June
Cleaver.

"I got a lot done and I may have learned some vital information. Sesame chicken?"

"Extra spicy?"

"Just like you," he smiled as he handed me a plate of food. I munched on an egg roll as he shared his morning. "First thing you should know is that I put motion sensor cameras in your apartment."

"Marshal Jameson," I feigned shock, "I am not that kind of girl."

"I was hoping to make you one of those girls," he teased, pointing his chopsticks at me. "And in the meantime, I thought it would be a good idea to see who keeps breaking in if it happens again."

"Brilliant. Makes me almost hope someone decides to ransack my place again," I rolled my eyes and took another bite of chicken.

"Moving on," he flipped open his notebook. "I pulled up the records of the past few years on the gambling investigation and pulled the names of all the officers involved. I've been comparing them to the decrypted list. We have a few matches. I also found out that the Marshals were brought in to protect a witness who has since disappeared. Guess who was in charge of that detail?"

"Chief Deputy Marshal Dan?"

"Nope, Deputy Marshal Kyle Clarkson. Not only that, he is cousins with two Peoria officers that are on the list."

"Hmmm, small town."

"There was more, but it's all circumstantial, I don't have anything concrete. How does this get us to Nevada? And what's really going on? The gambling seemed to be

Shiedeger's thing. It may have very little to do with the overall conspiracy that involves Mike and your father."

"Oh, speaking of my father," I said before taking another bite and chewing carefully. Colby waited, eyebrows raised. "I think he sent me an email today." I turned to my computer and pulled up the email and slid over so Colby could read it.

"Well, damn, man, couldn't you spell it out for us?"

I laughed, "That's what I said!"

"Another cryptic piece of the puzzle. Did you try replying to it?" I stared wide-eyed at Colby for a moment and shook my head. It hadn't even occurred to me. He smiled and started typing. "My guess would be this is a spoof account and a reply will be returned as undeliverable." He hit send and we waited. Sure enough, less than a minute later an "undeliverable" reply was in my inbox. "It was worth a shot."

I went back to my lunch, since it was the only thing not disappointing me at the moment. Colby's intel hardly felt worth the risk. I was beginning to think the entire city was corrupt and couldn't wait to get out of Dodge. Colby interrupted my sulk. "I brought you a present."

My interest was piqued. I loved presents. Colby picked a leather bag up from underneath his chair and put it on the desk. I reached over, pulled it to me, unzipped it and looked inside. "What am I suppose to do with this?" I exclaimed incredulously as a bolt of lightning streaked across the sky. Thunder followed and the sky opened up.

TWENTY-ONE

There are so many things we've been brought up to
believe that it takes you an awfully long time to realize
that they aren't you. – Edward Gorey

I reached into the bag and gingerly pulled out a large gun. I checked to make sure the safety was on before turning it over in my hand. It felt heavy, not only physically, there was an emotional weight to it. This wasn't my uncle's rifle. It wasn't my cousin's shotgun I used to shoot skeet as a kid. This was serious. This was a cop's gun. I looked at Colby as I put it back into the bag.

"Looks just like yours."

"It is. It's my backup. I want to make sure you can use my weapon if you need to and I'll lock this one in the truck," he was all seriousness and concern, "just in case."

"I thought I was already familiar with your weapon," I sassed and was happily rewarded with that sparkle in his eyes and a leer.

"I have a buddy at the local range. He'll open the doors for us after hours tonight so I can give you a crash course. Is that okay?" I nodded again. He reached over, put his hand on my arm and squeezed. "I wish I didn't think this was necessary."

"I'm a quick study," I finally said after I was sure I wouldn't start to shake uncontrollably or worse, cry. "I want to make sure I've got your back if the worst should happen. I'll be all right."

We finished our lunch in silence. My mind was beyond forming thoughts, much less words. The dark clouds were gathering and I wasn't sure I could weather the storm. As Colby packed up our trash, his phone buzzed. He pulled it out of his pocket. Realizing it was the burner phone, he cursed under his breath and reached into his other pocket for his work phone.

"I disabled the GPS," he said in reply to my quizzical look. "Well, look at that, your car has been delivered to your apartment, evidently as good as new."

"Guess I can flee for parts unknown. Unless of course it has been upgraded with a brand-new tracking device." Colby didn't seem to find my dark humor amusing.

"I'll pick you up after work and we'll head to the firing range."

"Actually, can we stop at home first, so I can change into something more 'range-worthy'?" He nodded. Then he stood up, pulled me to my feet and kissed me.

"I'm hoping for something fit for a Guns and Ammo cover," he said when he released me. And with that, he was gone. I watched him walk to his truck, admiring his fine, tight ass. I bet jeans fought each other to be the pair wrapped around that butt.

The remainder of my afternoon was quiet and busy, so it passed quickly. I was grateful there were no more screaming family members. There was enough planning to do for the service that I was unable to obsess about everything else in my life. I did allow myself a brief interlude of fantasizing about Colby's fine ass and having his muscular arms wrapped around me. At five thirty, I shut down the computer and looked out the window to see if my ride had arrived. The rain had stopped and the sun was out. Colby was turning into the parking lot. As usual, my stomach fluttered and my breath quickened. I sighed, deciding it was useless to struggle against my hormones right now. I could only fight so many battles in one week. As long as the condoms held, at least my hormones were relieving a modicum of stress. I packed my bag and closed my door behind me. I didn't bother to buzz Dee and let her know I was leaving because for once, she had left early. I stepped out through the heavy oak doors and was hit with a blast of late summer heat and humidity. Good to know Hell hadn't frozen over.

I walked to the Silverado as Colby stepped out and opened the passenger door for me. I climbed in and then reached out, grabbed his shirt and pulled him in for a kiss. He returned it, but I could feel tension behind it. I suspected there was more to his trip this morning than we discussed at lunch. I settled into my seat and we drove in silence to my apartment. I'm not ashamed to say I was excited to see my little yellow Mini parked on the street in front of my building.

I changed my clothes quickly, filled two bottles of water and met Colby downstairs. He was going over my little SuzieV, checking for anything that shouldn't be there. I handed him a bottle and noted the concerned looked. His hand lingered on mine for a moment and he took a deep breath. I braced myself.

"The good news is, I found no trackers or listening devices."

"And…is there bad news?"

"Not exactly. I found this on your front seat." He handed me a sealed manila envelope that had my full name scrawled across the front in black sharpie. It was beautiful script and I suspected it hadn't been left there by the auto body guy.

"It's sealed," I said with surprise when I took it from him. I assumed he had already inspected the contents.

"It was addressed to you and with my keen professional skills, I ascertained it was not lethal, so I thought you should open it."

I crossed my eyes at him, turned the envelope over and peeled open the flap. I pulled out two sheets of paper. One had a diagram on it that looked like a genealogy chart. The other had a timeline. I handed them to Colby. "Think this is the rest of the story?" He took a quick look and put the papers back in the envelope.

"Could be. Let's head to the range and we'll decipher this new clue over dinner." He tucked the envelope into his jacket pocket, next to his holster.

The gun range was so quiet it was spooky. Our footsteps echoed as we walked down the hall to the lanes. The owner had let us in the back door and it was clear from his interaction with Colby that their relationship was born of shared experience. I doubt Colby had given him any details, but there was an acknowledgment that if Colby was asking for this favor, it was serious. He left us on our own with instructions to knock on his office door when we were done.

Colby set both weapons on the shelf in front of me. He walked me through loading and unloading the gun and general instructions on safety and firing. I spent the next thirty minutes obliterating little paper men. In the beginning, I was unsure and shaky. I was used to the length and weight of a shotgun or rifle but once I became used to the size and recoil, my hands steadied and my aim became deadly. After I discharged my latest clip, I ejected the cartridge and put the gun back on the tray.

"I think I've got it." I was exhausted. Firing a weapon takes focus and strength. I was out of both.

I couldn't face another pizza, so we picked up chicken Caesar salads and a bottle of wine on the way home. I moved SuzieV into the parking lot behind the building and set her alarm. Colby waited at the back stairs for me and we climbed them together. We made a point of detailing our evening to the listening devices sitting atop the washing machine. Although I doubted anyone was buying our ruse any longer.

We were both grateful to see that nothing had been disturbed while we were gone. I set up dinner in the dining area while Colby checked the video feed. Given that we were having wine, I even put out placemats. I dumped the salads on plates. Set the plates on the placemats, along with the wine glasses and forks. Colby opened the wine and poured, then pulled out the mystery envelope. He removed the papers, set them on the table and we sat down to dinner.

I picked at my salad. I wasn't really hungry. There was a feeling of foreboding knotted in my gut that I couldn't shake. I sipped my wine, but it tasted like vinegar. I pushed it aside and pulled the papers to me. The one that looked like a genealogy chart listed familiar names and at the apex was my father. Branching down one side were Mike and Colby, on the other side Clarkson and an unfamiliar name, at least to me. Smack dab in the middle: Chief Deputy Marshal Dan Strickland. Branching off underneath them were names from the decoded list, each linked to one side or the other. Underneath Mike and Colby's names, was my name. I was confident this was part of the missing information. It was probably what Mike was trying to put together before being killed. The other page was a timeline. Looking over it, I felt my stomach churn. It began with Mike arriving in Peoria. Next hash mark: meeting me. He didn't stumble onto whatever corruption was going on until after he met me, and then it was too late. I was on the radar and I became their target. But, why? Because of what Mike knew or because of who my father was? The last hash mark was Mike's death. I pushed my plate away, sick that Mike's murder somehow connected directly to me...to my father. I handed Colby the papers without a word.

"When I was at the Marshals office this morning, I dug into your father's history with the Marshals and the FBI," he paused and I braced myself for the worst. "These lists, the one we found and the one your father left for us, it's not just about corrupt cops. Many of the officers on the list have had interactions with your father on one level or another. Not surprising, given how long he was in WITSEC and then employed as a consultant. Somehow he's right in the middle of this."

"Do you think he took part in Mike's murder?"

"I don't know. I hope not. It's clear, though, that if he did, Mike's murder was a bridge too far and he's been trying to help you ever since."

"The light in my apartment, that night it was ransacked," I nodded, "was the first time."

Colby nodded. "I've been thinking that, too. I think he's been underground and watching their every move. I also think he's trying to protect you."

I wasn't sure how I felt about any of this. A week ago, I didn't even know my father was alive. The thought that he was suddenly my knight in dented armor was too much to process. "Do you think there are people on the list we can trust to help us?

"I'm sure there are, but until we can unravel this further, I'm not ready to risk it. What about you?"

"Until I know who shot Mike, everyone is a suspect as far as I'm concerned."

"Including me?"

I looked at him for a long moment before replying, "Depending on my mood, even you are suspect." I wasn't kidding.

"Fair enough." He took my hand, "Let's say we forget about this for a while and go have some fun."

"Seriously? What did you have in mind?"

"Didn't you say Nick was playing at a bar tonight? Let's go listen."

"Seriously?" I repeated, thinking the stress had finally broken my Sexy Lawman.

"Sure. It will do us good to get out, clear our heads. I'm armed and dangerous. We will be fine. Besides, maybe if your boss sees you out on a date, he'll stop trying to grope you in the supply closet."

An hour later, we were out at Jimmy's Bar, which was a stone's throw from my apartment and featured local musicians on the weekends. Despite harboring a suspicion that Colby was trying to lure the Bad Guys with this excursion, it did feel great to be out.

The bar teemed with happy, laughing, slightly intoxicated people and the energy was infectious. Nick's band was on the small stage in the corner of the back patio. The bar spanned an entire wall of the main room. Rugby and hockey banners hung from the ceiling. Sports memorabilia decorated the walls. Colby paid our cover and we dutifully obtained our hand stamp - the rugby team's mascot, a mean looking pig. I hoped it would wash off before the funeral tomorrow because it would clash with my outfit.

We ordered two beers and took them out to the patio. There were no open seats, but we squeezed in near the patio fence. We could set our drinks on the ledge if the music compelled us to get our groove on. I was surprised to find myself enjoying the band. Nick played guitar. A blond haired guy, who looked like an aging surfer, sang lead. The drummer was graying and shirtless. The bass player looked like he could be their son, years younger than the other members, with thick dark hair and intense eyes. Joe Perry in his prime, it was easy to pick out which were his groupies. The band played a mix of eighties and nineties rock covers, with a little seventies thrown in to round things out. Everyone was having a good time and I found myself letting the music and mood take me away. For a while, I was in the moment, just a girl in a bar with a good-looking date on a Friday night. At one point during the first set, Nick caught my eye, giving me a nod and smile. He sought me out during the set break and insisted on buying us a round of drinks. After that, he was quickly swept away by a sea of admirers before jumping back on stage for the second set. Halfway through "Jessie's Girl" I realized I was almost finished with my second beer and hadn't eaten anything substantial since lunch. I looked around. The prospects of getting food in less than an hour from the overworked waitstaff were slim, so I tugged on Colby's arm. We wound our way back into the bar and then outside before trying to talk over the din.

"Had enough?" he asked me as we stepped out front. People were still streaming in as we weaved our way to the parking lot.

"I'm hungry and I didn't want to risk another beer on an empty stomach."

We settled into the Silverado. My ears were ringing and I was exhausted, but the darkness had lifted, however temporarily. Now, I was hungry and horny. I planned to remedy both those desires before the night was over.

Later, lying naked in bed together, looking up at the stars, I dared to imagine a world where I was safe and happy. It felt good. However, in order for that to become a reality, people needed to stop shooting at me, trying to run me over and ransacking my apartment. I slapped Colby on the ass.

"Mmmmm," was all he said. I smacked him again, this time harder.

"Get up, we have work to do." I got up, slipped into spandex shorts. I topped it with an oversized t-shirt and left to make coffee. Colby appeared a few moments later, dressed only in basketball shorts that left little to the imagination.

"You sure know how to kill a mood," he said as he pulled mugs from the cupboard and milk from the refrigerator.

"My goal is to extend the mood to more than a stolen moment between attempts on my life. To do that we need to work this problem and come up with a plan."

I spread the papers across the kitchen table, including a printout of Mike's list. We started comparing names. When the coffee pot chimed, I poured us both a mug and we continued to analyze the lists. We started with Thomas Joseph's genealogy and then added more names from Mike's list, making intuitive leaps when it wasn't clear on whose side they belonged. Once we had it completed, Colby stepped back and looked at what we had created. I could tell from the look in his eyes, he didn't like what he was seeing. I topped off my coffee and waited. Colby circled a few names on the Bad Guy list. His green eyes darkened as something became clearer to him.

"TJ, this isn't good. I don't know everyone on our suspicious list, but these, here, that I've circled – Marshals Service, State Patrol, Peoria Police Department, and these two are FBI. The Marshals and the FBI agents I've worked with and all of them were on a joint task force about three years ago. When I was looking through your father's records, he was on the same task force."

"So we have Marshals, FBI, a gambler who overreached...and my dad."

"We can't be sure that Shiedeger had anything to do with any of this, he may have been the excuse for Mike to come to Peoria, looking for you."

I shook my head, I was frustrated. We had a list but nothing else, no evidence, no idea why anyone would kill Mike. I swiped the papers off the table and stifled a scream. Wouldn't want to wake Mrs. Cavaleri. I paced the kitchen. "We have nothing. It's all supposition and nothing tells us what is going on or who is doing this. This can't go on any longer, I'm done."

"I'm wondering if we should take you to your mom's house until I can figure this out. You'd be safer there."

"Fuck you. I'm not going anywhere and you're not doing this alone. Look what happened to Mike. No. Just no."

"We might have to take a leap of faith here and talk with Dan. See if…"

"Are you kidding? He pulled my detail. He believes that bullshit story that some drunken wannabe mobster tracked Mike down on an undercover operation and killed him with a single shot." I was near hysterical now. To hell with Mrs. Cavaleri, sleeping soundly with Could Have Been My Cat curled up next to her. The walls were closing in on me and I couldn't breathe. I felt like death was all around me, which could be because I worked at a fucking funeral home, but I'm sure having Mike die in my arms had something to do with it. My marriage was over and I didn't only lose a husband, I lost my best friend. Now I was stranded in a town where I didn't want to be and hardly knew anyone outside of work. Moreover, one of those openly loathed me. People were trying to kill me, breaking into my home and to top it off, I was sleeping with a guy I barely knew. I had no idea how I was going to get my life back, how I was ever going to get out of this godforsaken town and it was all too much.

I wanted to get in my car and drive. I walked out of the kitchen and to my desk. I grabbed my purse, rummaged through it for my keys and strode purposefully to the back door. Colby quickly blocked my path.

"Get out of my way."

TWENTY-TWO

*We never really know what stupidity is until we have
experimented on ourselves.– Paul Gauguin*

"I said get out of my way." I was not screwing around
here. If I had to resort to calling upon my martial art
skills, I would. I'd probably get my ass kicked, but I'd be
damn sure I made it out the door. More to the point, I had a lot
of pent-up anger and a good brawl would be welcome. One
can only relieve so much tension with sex, sometimes you
needed a good beat down. I stood my ground and stared at
him, daring him, goading him.

"You are clearly upset and if I were in your position, I'd
have cracked long before this," he started, his voice level, not
moving, barely breathing. He was in full cop mode. "But you
need to know, if you try to go down those stairs, I will have
you down and handcuffed before you land your first kick."

There was no anger, no frustration in his voice, just cold
professionalism. That only fueled my fire. Unfortunately, I
knew I was no match for him. Defeated I turned around and
went upstairs to bed. I would have slammed the door, but my
bedroom didn't have one. I settled for throwing his clothes
onto the stairs. I threw myself onto the bed and proceeded to

toss and turn until the sun peaked over the horizon. Colby never came to bed. He was not a stupid man. I got up, pulled my clothes out for the funeral and draped them over the chair. The service wasn't until early afternoon, so I grabbed a pair of jean shorts, a t-shirt, sports bra, panties and went to shower.

Colby was sitting at the dining table, looking like he'd been working on the lists all night. Since I was still in a foul mood and did not have the benefit of coffee, I ignored him. I peeked in the kitchen to make sure there was coffee. A fresh pot was brewing. I showered, dressed, grabbed a mug and sat at the kitchen table. I turned on my tablet. Since my files were safely on a flash drive and I was feeling rebellious, I re-enabled my Wi-Fi access. I mindlessly surfed the web. I opened up the app for job openings in the art world to see if there was anything promising. I virtually walked through the Museum of Modern Art and while I was staring at a Dalí, I heard Colby taking a shower. I toyed with making my escape, but the moment had passed. I was resigned. The only way out of this was through it and I was working on a plan. I wasn't sure how we could do it, but I was going to make whoever was behind this think I was going public with information that would implicate them. I was going to force them to make a move on me, bring them into the light. Otherwise, I didn't see how Colby and I would solve the puzzle, or survive another week in forced exile together.

Colby came into the kitchen and interrupted my thoughts. I was about to tell him my brilliant plan when his phone buzzed. He pulled it out and read a message. His face gave nothing away as he put the phone back in his pocket. He filled a travel mug with coffee and said, "I have to run a couple of errands. If you choose not to stay here and wait for me, don't go unarmed." He placed a taser and pepper spray on the table in front of me. "I won't be gone long." His voice was flat. He kissed my forehead and went into the living room. A few moments later, he was out the front door and gone. And I was alone. I looked around. I picked up the pepper spray, read the warnings and scared myself. The taser was probably more my style. I got up and poured another cup of coffee. Something didn't feel right. I paced. What errand could be so important Colby would leave me…unchaperoned…unprotected? I walked into the living room and looked out the front windows and I was surprised to see the Silverado still parked out front. Colby was standing next to it, talking on his phone. Every hair on the back of my neck stood up.

I admit to not thinking clearly. Sleep deprivation, stress and frustration left me reactionary. That was the only explanation for what I decided to do. Grabbing my purse, I tossed the pepper spray and taser into it and threw a towel over the bugs on my way down the back stairs. I jumped in SusieV, turned the key and slowly pulled out into the street. The parking lot was off the alley, so I could pull out enough to see Colby's truck, but hopefully not far enough that he would see me. He was pulling away from the curb just as I pulled out.

I waited, holding my breath, praying he didn't flip around and come this way. He didn't, instead, he turned onto Columbia. I waited long enough to talk myself out of following him. When that didn't happen, I slowly pulled out onto the street. I wasn't sure why I needed to follow him, but I had to do it. That little voice in my head could not be quieted by sitting at the old oak table drinking coffee. Something bad was about to go down and I needed to be there when it did.

A bright yellow car was not the best vehicle for tailing an experienced Marshal. It was too early on Saturday morning for there to be much traffic. The sole advantage I had was the Silverado was large and tall so I could see it from a distance and the Mini was small enough it all but disappeared behind a compact. I put whatever vehicle I could between us and held back a good quarter mile. I hoped he was going somewhere familiar, like the Marshals office. That way if I lost him along the way I had a chance of finding him again. No such luck. He was headed away from downtown and took I-74 east across the bridge. I was unfamiliar with this area, so if I lost him, I was sunk. The bridge was almost empty. I pulled off the road and waited until he was over it before I followed. Luckily, once over the bridge, there was more traffic. I could follow a few cars back and not miss the exit he took.

People must have been waking up, traffic picked up significantly as we drove northeast on Hwy 24. Still, I held back, tracking the roof of the truck. Suddenly a car swerved into my lane. I slammed on my brakes and narrowly avoided them. On a normal day, I would have laid on the horn and flipped them off. But I didn't want to draw any unwanted attention, so I swore under my breath and eased back into the flow of traffic.

The further Colby drove, the more residential and quieter the streets became, with fewer cars to hide behind. I took to stopping and waiting before turning when he turned. I could only pray he didn't turn again before I had him in sight. Once, I went around the block instead of turning after he did, because I felt I had gotten too close. As I was winding my way back to the street he was on, I told myself this was crazy and stupid. He had probably spotted my tail miles ago and was having a good laugh leading me around East Peoria. Yet, I couldn't stop. I continued following until he turned on Cedar Circle and slowed. Fuck. I stopped, not wanting to drive past the street in case he was parking or turning around. It was an older residential area, populated with large homes and old trees. However, it was new enough that there were no alleyways for me to slip down unnoticed.

There was no way I'd risk driving down the circle, so I made my second stupid choice of the morning, I parked the car and got out. I always kept a hoodie in the backseat in case the weather changed unexpectedly. It was black. I pulled it out, tugged it on and pulled the hood up over my curls. At least there was a nip in the morning air, so I didn't look too ridiculous: shorts, sandals and a hoodie. Who doesn't go out for their Saturday morning jog like that? Nothing suspicious here people, move along. I casually walked past the street, glancing quickly to see that Colby's truck was parked in front of a house about halfway down the circle. I continued walking, trying to look inconspicuous.

A half a block later, I doubled back and cut through the yard at the corner house. I slid between the house and the garage next door. I could hear the 911 calls now. Fortunately, there were no windows facing the neighboring garage, so I felt safe remaining there long enough to get a good look at the house where the truck was parked. I was hoping to get a house number and then get the hell out of there. I could go home and search the white pages or the county assessor's site to satisfy my curiosity from the safety and comfort of my kitchen.

Instead, what I witnessed was a kick to my gut. Suddenly, I feared for my life in a way I hadn't experienced since the night I ran from my damaged car. Standing under the tree in front of the house was Chief Deputy Marshal Dan Strickland. And Colby was taking an envelope from him as they spoke quietly.

I couldn't process this, couldn't think beyond escaping, silently praying Colby wasn't aware I followed him. I turned and began to retrace my steps. I slipped on the grass, still wet from the morning dew and landed on one knee before scrambling back up and walking quickly back to my car. I would have run, but I was afraid it would draw unwanted attention. As I dug into my pocket for my keys, I looked down and saw the blood seeping from my grass-stained knee.

I must have landed on a rock or other debris when I slipped. I hadn't even felt it. Impatiently I swiped away the trickle of red. I got into the driver's seat, started the car and slowly pulled away from the curb. I resisted the urge to gun the engine. Instead, I moved slowly out of the neighborhood. When I felt I was far enough away, I stopped in the parking lot of a small church and dug my burner phone out of my bag. I opened up the back and pulled out the battery. Then I began to cry, deep, ragged sobs.

A few moments later, I took several deep breaths, angrily wiped away tears and put the car in drive. I decided to wind my way back a different way, in case Colby was not far behind me. I eschewed the interstate for Washington Street and cruised through downtown, past the now familiar Marshals Service building and back to my apartment. The entire drive I replayed the morning. First the text, then the call, then the meeting - I struggled to put the puzzle pieces together. I searched my memories of the past week. Were there other signs I missed? Indications the man I was trusting with my life, my heart, my body, was not who he seemed. By the time I pulled onto my street, I was no closer to an answer. However, alarm was setting in.

Colby's truck wasn't parked on the street or in the back parking lot. I parked in my usual spot, scoping out the lot and alley for anything suspicious before getting out. My back stairs felt too secluded, so I took the walkway on the street side of the building and used the front entrance.

I opened the door and stepped into the entry. The building was bustling with life. I could hear Jeff tuning up his cello and wonderful smells were wafting from Mrs. Cavaleri's apartment. It would not surprise me if she knocked on our doors mid-morning with some freshly baked treat. Just a typical Saturday morning in Peoria. I marveled at the ordinariness of it, in such stark contrast to my life, which was spiraling out of control. I climbed the stairs. Once inside, I shut and locked the door behind me. I dropped my bag on the couch, stripped off my hoodie and tried to formulate a plan. Colby couldn't be far behind me and I didn't want to be here when he arrived. I was done playing.

I walked into the laundry room, pulled out the listening devices, dropped them to the floor and smashed them into tiny bits with my shoe. Huh, that felt good. Then I went upstairs. There I pulled the shoes I would need for today's service out of the closet. I also pulled out the box where we were keeping the flash drive and the charts. I tossed it on the bed. I dug in the back of the closet and found a duffle bag. I put the papers, flash drive, shoes, makeup and hair products into it. I changed into jeans and my favorite sleeveless black sweater, grabbed my service clothes and went back downstairs. I added my tablet to the duffle and in a moment of sheer audacity, picked up Colby's laptop and put it into the duffle before zipping it shut. I glanced out the front window for any sign of the Silverado, but the street in front was still empty. I gathered everything and left by the back stairs, stepping over bug crumbs as I did.

When I arrived at Butterfield, I parked in back, assuming that they would need all the front parking for today's guests. I hiked the duffle and my purse over my shoulder and draped my clothes over my arm before beeping SusieV's alarm. I stumbled over the parking curb as I struggled to keep everything balanced. Too late, I realized that with my arms full I was leaving myself vulnerable in the already secluded area. Anger was making me stupid. I scanned around and then continued to the back door.

I still had my keys in my hand as I awkwardly attempted to turn the doorknob. It wouldn't budge. I juggled my keys to my other hand and tried again, it still would not turn. Of course, it was locked. It was hours before anyone needed to be here for the afternoon service and even if Tom had a call last night, he would have locked the doors as he worked alone. Funeral homes are prime targets for bizarre embalming fluid thefts. I tried not to imagine why.

I scrabbled with my keys to isolate the one for the back door and managed to get it into the lock, turn it and the doorknob without dropping any of my cargo. I pushed through the door and used my backside to close it behind me. I hung my clothes on the wrought iron entryway hooks and turned to lock the door. I walked down the long hallway, passing the stairs, one set leading upstairs, the other down to the embalming rooms. I continued past the door that led to the basement, until the hallway opened up to the casket room, the office and the bright window-lined hallway that led the way to my office and the viewing rooms.

The quiet was unsettling and I was reminded once again that there was nothing quite as eerie as being in a mortuary all alone. I opened my office door and dropped the heavy duffle off my shoulder onto the chair that was against the wall. I tossed my purse on the desk and booted up my computer. I picked up the phone and buzzed the embalming rooms in case Tom was here. I didn't want to risk being suddenly startled and tasing him unnecessarily. There was no answer, so I assumed it was only me and the overnight guests. I started my email program and went upstairs to put on a pot of coffee.

As the coffee brewed, I rummaged around for something to eat. The rush of adrenaline had worn off and I was suddenly ravenous. I found the leftover donuts and popped an apple fritter into the microwave. I poured my coffee and when the oven dinged, took my coffee and fritter back to my office.

I settled in and scanned my email. Most of it could wait until I was in a better frame of mind, but I opened the one from Jacob regarding today's schedule. I read it while I sipped my coffee and enjoyed my stale, but warm pastry. It all looked straightforward and I wouldn't have much to do except wander around, hand out tissue boxes and assist the bereaved.

I printed out the schedule, closed my email and opened my browser. I typed Chief Deputy Marshal Dan Strickland into the search bar. I wasn't sure what I was looking for – was I expecting to find a search result that described how he betrayed his badge and murdered my friend? I hit return. No luck on the corruption results, but I was surprised to see he had been awarded several commendations in the past few years. He was originally from Crab Orchard, Tennessee, was married and had three children. Peoria was his first command as Chief. He coached soccer and Pee Wee football. That was it. No suspicious activity, no photos of him with the crew at the River Dogs stadium. He was a small town dad doing his job.

I sat back and stared out the window, no sign of Colby yet. I was confident it wouldn't be long before he tracked me down. I went back to the computer and began typing: Colby Jameson. I hesitated and then hit return. Before I could begin to read, the phone rang, fracturing the stillness. Startled, I hit my coffee cup as I reached out to silence it, sloshing coffee onto the papers I just printed out. I cursed, looked at the Caller ID and surmised it was someone calling about today's service, hit the mute button and let it roll over to the answering service. They'd call Tom if it was urgent. I mopped up the coffee and took a deep breath. I checked the phone, the ringer was on the lowest setting, which meant that unless I put it on silent, I would have to get hold of myself. It was too quiet, that was the issue. I reached over and flipped on the small radio that sat on my desk, a remnant from my predecessor, and turned it to a Top 40 station. Then I returned my attention to the computer search.

On the first page of results, there were five Colby Jamesons. None of them were under the age of seventy. Adding Deputy Marshal and Marcus to the mix only gave me a garbled outcome of senior citizens and descriptions of the Marshals Service. I gave up and instead pulled the cheat sheets out of the duffle bag. I highlighted all the Peoria names. I propped the sheets up on my document holder and started typing in Strickland's name on my computer paired with another on the list. I hit return when a reflection in the window caught my eye. Someone was standing behind me. I spun around to find Colby leaning against the doorjamb, looking cold and menacing.

TWENTY-THREE

Mistakes are almost always of a sacred nature. –
Salvador Dali

Neither of us said anything. My heart was racing. I willed myself to keep my breathing normal and my expression placid. I was prepared to bluff my way through until someone, anyone showed up.

"You've had a busy morning."

"Wanted to get an early start," I said as I turned back to my computer and closed down the open search window. I was under no illusions it went undetected. "I made sure to pack my defense kit." I reached over and pulled the pepper spray and taser out of my bag. I turned around to face him, still radiating pleasant coolness. He wasn't buying it.

"Doing more homework?" He nodded toward the papers.

"Quiet place where I could concentrate...uninterrupted," I replied pointedly.

Colby moved into my office and I willed myself not to recoil. He took the duffle bag off the chair and moved the chair over to my desk. "This might help." As he sat, he pulled a folded stack of papers from his jacket. "Dan gave these to me this morning." He unfolded the papers. "There was a tip, to the Director's office in D.C. There were several law enforcement officers working with WITSEC participants on a large scale counterfeit operation. These are the names of those people."

I took the papers from him, scanning him for any indication he was aware I had followed him this morning. He gave nothing away, I took nothing for granted. I spread the papers out on my desk before turning back to him.

"Mike was under a cloud of suspicion because there was significant damning evidence found on his computer here and in his desk files in D.C. Once these names came to light, that chain of evidence came into question." I was holding my breath as he related this. I wanted it to be true, I wanted to believe him, but my world had been turned upside-down for weeks now and what little faith I had left evaporated this morning. This could all be an elaborate ruse to distract me from continuing my search for the truth.

"How do you know you can trust anything Strickland says? How do you know he's not just feeding you what you want to hear so you'll divulge information?"

"I don't, which is why I took the papers and listened to what he had to say, but didn't share anything with him, except that I'm sticking close to you. He thought that was for the best," he paused, "because the ballistics came back yesterday on all of Himmel's weapons, none of them matched the bullet that killed Mike."

"Well, that's not a surprise."

"No, not to you and me, but to a by-the-book guy like Dan, it was significant and he does not appreciate being manipulated. I think you'll find one of the names on that list interesting."

I began to examine the pages and one name immediately jumped out: Kyle Clarkson. He had now shown up on all three lists. I tried to recall what he looked like the morning I bumped into him at the Marshals office. Big, unmoving, but nothing said corrupt murderer in that brief encounter.

"How well do you know Clarkson?"

"It's a small office, I see him, but we haven't worked together much. He handles a lot of prisoner transfers and the Federal Court detail. My jurisdiction is primarily fugitive retrieval and various task forces." He paused for a moment and picked up Dan's list. "But if you're asking me what my gut says, he wasn't high on my list of Marshals I wanted to work with on a detail."

"What about these other names, Sandoval and Lapp?" Those were two other Marshals names that came up on all three lists.

"Only what their personnel file says, Lapp is the one who booked Mike's desk contents into evidence. He doesn't do much fieldwork. He handles a lot of the coordination of the asset forfeiture program. Sandoval works long distance prisoner transfer. The sole connection I could find was that five years ago, they were all working on a joint task force with the FBI that included your father." He shuffled through the papers until he found the sheet he wanted.

"Counterfeiting?"

"Counterfeiting almost exclusively falls to the Secret Service. No, this was a drug bust, lots of money being laundered, heroin being transported across state lines, multiple agencies."

"My father was involved with drugs?"

Colby shook his head. "I'm not sure why they brought him in on the task force. As a consultant, his participation is a bit murky, but there isn't anything I've read about him to indicate he was ever involved in drug trafficking."

"Something happen on that operation?"

"Hard to say. It looks routine, good bust and solid convictions." He handed the sheet to me. "I think it may be where they met. Maybe one night on a long, dreary stakeout they got to talking and that planted a seed. Until we know what this is all about, I don't think we'll know how everyone fits in, including your father."

I picked up the paper. It listed the members of the task force. It was long, but there were two more names I recognized. Two FBI agents that were on the list my dad gave us.

Three Marshals and two FBI agents on three lists, Strickland's name was on two of the lists. My father was on two of the lists. Additionally, we had confirmation he worked on the task force with the Corrupt Five.

"What about all the other names, the ones that Mike left for us? State Patrol and Peoria Police, how do they fit in?"

"Only a guess, but as the operation grew, they needed more people to help them cover up and run interference." Colby shook his head, "There has to be a lot of money involved here."

"Enough to murder one of their own," I looked at Colby. He met my eyes and all I saw was an honest cop trying to do the right thing. Unfortunately, I did not trust my ability to discern truth from fiction at this moment. I stacked all the papers together and put them into an empty file folder. I dug the flash drive out of my duffle bag, piled it with my tablet and the folder, pulled open the top file drawer, put them inside and closed the drawer. I opened my middle desk drawer, flipped through the paperclips, pens and rubber bands until I came up with a key. I inserted it into the lock on the filing cabinet and of course, it didn't fit. I continued my search, lifting up the drawer tray and finding another key. I had better luck with that one. It fit into the lock, so I pushed the lock in and turned the key. I attached the key to my keychain and tossed it into my purse.

"The file cabinet isn't all that secure, but I'll lock my door during the service." Next, I retrieved Colby's laptop from my duffle and handed it over to him. "I didn't want to leave it unattended," I lied unconvincingly.

"Lock it in the file cabinet and then let's go over this afternoon's events." I unlocked the file cabinet, added the laptop to the drawer, relocked it and turned to my computer. I pulled up the schedule for the day. There was no further discussion of our morning exploits, not then, not ever.

We went over the schedule, after which Colby wanted to walk through the funeral, ostensibly so he could make an action plan. I walked him around the chapel, remembering how barely a week before I had given Mike the identical tour. I showed him the family room, where members of the immediate family waited in private until the time of the service. After that, I accompanied him to the reception area where mourners would greet the family before departing to the cemetery for internment. At which time I would be released from my duties and we could continue on the hunt for our mystery contestants. Would the real killer please come on down?

"It looks like you'll be safe here unless a gunfight erupts between the Himmels and the Shiedegers. This, from what I have heard, is a distinct possibility."

"Let's hope not. I've already had to deal with the screaming widow and her mother-in-law, which was traumatic enough."

"I want to do a sweep of the entire building before people start arriving."

"What are you looking for?"

"I don't know for sure, but too many people know you're here today. I don't like it. Something smells in Peoria and all of this," he gestured toward the chapel, "is making someone extremely nervous. I don't know if Shiedeger's murder started the dominoes falling, or if it was your father going off the grid, but people are getting careless and making mistakes. Shooting Mike and coming after you are acts of desperation. You'll be safe here with all the people, but for my own peace of mind, I need reassurance that there won't be an ambush later."

"Let's start in the kitchen, I need more coffee," and possibly another donut, "and then I'll give you the grand tour."

Thirty minutes later, we had surveyed the garage, the tool shed, the alley and were now back inside the old mansion, upstairs in Nick's office. I wanted Colby to see that the windows in the corner office allowed him to observe much of the surrounding area. After that, we checked every room, closet and alcove on the third floor. On the way down to embalming area, I heard Dee on the phone in the main office. I pulled Colby aside and told him to scrutinize the lower level on his own and meet me back at my office. After I made my presence known to Dee, we could make a quick sweep of the basement. He took the stairs down and I walked the hall to the office. I poked my head in as Dee hung up the receiver. I raised my coffee mug in what I hoped was a friendly gesture.

"I made a fresh pot of coffee if you need one." As there was no response, I rolled my eyes as I walked back to my office. On the list of things I had to worry about, Dee came in below dead last. I unlocked the door and slipped in, closing it behind me. I sat at my desk and sipped my now cold coffee. My thoughts should have been sifting through the new information handed to us, but instead, they were solidly centered on Colby. The meeting with Chief Strickland replayed in my mind and I came back to the same question. Why not tell me about the meeting before he left? If there wasn't anything untoward going on, why keep it a secret?

Until this was over, until I knew all the facts, I needed to be cautious and not let my feelings for Colby overshadow my instincts. And my instincts told me there was something more here, a thread I was missing. The question I kept coming back to: was Colby withholding information? And if that was the case, was it to deceive or to protect? If they were willing to silence and smear a fellow Marshal, why would they hesitate to eliminate me? What better way than to have Colby become my shadow to learn what Mike had shared with me. Then feed me whatever information they wanted to distract me from what was actually happening.

I closed my eyes and shook my head. I was being paranoid. Whatever Colby's reason for slipping out today, nothing would make me believe he had been playing me from the beginning. I might be exhausted, traumatized and fearful, but not so dazed by events to not recognize genuine concern and desire. I would be cautious, but I wouldn't be stupid. A knock on the door cut short my mental gymnastics. Nick opened it and leaned in.

"Not interrupting am I?" he asked with a smile. Given that I was staring out the window when he arrived, the answer was obvious. With that, I pushed aside thoughts of Colby and focused on my job. He would have to check the basement without me. Twenty minutes later, I had changed my clothes and met everyone in the chapel to go over final details. Everything appeared to be set to go, I had my assigned tasks, all that was left was to wait until the family and mourners began to arrive. I chose to await that moment in my office. Colby was waiting for me.

"I don't think you should look that sexy at a funeral."

"Technically it's a memorial service," I said before giving him a quick kiss. What the hell, life was short.

"When do you have to start doing your comforting-the-bereaved thing?" If I had been hoping for a sexual interlude, I was disappointed. His motives were strictly business. "I want to wire you up." He pulled out a small case from a black leather bag on my desk and opened it. I froze.

"I can't."

"No one will see them," he held up an earpiece and I felt the room spin. Then he reached for the tiny lapel camera and the air left the room.

"I can't."

"TJ, what's wrong?" He reached for me and I flinched, but he ignored it. He brought me into his chest and wrapped his arms tight around me. "Tell me," he whispered in my ear.

I tried to find air, to talk without breaking into sobs. My mind involuntarily flashed back to my last day with Mike, laughing, joking and then that awful sound in my ear. Not understanding as I rushed to him. Finding him slumped over, hearing the echo of my own voice in my earpiece as I called out to him, trying in vain to get him to answer me. I leaned into Colby, unable to control the fear and grief that gripped me. Finally, I took a deep breath and pulled away.

"I can't. I can't wear those. You'll have to be satisfied with watching over me." I couldn't explain it to him, couldn't verbalize the turmoil inside, but somehow he understood. He closed the box and put it back into the bag.

"It's okay. I'll be close by if anything happens. If at any time you feel threatened, pull the fire alarm. There is one in the chapel and one in the reception area."

I smiled at him, I had never noticed them. I was beginning to feel better now that the electronics were out of sight, even a bit foolish reacting that strongly. I was relieved we had an alternative plan of action. I looked out the window and saw the family was beginning to arrive. "I have to get out there. Do me a favor and come up with a strategy to flush out these guys. I'm tired of this game. I want to play a new one." He nodded, leaned down and kissed my cheek before I went out to do my comforting the bereaved thing.

The chapel filled quickly. Nick and Jacob were ever watchful for signs of a rumble. Thankfully, everyone kept to neutral corners and appeared to be in attendance either out of respect or to gawk. I stood in the back, boxes of tissues at the ready in case anyone ran out. I was superfluous, there was very little crying with this crowd. The deacon who drew the short straw kept his remarks brief and to the point. It looked like we would be out of here in record time.

As things were wrapping up, Jacob came forward and asked the dreaded question, "Does anyone want to say a few words about Dale?" I cursed under my breath and glanced over at Nick. His face said it all, Jacob may have lit a fuse and now Nick was scanning the mourners for anyone who looked like they would detonate the bomb. Moments passed, Jacob seemed to realize his mistake and jumped quickly into the silence and wrapped up the event. Crisis averted.

Nick, Dee and Jacob led the crowd out row by row as I stood by the double doors and directed the family to the reception area. Once the remainder of guests were securely following the designated path, I ducked back to my office. I was surprised that Colby was not there waiting for me. I dug through my purse and pulled out both my cell phones. There were no messages on either one. Then I realized, duh, I had pulled the batteries. After I replaced them, I dialed Colby's number on my burner phone. Colby picked up on the first ring.

"Hey, the service is over, where are you?"

"Out in the back parking lot, are you in your office?"

"Yes. I'll grab all of our stuff and meet you outside."

"No," Colby said too quickly. "I'll come get you. Stay put."

"Okay. But hurry before someone finds something for me to do." I tamped down the lingering feeling of uneasiness and began pulling my things from the filing cabinet and put them into the duffle bag. A rap on my office door startled me and I almost dropped Colby's laptop. My door opened and Jacob leaned in.

"Sorry to bother you, but Mrs. Himmel, Sr. is making a fuss about the guest book. She's distraught because all the gawkers signed it. I think in the interest of peace and safety, it would be best if we gave them another one and let only family and close friends sign it."

"That seems prudent."

"Could you grab one out of the supply closet in the casket room? It's the Forever In My Heart one, with the butterflies on the cover."

"Not a problem, should I bring it to the reception area?"

"I think it would be best if you left it in the Family Room and I'll direct the appropriate people there to sign before they leave."

"On it." I followed him out my door, no time to put the duffle bag into the filing cabinet. I paused a moment to lock the door before I walked down the hall, past the main office to the casket room. The supply closet was at the far end of the room, tucked behind decorative drapes. As I walked across the soft pile carpet, I realized I left both my phones in my office. Oh, well, this wouldn't take long and the office phone sat on a table next to an overstuffed chair if I needed it.

I pushed aside the curtain and slid open one of the bi-fold doors. The top shelf held blank memory cards, service cards, bookmarks, prayer cards and thank you notes. Below that were candles, rosary beads and other memorabilia. The bottom two shelves were boxed guest books. The name of each book was printed on the outside of the box. A quick scan revealed five On the Wings of Love, three Bridges of Faith, seven Messenger of Peace and two Eternal Spring. But, not one damned Forever in My Heart. I slid the door shut and opened the other side, nothing but boxes of tissues, extra flower stands and altar cloths.

I looked over at the phone. I could buzz Jacob and tell him he was out of luck, but I worried if a skirmish ensued I'd never get out of here today. I'd have to go down in the basement where there was sure to be a whole stack of them in the storage room.

I walked through the casket displays and into the adjoining memorial room, where you could choose everything from urns, to jewelry, to memory boxes, to personalized sculptures to remember your loved ones. I hurried across the hall, worried both about averting the crazy family drama and making it back to my office to meet Colby.

I opened the door, and as always, was confronted by musty, basement smell that the late summer heat intensified. I reached in, flipped on the light switch and stepped carefully down the narrow stairs. Luckily, there was an outside cellar door, near the back parking lot for them to bring the extra caskets in and out because they would never fit on these stairs. I reached the bottom and had to stop for a moment to think if the extra stationery supplies were to the left or the right. That's when I heard the voice behind me.

"Don't turn around."

TWENTY-FOUR

What is, is, and what might have been could never have existed. — Edward Gorey

Time froze. I think my heart might even have stopped beating. I felt the hard barrel of a gun pressed into my back. Actually, to be more precise, just below my shoulder blade. Fear crept from my gut and made its way up my spine to my brain. I took a slow, deep breath to calm myself and gather my thoughts. Slow, deep breaths also have the benefit of unnerving an assailant. Slow, deep breaths are an indication of preparation and action. Assailants rely on panic and fear.

I felt the gun press harder against my back. Ah, someone was getting nervous. I took another deep breath, the beginnings of a plan pushed back at the welling panic. Overtaking someone with a gun is rarely smart or practical. Especially when he was behind me and I had no sense of his size or vulnerabilities. I assessed my location. There were two rooms to my right and three to my left. None of the rooms had locks and all the windows were small and probably painted shut. The only other door was the double cellar door that was padlocked from the outside. My captor stood between me and the stairway I had just descended, blocking my only feasible escape route.

"Where is the flash drive?" he rasped in my ear. I shuddered involuntarily as I felt his breath against my neck. His voice was barely a whisper but it felt like a shout and I had to take another breath before answering him. In that brief moment, I made the decision to stall, fearing if I told him it was up the stairs and easy to obtain, his need for me would evaporate.

"Everyone knows I'm down here and they'll be looking for me," I said loudly and with as much confidence as I could muster, ignoring his demand completely. He responded by using the gun barrel to push me further down the narrow hallway. I'm sure he thought it would offer him cover, but what I saw was a gap between him and my escape route.

"Where's the flash drive?" He pushed me again and I used the momentum to turn myself at a right angle into the wall, inching me a bit closer to freedom. At the same time, I answered his question with a question, hoping it would distract him enough that he wouldn't notice my tactic.

"You mean the flash drive Mike…Marshal Fraser…left for me? We printed the information out and left the drive in a safe deposit box at the bank." My mystery guest laughed quietly. It was a sick, menacing sound.

"That fool didn't know anything worth chasing after. I'm talking about the drive your father gave you."

Suddenly the basement felt like ice. I forced myself not to shiver. I did not want to give this creep any indication of fear or weakness. But my mind raced. My father possessed information worth killing for and Big Bad here thinks I have it. Why would he think that? Did my father tell him he gave it to me? Did he try to give it to me, but someone – Colby jumping to the head of the list – intercepted it? Why would my father put me in danger like that?

Having more questions than answers, I pushed them aside and refocused on getting out of the basement. "My father is dead."

"Not yet he's not."

I ignored him and continued, "He died when I was very young. I can take you to his grave if you like."

Big Bad apparently did not like my answer because he shoved me hard into the wall and hissed into my ear, "I'm going to make sure he regrets ever involving you in this. I want that flash drive and you're going to take me to it, NOW." Well the joke was on him, wasn't it?

I wanted nothing more than to do that since it would get me out of this basement. But there were two problems that I could see: one, I didn't have what he was looking for and two, taking him upstairs could put a lot of people in danger. Colby had to be looking for me, I'd have to stall until he found me or I managed to get away. "How do you propose we do that? The funeral home is crawling with people." I felt the gun move lower and Big Bad closer.

"They'll be gone soon enough and if not, I'll shoot you and anyone else who gets in the way."

"That's serious shit. What's on that drive that's important enough to go all Hans Gruber on a funeral home?"

"Ignorance is beneath you, Tammy Jean." I cringed at the familiarity. "You and your squeeze have it all figured out. We know you're just biding your time with your daddy there, until you can take what is ours."

"What makes you think that?" I had no idea what the hell he was talking about, but it would make sense that my father was staying underground so he could capitalize on whatever this was.

"Don't think you can fucking play me. All your father ever did was talk about you. There is no way he would end up in Peoria and not bring you in on this."

My head was spinning. It appeared that what Colby and I had discovered was only the tip of the spear. My father was in deep and it looked like the Corrupt Five believed he had read me in on the entire scheme. "What reason would he have to involve me in your criminal activity?"

Big Bad laughed. "Money. It's always about money." He laughed again and then put his hand roughly over my mouth and pushed me into the wall. He was very still. It was then I heard what he must have heard, voices in the hallway, getting louder as they moved closer to the basement door.

"Why are you surprised she disappeared? Like it's the first time." Dee, complaining to someone about me. I closed my eyes and prayed silently that she wasn't headed down here to retrieve the guest book. "She probably went home with her cop boyfriend." Oh, great, I'm being held by a deranged gunman and gossiped about by the world's bitchiest receptionist, this day couldn't get much worse.

"Her car is still here, she has to be here somewhere." That was Nick. I imagined Dee rolling her eyes at his concern. "Try her cell again. I'm going to see if she's in the basement." There was a pause and I tensed my body, ready to do whatever I had to, in order to keep Big Bad from shooting Nick. Then I heard him again, "What's up? Oh hell, no, I'll be right there." With that, the basement was quiet again.

That was too close. I had to get us out of the basement and out of the funeral home before this guy got trigger happy. When he eased his grip and I could speak again, I swallowed and hoped my voice didn't shake as I spun my lie.

"The drive you want is back at my apartment."

"Tell me where."

"Why would I do that? You'll just kill me and go and get it."

"You could be lying to me. Where would I be if you're dead? You're going with me and making sure I get what I want." His voice was low and sinister. I was under no illusions that getting what he wanted ended with the missing files. I could only hope and pray that Colby was outside waiting before this creep got me into a car. Impatient, he wrenched my arm back until I gasped in pain. "Stop stalling."

"If you want me to tell you anything, you'll let go of me, now." My voice was firm and calm. I stood still, breathing deep and steady. I was playing a hunch. He thought I was working with my father, as well as Mike and Colby. He thought I knew more than I did, that I was colluding with his enemies, so that was the role I was going to play. He released his grip on my arm. I pulled away from him, putting enough space between us that he could still hear my whisper, but I could no longer feel his breath on my neck. "The drive is well hidden. If something happens to me, Colby is the only other person who has any knowledge of its location. But even he would just be guessing. Because I'm not exactly sure where his loyalties stand." I didn't think it would hurt to plant a seed of future collaboration with my captor.

Big Bad laughed. "Never trust a cop." Very funny asshole. It took all my restraint, and the gun, not to pivot and break his nose. "I think you're lying. I think the drive is here and I think you're trying to lead me away from it."

"Do you know anything about the history of architecture?"

"What the fuck are you talking about?"

"That beautiful castle I live in was renovated during Prohibition." I paused for effect, making it clear I was convinced of his ignorance. "Do you know what every wealthy homeowner added to their homes during that time period?" Pause. "They put in a secret bar, a place to stash their liquor where no one could find it. Architects and builders had all kinds of tricks: secret panels, hidden cubbies, even completely hidden rooms. If you were willing to pay for it, they could build it." I paused again and waited for my words to paint the picture in his mind. If I got out of this alive, I was going to personally thank my modern art professor for his fascination with Prohibition period architecture. "Without me, you won't find anything." I finished with a confident shake of my head. "Nothing."

I must have convinced him because he grabbed my arm roughly and turned me toward the stairs. "Upstairs," he demanded, jabbing me with the gun. "It won't take much for me to shoot you and everyone here, so don't fuck with me."

I had no intention of doing anything except get him out of the building. After that, all bets were off. I still had no idea who I was dealing with, but as he pushed and pulled me, I was getting a sense of his size. He was about a head taller than me, with a good sized paunch. His arms were strong but doughy and he wore no wedding ring. I was not fooled, he might be a bit overweight, but nothing in his movements indicated he was out of shape. We were ascending the stairs quickly. Big Bad pulled me in close to him, while simultaneously propelling me upward. My arm was beginning to ache as he tightened his grasp and pulled it backward. I was going to need that arm eventually if I was to devise some sort of escape.

"Can you ease up on my arm? You're hurting me and …"

"Tough shit."

With that, I stopped my forward momentum and stood perfectly still. He wasn't expecting that and almost lost his footing. He bent down and I felt his stubble against my ear.

"Keep moving," he rasped. We were near the top and he was careful not to be overheard.

"Not until you stop hurting me." He wrenched my arm back, but I stood stoically, refusing to flinch even though it hurt like hell.

"Move, bitch." He wrenched my arm again. I didn't move or speak. Basically, I became granite. Without a word, he relented and loosened his grip on my arm.

I continued to climb the stairs with him close behind. Once we were on the landing he pulled me into him to stop. He turned me toward the wall, pushing me into it as he maneuvered around me. He opened the door, paused for a moment, and then pulled me back in front of him and pushed me out into the hallway. At that very moment, Colby came around the corner from my office. Everything went into slow motion. Colby pulled his gun from his holster. Big Bad pulled me into him, wrapping one flabby arm around me. The gun was in his other hand, which he pulled up and pointed at my head.

"Clarkson, drop it."

"I'll kill her. I'll kill your little girlfriend unless you back out of here. Now!"

At least I knew who I was dealing with as he dragged me backward toward the back door.

"Stop! You've got nowhere to go Kyle. Let her go."

"I am going out this door and if you try and stop me, I'll put a bullet in her just like I did with Fraser." To emphasize his threat, Clarkson pushed the barrel of the gun into my temple. His hand was steady, but I could feel the sweat seeping through his shirt. He was cornered and I feared he was becoming erratic. I needed him out of the building. I made eye-contact with Colby, looking for reassurance and counting on him to read my thoughts. I pushed back into Clarkson, to hasten his exit, praying Colby wouldn't stop him. Not yet.

Clarkson heeded my momentum and quickly dragged me to the back door. Once there, he was presented with a problem. The door swung inward and there wasn't an easy option for opening it. With both his hands engaged with terrorizing me, the closed and locked door posed an almost insurmountable conundrum. I closed my eyes and made a calculated decision. I reached behind him, unlocked and opened the door, giving Clarkson the opportunity to elbow it open wide and pull us outside. I opened my eyes in time to catch the "what the fuck" look from Colby. I didn't have time to worry about that, because once outside, I needed to distract Clarkson, so Colby could follow us out without getting shot when he crossed the threshold.

"My keys are in my office, so we can't take my car. Where is yours?" I asked him while turning my body away from the back door so he had no option but to turn with me. I was being stupid and reckless, but I was desperate. I knew someone who so easily shot a fellow cop had nothing to lose and wouldn't hesitate to shoot up the entire funeral home. I started to walk toward the alley, pulling him with me. Hampered by the gun, he couldn't keep a tight grip with only one arm, so I diverted his attention just long enough for Colby to slip out the back door. He found cover by the big maple tree as Clarkson regained his footing and put a stop to my shenanigans. He grabbed me roughly, pushed the gun into my side and swung around to locate Colby.

"Stop fucking around. I can do a lot of damage before I kill you." He dug the gun in deeper and wrenched my arm behind me. I cried out in pain. Colby stayed behind the tree. I took a deep breath and steadied myself against the assault.

"You sure are being stupid. I thought you wanted the flash drive. Why are we standing around?"

"You think your boyfriend is going to let us just walk out of here?"

"I'm betting Colby is busy securing the civilians inside so they aren't endangered." I maneuvered myself so we were facing the garage. "We could take the town car. The keys are usually in it," I lied through the pain. No way would Jim leave the cars unlocked, much less keys in the ignition.

"See, I think you're too eager to get away from here. Why?" He tightened his grip. "Maybe we should take a look in your office." He tried to turn me back toward the door, but I twisted myself back to the garage. I didn't know what Colby had planned, but I needed to keep Clarkson from seeing him.

"You think Colby is going to let you get ten steps inside, much less my office? My motivation for getting us away from here and getting you the flash drive is to avoid anyone else getting shot. Period." I threw my weight in an effort to propel us toward the garage and away from Colby. It was like trying to move a refrigerator. I knocked Clarkson off-balance and he lost his iron grip on my arm. But in a skirt and heels on soft grass, I miscalculated and before I could move out of his grasp, he grabbed my hair and almost pulled me off my feet. Colby must have seen the fire in his eyes, because before I could regain my footing, he was in front of us, gun drawn.

"Fucking drop your gun, Kyle. Now!" He was going to shoot him. I could see it in his body. He had the shot and he was going to take it. I braced myself, prepared to hit the ground as soon as Clarkson took the hit. And then I heard the gunfire. It was deafening. Reflexively I ducked my head and raised my hands to my ears to ineffectually lessen the sound. Clarkson still had his hand tangled in my hair, and he jerked me back. That is when I saw Colby thrown back by the shot, hitting the stone birdbath and going down. He lay there motionless.

Not again, not again, not again, I repeated over and over to myself, panic threatening to drown me. Then my brain went blank and all my training kicked in. The world began to move in slow-motion. I dug my high-heel down into Clarkson's foot, causing him to loosen his grip enough that I could slam my elbow into his solar plexus. He let out an "oof" before doubling over, trying to breathe. As he moved forward, I turned around and struck his nose with the palm of my hand, hoping to bury it into his skull. He went down on one knee, yelling something at me I did not hear. My entire focus was to get to Colby. Clarkson began to stand up, firing his gun blindly as he did.

I was so fucking sick and tired of guns and blood and corpses. I spun around and landed a roundhouse kick to his temple. The spiked heel of my shoe tore through his flesh, leaving a bloody gash before connecting with his eye. His eyelid was torn away and blood dripped into his eyes. He stumbled and went down again as my shoe flew across the driveway. Still, he held onto the gun. He crawled to his knees and raised his weapon. I scrambled to Colby. Like a runner sliding into home plate, I landed next to him. I grabbed the gun lying next to his head, rolled over, closed my eyes, and fired.

TWENTY-FIVE

You will see, in the future I will live by my watercolors.
– Winslow Homer

I had to drive myself to the hospital, following the ambulances that carried both Colby and Clarkson. I was shaking, struggling to stay composed and not break down into hysterical tears. I forced myself to pay attention to the road. I could not let my mind dwell on Colby's blood-soaked shirt or Clarkson's lifeless body lying in a pool of his own blood. The yard was filled with police within moments of shots fired. The ambulances followed. Officers wanted to interview me and then drive me to the hospital. Knowing what I knew, I told them I would only talk with a lawyer present. There was not a chance in hell I was getting into a vehicle with anyone Colby hadn't vetted. I was still in danger and Colby could no longer protect me.

Once at the hospital, it was chaos. I found a sympathetic nurse who kept me informed on Colby's condition. He was stable, the bullet had only grazed him, but they were doing a CT scan. He hit the birdbath pretty hard. Before I left for the hospital, I had made sure to go back to my office for our things and locked them in my car. Not very secure, but it was the best I could do.

So now, while I waited, I went to the restroom and changed out of my torn and bloody work clothes and back into my jeans and sweater. Then I grabbed a diet soda in the cafeteria and paced the hallways waiting for word on Colby. When they finally moved him to a private room, I made a beeline there, avoiding any cops I saw along the way. I don't think anyone realized I was the one who shot Clarkson. Otherwise, I assumed I'd be in handcuffs, not wandering the halls of the hospital. I shot a U.S. Marshal. Every time I tried wrapping my brain around that, the walls began to close in. I found Colby's room and tapped lightly on the door before entering. I was surprised to see Dan at his bedside.

"TJ," he greeted me warmly. "Just the person to fill in some of the missing pieces from this afternoon's activities."

I smiled weakly at him and looked to Colby for clarity. I was happy he appeared in good shape, considering the last hour.

"It's all good, TJ. I'm okay and Dan is on the right side of the tree." He grinned at me and my heart melted. I wasn't convinced of his judgment, though, he could be heavily medicated.

"If you're okay, why did they admit you?"

"Technically, they didn't. I wanted him to have a private room while we waited for his test results. We needed to talk."

"Dan has been filling me in on some details you'd be interested in hearing."

"But first, can you elaborate on what happened this afternoon? The Marshal here is a bit fuzzy on the details."

"Okay," I replied as I moved to the bed and sat next to Colby. I didn't much care what his Chief thought, I needed him close. I didn't think I could recount the events of the afternoon without support. The adrenaline was wearing off and I wasn't confident I'd get through my story without tears. Or vomiting.

Slowly and deliberately, I walked Dan through Clarkson accosting me in the basement and the standoff in the backyard. When I got to the part of the shooting, I once again closed my eyes. Then I described grabbing Colby's gun and pulling the trigger. I had not yet been able to bring myself to ask anyone if Clarkson was dead, but now I opened my eyes and looked at the Chief.

"Did I kill him?" Colby squeezed my hand and I braced for the worst.

"No TJ, you didn't. He has a significant wound, but he'll recover. He is securely handcuffed to his hospital bed."

"Dan let him think he was dying though, didn't you Chief." Colby raised my hand and kissed it. I didn't want to imagine what Dan thought of all of this. Probably very bad Marshal form to sleep with your charge.

"I can neither confirm nor deny that. But I did get a dying declaration from him. He had some interesting things to say. Most importantly, he admitted to shooting and killing Marshal Fraser." Tears welled in my eyes and I willed them to stop. Now was not the time. I needed to focus on what Dan was saying. "He also admitted to the attempts on your life and gave us the names of the thugs he recruited to go after you." Colby wrapped his arm around me and pulled me closer while Dan continued, "We were already in the process of identifying the corrupt officers. With Clarkson's details and the information Marshal Fraser gathered, we've been able to begin arresting them." I looked at Colby, wondering when and how Strickland got that information. "Next, we are going after civilian accomplices. The short of it is, TJ, you are safe now. I can't tell you how sorry I am for everything Clarkson and the others put you through."

"Why did they do it?"

"Money, a lot of it. Clarkson and his partners ran the biggest counterfeiting operation we've ever seen. They recruited police, parolees and low-level politicians to pass the fake bills. They hit a lot of people who wouldn't report it to the authorities – drug dealers, gamblers, fences – and if they did decide to report it, that's when they bought off the local cops. It was sophisticated. And we owe a debt to Marshal Fraser for discovering it."

"Once they knew Mike's murder investigation was tainted, they began to look deeper. Things started to fall apart." Colby explained.

I was trying to absorb all of this. It still didn't explain why I was targeted. "How do I fit into this, why did Mike seek me out…and my father?"

"We are still putting the pieces together, but it looks like Shiedeger was passing counterfeit bills to pay out gambling winnings. Las Vegas is where it all went off the rails for him." Strickland explained. "He tried to take his gambling party to the big leagues, spread around his counterfeit bills and it started the dominoes falling. He pissed off the wrong people, put himself and his gambling organization on law enforcement radar. He was hit with an illegal interstate gambling charge."

"That was when Mike decided to travel to Peoria. He had tracked Thomas Joseph here and assumed it was to connect with you. He used Shiedeger's case as a cover," Colby added.

"Clarkson assured Vegas law enforcement that Peoria would continue the investigation, he'd take point and coordinate the efforts. What he coordinated was a team of officers across multiple departments who began to cover things up to get Shiedeger out of the mess he was in." I could tell Dan was angry, understandably.

Colby pulled me in close and elaborated. "We are assuming that was what Mike stumbled upon, and began to gather evidence on, after Shiedeger was killed. He probably thought the murder was orchestrated by Clarkson or someone else involved in the organization."

"But how does my father play into all of this? I mean, he knows things. Clarkson was demanding that I give him information he thought my father had that would expose him."

"Whatever that information is, it must be damning, because Clarkson wouldn't give it up. Refused to say how Thomas Joseph was involved. We do know that according to the files Marshal Fraser kept, the ones Marshal Lapp omitted from his reports, he had been contacted by your father and he felt your father was in trouble, so he started to look for him. He kept hitting dead ends, but in the process located you. It appears sheer dumb luck that your life and Shiedeger's collided. "

"Why didn't Mike tell me he was looking for my father?"

There was a quiet rap on the door and an older, balding gentleman, in a white lab coat, entered the room. Colby's doctor. He gave us the good news that Colby only had a minor head injury and handed him a prescription for antibiotics for his bullet wound. With that, he was told he could go home. After the doctor left, Colby got up and began to get dressed.

"To your question, TJ," Dan continued while Colby tracked down his pants. "Thomas Joseph spent many years in WITSEC and Mike probably realized you had no idea he was alive."

I thought back over our dinner conversations, I didn't remember telling him about my family, but I could have, so much had happened in such a short time. But I was suspicious of why he would conceal his intentions.

"Until your father comes forward or we find the information Clarkson was worried about, we may never know how your father ties into all of this."

I nodded. Now that he was once again in danger and in all likelihood, deep underground, I doubted I would ever meet my dad. "Let's go home, Colby." He still hadn't located his pants. "Well, after you find your pants," I said with a laugh.

Once in the parking lot, I unlocked the doors and waited for Colby to settle in. I wondered where exactly I was taking him – my apartment or the Batcave – since that's where I assumed he lived.

"So, do you have to wind this car up before you start it," he joked as he squeezed himself into the Mini.

"Yuk it up funny guy and you'll be walking."

I slid into the driver's side and buckled up. I put the key in the ignition and turned to him. "Where are we going?" He looked at me, not understanding. "Am I taking you to your house or are we going back to my apartment?"

"Your apartment feels a lot like home." He leaned over and kissed me. Great, he's got a wife and two kids stashed at his house. Or it is the Batcave.

I turned the key, started little SusieV and maneuvered us out of the parking lot. It was odd, being in the driver's seat and Colby next to me. I stole a look at him. It might have been the bullet wound, but he didn't look very comfortable, folded into the passenger seat.

"So how are you doing?"

"Me?" I asked as I turned onto Glen Oak and eased into light Saturday traffic.

"Yeah, you. You had quite the afternoon."

"At least I didn't get shot. Or fall head first into a birdbath." Humor – my secret weapon. Colby waited. "I can't...I can't process any of this right now. I need a hot shower, a good dinner, lots of wine and maybe throw a Rom-Com in the DVR before I can even begin to digest what has happened today."

"I know something that might help you relax..." He grinned at me and I gave him the side-eye.

"You have a concussion. And a bullet wound."

"Takes more than that to stop me from enjoying your p..."

"CAT. I think now that this is all over I'm going to go to the animal shelter and get a cat."

"A cat, huh?."

"Yup. What every divorced woman should have, a cat. Matter of fact, they should be issued with the divorce decrees."

"Okay, I think there's a message here and I'm not getting it." Colby put his hand on my thigh.

"The only message is, you have been wounded and need to rest." Which was a half-truth, but I wasn't ready to face our new reality. Luckily, our conversation was preempted because we had arrived at the castle. I parked on the street in front.

The stairs were not as steep as the back entrance and I could also check my mail on the way in. I couldn't remember the last time I actually did that and I was sure there must be bills to be paid. We climbed the stairs in silence and I was looking forward to collapsing on the couch, watching several hours of bad television and eating takeout. As we reached my landing, I saw it. The door was open. Colby grabbed my arm to pull me behind him, but I was having none of it. I was freaking sick and tired of people breaking into my apartment. Danger or not, I was putting a stop to it. I pulled away from Colby and charged into the living room. There I froze in my tracks.

"This looks personal," Colby said quietly as he moved in beside me.

I surveyed the damage in the room. The sofa cushions were slashed and fluff littered the floor like cotton candy. What looked like acrylic paint was smeared on everything. "Cunt" was scrawled on the wall in black paint. My legs felt like rubber as I walked toward the dining area. More paint on more walls. Everything that had been on my sideboard was thrown to the floor. Drawers were pulled out, dumped and tossed into the heap on the floor. Multi-colored paint was smeared across the table, "bitch" clearly spelled out in the red. Tubes of my acrylics were tossed on the floor next to the chairs. Each chair displayed its very own smeared handprint on the seat and back. The entire area looked like it had been ravaged by an enormous toddler. "DIAF" was painted on my big mirror.

I looked at Colby, puzzled. "What do you think that means?"

"Die in a fire."

"Oh."

I could see my desk from where I was, no need to get closer. It had been overturned and the painting that had been on my easel was thrown on top of it, slashed beyond repair. I braced myself and walked into the kitchen. It was relatively unscathed. Must have run out of paint. But there, in the middle of my beloved Grandmother's oak table was a huge butcher's knife, the blade jammed deep into the center of it. I pulled out a chair and sat down. I reached over to pull the knife out.

"Leave it. We can pull prints from it."

I looked at him, tired and defeated. "We don't need prints, I know who did this," I said, but left the offending utensil where it was. "I can't bear to go upstairs," I said, wondering when this was all going to finally end. "Can you..."

"I'll be right back." I watched him pick his way over the desk and easel that were blocking the stairs and disappear from view. He was back a moment later. "I am happy to report, your bedroom is intact."

I didn't say anything. I stood up, went to the living room and retrieved my purse where I had dropped it. Colby had followed silently behind me. I dug through my bag and found his prescription. "You should get some rest. I'm going to get this filled for you."

"We should pull up the video feed and call the police."

"You are the police."

"You know what I mean. They need to find who did this."

"I've had enough police today, thank you very much. Right now, I need to clear my head. Go lie down. I'll be back in a little bit."

I don't know why he let me go, I thought he'd put up more of a fight. Maybe it was the look in my eyes. The look that said, *make one wrong move and I might use the knife conveniently located in my kitchen table.* Whatever it was, he kissed my forehead and went upstairs. I pulled the phone out of my bag, realizing for the first time I no longer needed the burner phone. I set it on the end table next to the couch and burrowed a little deeper and found my phone. I looked up the pharmacy and checked their hours. Plenty of time to pick up the antibiotics, grab takeout and still make it home in time to once again begin cleanup before dark.

I buckled myself in, put the key in the ignition, but didn't start the car. The late afternoon sun was blinding. I stared out the windshield, unseeing. Finally, I took a deep breath, turned the key, pulled away from the curb and drove to Butterfield. See, I recognized the handwriting, however badly scrawled on the walls in paint. I had seen it every day for the past few weeks. Angrily scratched out on little pink sheets of paper, detailing my phone messages. The same handwriting that neatly detailed the week's events on the kitchen whiteboard. I knew who, I just didn't know why. I needed to know why.

I knew she'd be there, so I wasn't surprised to see her car parked in the front parking lot. I drove around the block and through the alley. I wanted the element of surprise. If she was in her office she'd see me out front, so I parked in back by the garage. Crime scene tape still decorated the lawn. I walked to the back door, surprised to find it unlocked. Cautiously I opened it and quickly took a step back. The overwhelming odor of gasoline streamed out the door.

Concerned, I pushed the door all the way back and looked for something to prop it open. I decided on the small boxwood planter. I moved it inside and pushed it against the open door. The fumes were getting stronger. I was not registering what was happening. I stepped inside and the floor was damp near the threshold. Then I understood. As I turned to leave, I saw something. The hallway was dark with early evening shadows. I squinted, trying to make out what caught my eye.

And then I realized, it was a man's shoe. . .a man's leg on the stairs. I dashed in, not thinking, only reacting. It was Nick. I leaned down and was relieved to see he was still breathing. There was blood seeping from a wound on the back of his head, but no other apparent injuries. I started to shake him, to see if I could get him to respond. That's when I heard a whoosh and suddenly everything lit up.

Panicked, I grabbed Nick's arms and started to drag him off the stairs. Before I could move him I heard a scream, turned and saw Dee running down the hall, backlit by orange flames. She raised her arm and I could see something glint in her hand. It was a scalpel. I stood up and ran. The open back door was steps away, but I couldn't leave Nick behind, so I slipped into the utility room across the hall. I hoped I could use the door as a shield long enough to figure out what the hell to do next. Dee followed me, screaming for me to die.

"Die you fucking cunt! You bitch-faced whore!"

"Dee, you've lost your mind. What did I ever do to you?" I yelled as I pushed the door into her with enough force that she stumbled backward.

"I HATE YOU!" She screamed as she headed toward Nick.

I grabbed the push broom from the hook on the wall and rushed out after her. She turned and began slashing wildly at me. The broom was long enough that I could use it to keep the scalpel away as she lunged for me. The air was thick with smoke and I wasn't sure how much longer we had to play this game. It was time to act instead of react. I plunged the end of the broom into her solar plexus. She screamed, but this time it was in pain. I then turned the broom in my hands and swung it like a bat, connecting with her head, leaving a gash and causing her to drop the blade. I swung again and again until Dee turned and ran screaming out the back door. I dropped the broom and ran over to Nick.

Still unresponsive, I grabbed his arms, turned him, and began to drag him down the stairs. He was dead weight once he hit the hallway floor. The smoke was billowing from the front rooms, I didn't know how long we had until the hallway was engulfed. I gathered my strength and began to drag him toward the open back door. Only a few feet to safety.

"I cannot..." I panted and pulled, "wait to..." I panted and pulled some more, "get the hell..." more panting, more pulling, yet the door did not seem any closer, "out...of...Peoria!" And then we were outside. I could hear sirens getting closer. I wanted to drag Nick to the grass but was afraid Dee might be lying in wait for us. I stood up and looked around. No Dee, that was good. Then I saw Jacob come running up from the garage.

"Are you all right?" he asked as he helped me move Nick to the grass, safely away from the building. "What happened?"

"Dee happened. She tried to kill the boss and burn down the funeral home. Did you know she was a few roses short of a bouquet?"

"No, but somehow that doesn't surprise me."

Back at the apartment, Dan and Colby were waiting for me in the kitchen.

"Couldn't wait, you had to confront the deranged lunatic by yourself."

"I knew she didn't like me, I didn't know she was homicidal."

Dan handed me a beer. "They located the suspect running down the alley, bloody and with one shoe. She confessed to everything. Seems she was having an affair with the boss and he broke it off right after you were hired, so she blamed you."

"I had no idea. Although with Nick, I shouldn't be surprised. He has a concussion to rival yours, by the way. But he should be fine. I can't say the same for the funeral home." I took a long sip of my beer, not wanting to tell them how close Nick and I came to being cremains.

"Dan here was sharing some interesting developments before we were so rudely interrupted with phones calls regarding your latest escapades. Seems that flash drive Kyle was desperately looking for was inexplicably found in his home when the State Police searched it."

"Right on his dining room table." Dan leaned against the counter.

"You're kidding."

"Nope. And guess what they found on that flash drive?" Colby asked as he pulled me down onto his lap.

"Location of Johannes Vermeer's *The Concert*?" They both smiled at me. Gotta love working with Marshals, they understand art theft jokes.

"Better. It outlines the entire criminal operation. Names everyone, provides timelines, and spells out where to find money, equipment and assets. Pretty much everything the prosecutors need to know."

"Well, that's expedient."

"Some excellent and effective detective work was done."
Dan smiled at me, knowingly.

"How could they do this? I mean, they're cops."

Dan sighed. "Money corrupts, TJ."

"Says the Marshal to the woman whose father counterfeits money."

Dan and Colby looked at each other.

Colby rested his chin on my shoulder. "TJ, your father didn't counterfeit money."

"Thomas Joseph was one of the best art forgers in the world," Dan explained. I looked at him and then craned my head around to look at Colby, not comprehending.

"He forged a Renoir for a big-time collector who used it in an insurance scam. Your father testified in exchange for immunity and went into witness protection. He had a good eye. He could spot a counterfeit bond or bill better than anyone. Not to mention forged artwork. That's how he came to work with law enforcement. I'm sure that's how he figured out this entire enterprise."

I stood up and walked over to the trash can. I dropped my empty bottle in it. My dad was an art forger. Colby stood up and kissed the top of my head. He and I walked Dan to the door. Monday I'd have to go to the office and give an official statement, but for now, we were done. I closed the door and started to laugh. My dad was an art forger. I laughed as I walked around and turned off lights. I laughed while I closed all the curtains. I laughed as Colby guided me upstairs. There he started to undress me. Then I stopped laughing.

EPILOGUE

O nce again my apartment looked like angry raccoons lived here. Closets and drawers were empty, their contents strewn everywhere. No malicious mischief this time. I was packing. The dining room table was covered with packing boxes yet to be assembled, packing tape and bubble wrap. I went old school and had Shania Twain cranked up. It was time to clean house. Physically and emotionally.

Turned out, my mother knew all along my father was alive and in WITSEC, although she didn't know he had left the program. With that fresh betrayal and the not yet healed wound of my broken marriage, I made the only rational decision I could. I accepted a job in the last place I was happy, Boston. I would be working at a small art gallery and design showroom. Not my dream job, but it would get me the hell out of Peoria.

I spent the last month helping Nick organize insurance, cleanup crews and the rebuild of the funeral home. It didn't quite burn to the ground, but pretty darn close. And though it was tempting to build a new, state-of-the-art facility, I was pleased the family decided to restore the old mansion, with some fancy new upgrades. Dee was being held in a state mental facility, awaiting trial. She refused to accept any type of plea deal. I wanted to feel sorry for her, but the thousand dollar insurance deductible I had to pay after the restoration of the floors and walls in my apartment only fueled my anger. Bitch tried to burn me alive.

Colby had spent most of the last month shuttling between Peoria and D.C. This week he was in D.C. He was put in charge of the corruption investigation and was doing his own restoration and cleanup. He said they just about had everyone rounded up and arraigned. Everyone but my father, they still couldn't find him. But the flash drive provided enough details and breadcrumbs to actual evidence, they didn't really need him. I suspected he would turn up when they needed his expertise again. For his part, Colby was looking at a significant promotion and a prime assignment in D.C.

I missed him, but was being disciplined and refraining from calling or texting him. I had made a decision and I was sticking to it. Time with him was intense, the sex was hot, and his presence was exhilarating and reassuring. I doubted I would ever have an experience like it again. But I needed breathing room. I needed to find my own way. I needed to figure out who the hell I was anymore. He wasn't happy when I told him, but I think he understood. Our lives were taking us in different directions. I was sad to let him go but excited to see what new adventure awaited me. As long as there were no more people trying to kill me, the future looked promising.

I began sorting another pile between donation box and packing box. A week from now I'd be in Boston. My phone buzzed. I picked it up and read the text. It made me smile.

"I'm not giving up on us. XO"

ABOUT THE AUTHOR

Annie DeMoranville has lived all over, including Boston and
Los Angeles. She now resides in the shadow of the Rocky
Mountains with a menagerie of critters. She loves to travel
with a goal to see the most beautiful beaches in the world.
Run Aground, the first book in the **TJ Wilde Trilogy**, is her
debut novel.

For more information on her upcoming novels, visit
www.AnnieDeMoranville.com

And connect with her:
Facebook/AnnieDeMoranville.com
@AnnDeMoranville on Twitter

ACKNOWLEGMENTS

This book wouldn't have progressed beyond a few chapters without the enthusiasm of family and friends. They read the first few chapters and wanted more, so I wrote more.

Special thanks to Lari and Larissa for reading the book many times and offering thoughts and suggestions. Couldn't have done it without their support.

Coming Soon

UNDERWAY

Second book in the
TJ Wilde Mystery
Trilogy

TJ finds herself back in Boston, working in the Art District. She finally feels her life is back on track. That is until there is a break-in at the Cuban Art Gallery. Now she must find a missing painting in time to save a life.

And what of her Sexy Lawman, Colby Jameson? He's not going to let her go without a fight.

Don't miss the next adventures in TJ Wilde's ever complicated life. Sign up for the newsletter at
www. AnnieDeMoranville.com

www.ingramcontent.com/pod-product-compliance
Lightning Source LLC
Chambersburg PA
CBHW022020240626

47154CB00007B/2182